# KESSLER WOMEN

# KESSLER WOMEN

N.R. KING

LUMINARE PRESS
WWW.LUMINAREPRESS.COM

Kessler Women


Printed in the United States of America

Cover Design by Claire Flint Last

Luminare Press
442 Charnelton St.
Eugene, OR 97401
www.luminarepress.com

LCCN: 2020919920
ISBN: 978-1-64388-462-2

*To Andy*

# Contents

## PART ONE

Ada in the New World . . . 3
Emma Finds Love . . . 43
A Woman with Ordinary Intelligence . . . 66
Borrowed Sunshine . . . 89
The Child of Her Old Age . . . 114

## PART TWO

The Promised Land . . . 147
Lillian and Anshel . . . 168
A Married Woman . . . 217
The Muse . . . 232
Clara's Legacy . . . 241

## EPILOGUE

The End Is in the Beginning . . . 271

*Acknowledgments* . . . 281

# PART ONE

# Ada in the New World

*1937*

THE MOMENT SHE BOARDED THE SHIP, ADDY ANNOUNCED that she would no longer answer to her childhood nickname. From now on, she was to be known by her given name, Ada. Douglas laughed and promised to call her Ada, and his parents followed his lead. Ada smiled. The voyage was off to an excellent start.

As it turned out, the voyage was better than excellent. It was glorious. Ada carried herself as Mrs. Kessler, the wife of a doctor, and no one was permitted to overlook her status or that of her new husband. She doted on Douglas and was formal and kind to her in-laws, Max and Clara, addressing them as "Mom" and "Dad" in keeping with the family custom. Even in the face of her mother-in-law's loud laughter and lack of refinement, Ada managed to maintain her composure. She genuinely appreciated her father-in-law's courtly manners, however, and enjoyed his attentions, though she could see that he annoyed Douglas.

"Don't let him get too chummy," Douglas warned after his father had taken her arm for a stroll around the deck. "It's my mother who's the good person. He's a bum. Don't forget that."

"I'll remember, but really, Douglas, I'm your wife and he's your father. Don't be silly." Silly or not, Ada noticed that Douglas didn't leave her alone with his father again.

More than anything else, Ada loved recounting the story of her courtship and was pleased to find ready listeners among the other passengers. She used the lilt of her Scottish accent to her advantage when she realized how delightful they found it and spun a story that always began with the claim that she had seen Douglas first. But that was a lie. Her mother, Bess, saw him first and was charmed by the new medical student from the States, just off the boat and so inexperienced that he couldn't count the money or open a bank account. Ada also lied when she said she was the one who invited him to dinner. In fact, that was Bess, again. Her lies continued as she recounted that evening, including the assertion that Douglas couldn't take his eyes off her when, actually, he had talked to her mother and to her sister, Rose. Ada insisted that, though she was merely a child of fifteen at the time, Douglas had loved her immediately, and had eagerly waited for her to come of age so he could announce his intention to marry her. She said she was the only woman he had ever loved. When Ada said that, she tried not to think about Rose.

Douglas looked surprised and amused the first time he heard the story. But he didn't contradict her, and Ada became more and more bold with each retelling. Soon theirs was the perfect courtship, with Douglas cast as the knight in shining armor who rescued her, the radiant princess, from the wicked queen's castle, a gloomy, forbidding place where she toiled ceaselessly in the hot kitchen. Her one refuge was the garden she secretly filled with fragrant flowers in defiance of the queen's edict against any new planting. At last, the handsome knight whisked her away from all of that, and now they were on a voyage to their beautiful home where they would live surrounded by the love of their family and the admiration of their friends and neighbors.

By the time the family disembarked in New York, Ada had developed her persona to the degree that even old friends would have been hard-pressed to identify the schoolgirl they had known, and customers would not have recognized the helpful, obsequious shopgirl who sold them ribbons and buttons and other sundries. Ada was very pleased with herself.

Ellis Island and the train ride were tiring, but as she neared her new home, Ada forgot her exhaustion. She couldn't wait to be part of a big family, to be welcomed and admired as Douglas's lovely wife, to be adored by his two younger brothers and his little sister, to be loved by all her new relatives and envied by everyone who knew them.

THOUGH DOUGLAS HAD DESCRIBED THE HOUSE TO HER, Ada was unprepared when their taxi stopped in front of a shabby two-family structure with a scrubby front lawn. Before she could react, even before they were all out of the car, a young girl rushed out the front door and ran to the curb. "I'm so glad you're here," she said, hugging Clara and Douglas and then hugging and kissing Max. "I thought you'd get here today, but I wasn't sure and I didn't know what time, so I've been ready forever. The boys went to school, but I stayed home because it is such an important day, so you need to write me a note for tomorrow. And I didn't let anybody else come over like you said because you would be tired and I told them that you would call when they could come by, but I don't know that they won't be here any minute." Lillian took a breath. "Hello, Addy," she added more quietly. "I'm glad to meet you."

Ada smiled at her. "I'm glad to meet you, too, Lillian. Please call me Ada."

Lillian blushed and looked confused. Ada could see why when she walked up to the front door and saw a colorful banner decorated with crayon announcing "WELCOME HOME, ADDY."

"You've only to take that down and no harm's done," Ada said, and Lillian hurried to comply.

When Max opened the front door, Clara stepped inside, took a deep breath and smiled at Lillian. "You did a good job keeping the house nice, Lilly," she said. "I'm proud of you."

Lillian grinned. "Aunt Ann and Aunt Molly helped a lot, but I did all the cleaning up," she said and stepped aside as Ada came in and looked around.

The front door opened directly into a small living room crowded with furniture. A faded blue couch, a big chair covered in the same worn fabric, several smaller chairs, and lamps on little round tables filled the space. Small knick-knacks were scattered everywhere. Ada noticed a chipped, white china candy dish, a plastic dog carrying a basket of flowers in his mouth, and two glass domes labeled Niagara Falls. Lillian picked one up as they walked past to show Ada the snowflakes that fell when she shook it.

A row of ten identical, plastic baby dolls stood naked on the mantelpiece, each with a curl of yellow hair on top of its head and a heart pasted on its chest.

"Harold won them throwing darts at balloons at the State Fair last year," Lillian proudly explained. "He said he could have won more, but he ran out of nickels.

"That was the living room, and here's the dining room," Lillian continued, pulling Ada by the hand with Douglas right behind them. The dining room had just enough space for a heavy wooden table, six chairs, and a low dresser with a large silver candelabra on it. "The kitchen is back here, and this is where the boys sleep," Lillian said, pointing to a room on the right beyond the kitchen.

It was a large space littered with schoolbooks, magazines, sports equipment, clothes, and trophies. The mess and the fact that the odor of disinfectant, obvious everywhere else in the house, was missing here told Ada that this room hadn't been cleaned in some time. She wondered how the boys made their way across the floor without breaking an ankle or how they found space to sleep once they reached their beds. Was this how teenage boys in America lived?

"Harold is a big sports star and lots of this stuff is his," Lillian said. "Ira complains all the time that Harold takes up more than his half of the room. I'm never allowed in there, and they don't even like it if I look from the doorway. Which is fine with me because that's one less room to clean."

Lillian closed the door and led Ada back through the kitchen and down a narrow hallway off the dining room to a bathroom with a bedroom on either side of it. "This is the bathroom, and that is where my parents sleep," Lillian said, indicating the bedroom on the right. "But I'll sleep in there, too, when Douglas isn't at the hospital so you and Douglas can have my room because Mommy said you will have things to talk over."

Lillian turned to the bedroom on the other side of the bathroom. "When Douglas is at the hospital, this will be our room."

Our room? Surely not. Ada knew that Douglas would have to sleep at the hospital for days at a time when it was his shift, but she hadn't known that she wouldn't have a room to herself when he wasn't home. Don't they understand that I'll need my privacy as much when he's not here, she thought. I'm a married woman. I can't be expected to share a bedroom with a nine-year-old.

"I hope you don't think it's too small," Lillian said.

Ada looked around. Barely large enough for twin beds and two little dressers, it would be generous to call the room small. Neither the beds nor the dressers matched, and it was clear to Ada that one bed and one dresser had recently been bought or borrowed for her.

When Ada didn't respond, Lillian went on, "Mommy says if we keep it neat, we can manage. And I promise not to take up more than my share of the space."

Lillian's hard work was obvious. The room was clean and tidy, and she had set aside as much space as she could. Ada appreciated her effort.

Still, it was oppressive. There's no place for my lovely things and no chance of privacy at all, Ada thought. There's no chair to sit in or desk to use. This is impossible. She looked around the room again. Can I live here for a year?

"And look at this," Lillian said, picking up a doll like the ones on the mantel. "Harold said I can keep one of the Kewpie dolls on my dresser. I was going to put one on your dresser, too, till Mommy said only you can put things on your dresser. But I bet if you ask Harold, he'll let you take one from the living room like he did for me."

Ada looked with distaste at the doll. She certainly didn't want one on her dresser and would prefer that Lillian didn't display one in the room, either.

"Ada will need the space for her own things, Lillian, though that's a thoughtful suggestion," Douglas said.

Ada was about to point out that there was no space for her own things, when Douglas put his arm around her waist and hugged her to him. Then she took a deep breath and reminded herself that Douglas was counting on her to make a go of it—that a little hardship now was a small price to pay for the lovely home she'd have one day. I've already crossed the ocean, she reassured herself, I can do this, too. It's not forever. It's only for a year.

Ada knew that Douglas was worried about her reaction by the way he followed her and Lillian around the house. After the tour, he suggested that he show her the backyard and led her through the kitchen and out the back door. Clara prevented Lillian from joining them.

"Are you okay?" he asked once they were alone and the door to the kitchen had been closed.

"Of course."

"I hope you aren't sorry to see the house. I know it's not as nice as your mother's house, and sharing a room with Lillian will be hard after having your own room all your life, but, right now, it's the best I can do. I promise we'll move as soon as we've saved a little money."

"Douglas, don't be daft," Ada said. "I'll be fine here. It's temporary, and your family is very kind. Besides, being married to you more than makes up for a little discomfort in close quarters." She smiled at him, proud of her brave, self-sacrificing attitude, and hoped that Douglas noticed.

Ada looked for a place to sit down, but the backyard was no more than a patch of dirt with a clothesline strung across it. "What's that?" she asked, pointing to a pile of cigarette butts in one corner.

"That's what my mother gets for not letting anybody smoke in the house. She says it ruins her sense of smell. Didn't you see her sniff when we came in? That sniff told her everything that went on the whole time she was away."

Ada smiled.

"Really, it's true. When we were little, we'd try to fool her. Once, without turning around, she knew that Ira was behind her wearing Harold's shirt. That's the last time we tested her."

Ada laughed, and Douglas pulled her to him. "Let's not think about anybody else right now. Let's think about each other. I love you, Mrs. Kessler. Thanks for coming with me across the ocean."

"I love you, too, Dr. Kessler."

After a little hugging and kissing that Lillian watched from the corner of the window in her brothers' bedroom and Max watched from a window in the kitchen, they came inside.

The very next day, Harold and Ira brought their high school friends home to meet their new Scottish sister-in-law. Ada delighted them by being just flirtatious enough to flatter them without losing her advantage as an exotic, older woman.

"Every one of them has a crush on you," Douglas complained.

Ada was pleased by her conquest of his brothers and their friends, but she didn't want Douglas to be unhappy. "I'm sure they see me as an old lady," Ada told him, though she didn't believe it for minute. "You're the only man for me, even when you're being silly. I'll not be trading you for a fifteen-year-old boy any day soon," she said and kissed him on the nose to make him laugh.

Ada managed to move into the space Lillian set aside for her by leaving most of her things in her trunk. She hung the clothing needed for the season in the closet and left the top of her dresser empty. She couldn't bear to see her pretty ceramic bowl and her graceful porcelain princesses crowded together on a tiny dresser in such gloomy surroundings or risk their falling and shattering on the floor.

Lillian showed no resentment at having to share her room, and she did try to keep her area neat and her things away from Ada's space. Every morning she smoothed her sheet and blanket, folded her nightie and put it under her pillow, and pushed her slippers under her bed. She kept her toys piled in her corner of the room and her coloring books stacked on her dresser. But she was a child and careless at times. It wasn't unusual for Ada to find stray socks and candy bar wrappers next to her dresser or Lillian's umbrella making a puddle nearer her bed than Lillian's. Whenever Ada found Lillian's belongings in her half of the room, she put them on Lillian's bed.

One afternoon, Ada discovered Lillian on her hands and knees about to crawl under her bed. "What are you doing?" she asked.

"I can't find my pink ball," Lillian explained.

"I'm sure it isn't under my bed, so stand up."

"Can I look a little bit more? Dotty and I want to play ball, and she can't find hers, either."

Ada sighed and sat on her bed while Lillian poked around. The ball was finally found resting against the back edge of Ada's dresser.

"Thank you for letting me look around on your side of the room," Lillian said. "I'll try to be more careful from now on."

But the next day, Lillian was in despair when she saw the hair ribbon, the jar of paste, and the red crayon Ada had put on her bed. "I'm never going to be good enough at staying in my half of the room," she sobbed.

Then Ada felt cruel. So, as annoying as it was, she threw the candy wrappers away herself, returned toys to the toy pile, and put errant socks in the laundry hamper.

THE RELATIVES STAYED AWAY FOR FIVE DAYS, BUT AFTER THAT, a deluge of aunts and cousins flooded the house. Every day brought somebody new.

"Clara," each one would shout from the front door, "I'm here to say hello for a minute." Then Clara would hurry to the door for a hug and a kiss and usher the newcomer into the kitchen to join the group already settled around the table, drinking coffee, eating rugelach, and staring at Ada. Everybody would greet the newest arrival with a hug and a kiss and a comment.

"How nice to see you looking so well."

"Is that a new hat? Wear it in good health."

"I could never wear that color, but on you it looks good."

"Sorry to hear about your little one. How does a person break a toe?"

Finally, Clara would introduce Ada. "My daughter-in-law, Ada, from Scotland."

And the newcomer would say, "Now I see why Douglas went all the way across the ocean to find a bride. Pleased to meet you."

It was gratifying to be the center of attention until Ada realized that they weren't interested in her. Listening to them talk as they sized her up was what was expected.

The worst part was all the hugging and kissing by people who might be family but were still strangers as far as Ada was concerned. Eventually, they seemed to understand her frosty look and stiff posture and left off grabbing her. The word must have spread because relatives who came later shook her hand instead of opening their arms for a big hug.

Douglas spent the week before the beginning of his internship showing Ada around the city. He always held her arm and guided her along the crowded sidewalks and across the busy streets. Ada loved it when he took charge that way and made her feel protected and safe. They went to the movies and out to dinner and, even though she felt a little guilty about spending the money, he insisted that she buy herself a new outfit. It was also his idea to take her picture wearing it and send the snapshot to her mother. Ada thought he was trying to prove that he was taking good care of her.

Where Douglas had found the money for her outfit was a mystery to Ada, since it was clear that the family's finances were precarious. Douglas told her that his father contributed nothing to the family budget, though he dressed in a suit and tie each morning and left the house, not to be seen again until late in the evening. Some nights he didn't return at all.

Clara sold briskets, corned beef, and other cooked food to the deli around the corner. She worked in her kitchen from early in the morning to late in the evening, bustling among the pots and roasting pans, seasoning, stirring, draining, setting out to cool, and beginning the next order. The house smelled like boiling beef, roasting chicken, and pastrami spices all week long. Ada never saw her mother-in-law taste anything, and she could believe the family lore that Clara seasoned the food based on the aromas rising from the pots. Clara also did business out of her apron pocket, selling sandwiches wrapped in waxed paper to anybody who knocked on the back door between eleven and one in the afternoon.

By far the greatest source of income was the rent paid by the upstairs tenants, Mr. and Mrs. Brotkin. Mrs. Brotkin was a tall, pale lady, fifteen years older than Ada. Her husband was twenty years her senior. He was a huge man whose appearance alarmed Ada the first time she encountered him at the front door. But when he stepped back and held the door for her, and then nodded politely in response to her smile, Ada quickly replaced her first impression with a more favorable one.

One morning, Ada happened to be sitting on the front porch when Mrs. Brotkin walked up the sidewalk, carrying a bag of groceries.

"Lovely day," Mrs. Brotkin said.

Ada agreed and took the opportunity to introduce herself.

"I'm delighted to meet you," Mrs. Brotkin responded. "But please call me Sylvia, and my husband's name is Joe. I hope you'll come upstairs for coffee one day. Or would you rather have tea?"

"Tea would be lovely," Ada said, and, to her surprise, a little note on cream-colored paper appeared in the mailbox the next day. It was an invitation to tea the following afternoon at four o'clock. Ada wrote an acceptance in return.

Sylvia responded promptly to her knock and led Ada into a bright, airy room. The apartment was a replica of the one downstairs, but without the abundance of furniture and people. Here the rooms were open and quiet, and Ada relaxed for the first time in weeks. She hadn't understood before how overwhelmed and oppressed she felt by the crowding downstairs.

Ada could see that Sylvia was charmed by her stories of life in Scotland and, especially, by the story of her courtship, but she didn't want to overstay her welcome. After an hour, she thanked Sylvia for the lovely tea and rose to go.

"Perhaps you would like to have tea again next week," Sylvia said, and Ada readily agreed to visit again. They had tea every Thursday afternoon after that, and her visit with Sylvia became the high point of Ada's week.

Downstairs, Ada struggled to protect her time and her privacy. Only her bed offered a safe refuge from the family. If she tried to read in the living room or write letters at the dining room table, she was sure to be interrupted by the brothers' arguments, or by Lillian and her friends, or by visiting relatives. Ada was amazed by the number of women with nothing better to do than sit around Clara's kitchen table drinking coffee, playing cards, and gossiping. Clara always invited Ada to join them, saying, "You remember Toby, Aunt

Bertha's oldest," or "This is Celia. I'm not sure you've met her yet. She's Martha's sister-in-law." They would ask a few questions about how Ada liked married life, and then trade the latest family gossip. The same stories appeared and reappeared from different sources, polished to a high shine. One day, Ada heard about Uncle Al, a conductor for the transit system, and how he had given his wife a free ride. Two weeks later, the story had him throwing bags of money to her off the back of the trolley as she ran alongside the tracks. Ada also heard about the latest abortions and about an old lady who gave a discount if two women came in for abortions together. Ada was shocked and didn't know what to believe.

Sometimes the gossip struck close to home. Like the time Ada heard Cousin Vera say, "I saw Max strolling along Fayette Street today, looking like a million bucks. That man cuts a fine figure."

Ada thought it a cruel thing to say to Clara, sitting at the table in her shapeless housedress with her hands smelling like cooked meat.

But Clara chose to take it as a compliment. "It's nice to be married to a man who turns all the girls' heads, including yours, Vera."

"Oh, he does that alright," Vera said. "That man turns heads."

Clara leaned forward. "Anything special on your mind, Vera?"

Vera shrugged and sipped her coffee. But a moment later, she added, "Harold's the one most like him, taller and even better looking in his way. Your other boys don't favor him."

Clara let the comment pass. But Ada didn't like hearing that Harold was, in any way, better than Douglas. She wondered what these people said about her when she wasn't at the table and worried that one day, they might even say something unkind to her face.

To her surprise, Ada found herself wishing for the peace and quiet of her mother's house. When she lived there, she couldn't wait to escape the tedium of life with her mother and her sister, but now she longed to be with them for a quiet evening in the parlor around the radio. Then, the only discordant notes had been the ranting of Hitler from Germany and her mother's constant worries and laments about the threat he posed. They paled now in light of the incessant chatter and turmoil in her mother-in-law's house.

More than anything else, Ada longed for the solitude of her old bedroom, for its cheery bedspread and curtains, for the woven rug her mother taught her to make with fabric scraps, and for the dressing table with its round mirror and lovely little red plush seat. Ada had never given her bedroom two thoughts, but now she remembered it as beautiful beyond compare.

Telling herself they were boring and crude, Ada took to avoiding the family as much as possible, and rarely joined their conversations at the kitchen table. Once, as she retreated to her bedroom, she overheard Clara saying that Scottish people sometimes seem a little standoffish, but they are really very nice.

Good, Ada thought. I hope they think I'm aloof and have better things to do than listen to their gossip. Perhaps that will encourage them to leave me alone.

If Lillian was already in the bedroom when Ada came in, Ada noticed that she tiptoed out without speaking. The third time it happened, Ada asked for an explanation.

"Mommy said I'm not to bother you," Lillian answered. "And the boys aren't to bother you, either. We have to respect your privacy and remember that you aren't used to so much noise."

Eventually, everybody learned not to bother Ada when she was reading or writing letters, and not to expect her to be out of the bathroom quickly if she was taking a bath. But her solitude was hard-won and turned out to be as oppressive as the chaos and crowding in the house.

Douglas came home once or twice a week, so tired that he had no interest in conversation and no patience with her complaints.

"There's nothing I can do about it, Ada," he said. "The family is doing the best it can. I'm doing the best I can, and you need to do the best you can, too. The house isn't going to magically grow another room for you."

"But you do understand how I feel, don't you? You do see that it's difficult for me."

"I see that it's difficult for everybody. Don't forget that I'm working around the clock, delivering babies at all hours of the night and day, caring for my patients, and barely getting any sleep, myself. I'm doing all this for us and for our future. All you have to do is share a bedroom with my sister and write letters. Can't you manage that without complaining? Can't I have a few peaceful hours with my wife when I come home?"

Ada didn't answer him. There was no point.

Early one evening, after Douglas returned to the hospital and before the family came back from wherever they had gone, Ada had a precious hour to herself in the empty house. She made a cup of tea and sat alone at the kitchen table. I don't know him anymore, she thought. I'd never have married a man who wants me in bed but can't be troubled to talk to me. He worries about his patients while I'm left here to fend for myself. He's abandoned me, that's what he's done.

Ada's sense of loss was different from the rages she sometimes felt when she blamed Douglas for everything and called him names and cried into her pillow while Lillian breathed lightly in the next bed and Clara gargled in the bathroom. This was much worse.

Ada sipped her tea and warmed her hands on the hot cup. I'm descending into self-pity, she thought, and that will never do. What would my mother say?

THE NEXT MORNING, ADA DRESSED IN HER NEW OUTFIT and, without telling anybody her plan, took the bus downtown by herself. She strolled slowly along the streets and then sipped a cup of tea at Schrafft's while considering the help wanted signs she had seen discreetly placed in the windows of three stores. I know the most about selling clothes, she reasoned, and decided to apply at the large department store first. If I don't get that job, I'll apply to the jeweler and at the card shop. Secure in her plan and the fact that nobody would know if she failed, Ada walked to the department store and asked for the manager.

The girl behind the counter asked, "What do you want him for?"

Ada thought her terribly rude, but answered nonetheless. "I'm here to apply for a job."

"Then you want personnel. Go up to the third floor and walk to the back of the store."

Ada made her way to the third floor, hoping the next person she met would be more pleasant. At the personnel office, she was given a form to fill out and told to wait. As Ada sat in the outer office, a short lady came in. Though she herself could only be called homely, her clothing was exquisite and perfectly tailored to her small frame. The silk scarf at her neck picked up the colors of her suit and blouse and draped gracefully over her shoulder. Ada admired her taste and pitied her looks.

The receptionist looked up. "Good morning, Miss Reifman. It doesn't do any good to keep coming up here every three days. We don't have a new girl for you yet."

"I'm sure you are doing your best, but I need two replacements now. Becky's pregnant and won't be back after next week."

Ada listened carefully. She was amazed to hear a complaint expressed in such a soft tone with such a nice smile and knew this woman would have her two replacements before the receptionist noticed what had happened. Emboldened by her manner, Ada took a deep breath and spoke up.

"I'd love to work for you. I could help out for a time while you decide if I can do the job."

The receptionist looked at her in shock. "You haven't even seen Mr. Martin yet. You have to wait your turn."

Miss Reifman looked at Ada with interest and sat in the chair next to her. "Where are you from?"

"I'm from Scotland, and I've been living here a month. My husband is an intern at the hospital, and I need a job to help pay the bills. I've experience selling, and I'm a quick learner."

"I can see that, and I think you would work out fine." She turned to the receptionist. "Is Phil in his office?"

"Mr. Martin is too busy to see you right now."

"I'm glad to hear he's in," Miss Reifman said and knocked on the door marked Director of Personnel. Without waiting for a reply, she walked in.

"I hope you have a minute for me," she said.

"Emma. Come right in. I'm always happy to see you."

The door closed, and the receptionist scowled at Ada. Several minutes later, Miss Reifman invited Ada into the office.

"Emma here tells me you have selling experience and she would like you in her department," Mr. Martin said. "Let me see your application."

Ada handed it to him without a word, and after looking it over, he filled in her hours and salary, put his initials on the front, and handed it back to her.

"Tell Polly you will start tomorrow and to have the paperwork ready for you by nine o'clock. You'll come here, sign a few forms, and then report to Emma. She'll be in charge of your schedule. Any questions?"

"No, sir," Ada said, and followed Miss Reifman out of the office. Ada handed her application to Polly, and Miss Reifman delivered Mr. Martin's message. Then she took Ada to a small staff lounge on the second floor.

"We'll chat for a minute here," Emma said, settling herself on a small couch and inviting Ada to sit next to her. "You've been hired to work in the better dresses department. I'm the assistant manager, and we'll be working together. There are usually three of us on the floor, so you'll need to handle more than one customer at a time without letting anybody feel neglected. It would be easiest if you could take Becky's schedule. She had Thursdays off." Emma stopped and looked carefully at Ada. "Am I going too fast?"

"No, not at all," Ada answered. "I've experience selling to women in my mother's shop, and I know I can do a good job for you. Thursdays off suits me well."

Emma smiled and shook Ada's hand. "A pleasure to meet you, Ada," she said. "I'll see you tomorrow."

"It's my good fortune to meet you, Miss Reifman. Thank you for your help today. You won't be sorry."

"I'm sure I won't. And you must call me Emma. Everybody does, except Polly."

Ada fairly skipped to the bus stop. The thought of being out of the house and at work during the day lifted her spirits, and the fact that she would bring money into the household made her proud. She was also pleased that her day off was Thursday and her afternoon teas with Sylvia could continue.

Clara was thrilled with Ada's news and hugged and kissed her. "Imagine going off on your own and finding such a good job after just a month in the country. You're quite a girl, Ada," she said, and hugged her again.

Ada was so pleased with herself that she didn't resist when Clara wrapped her arms around her. For a moment, Ada was engulfed in Clara's warmth and the scent of pastrami, and she understood what Aunt Martha meant last week when Ada overheard her say "If you hug Clara, you aren't hungry for a week."

"Now I'll be giving you half my pay like Ira gives you half of his and Lillian gives you half her babysitting money," Ada said.

"Oh no you won't," Clara said. "There's two of you, so you need more for yourselves."

"Then I'll split it three ways: five dollars for you, five dollars for me, and five dollars for Douglas."

"You're a generous daughter-in-law," Clara said, hugging her again. "There's none better."

Ada felt rich with five dollars in her purse, and she could see that Douglas was grateful to her. Emma was easy to work for, and the department was a happy place. It wasn't always easy to deal with customers, but the lessons learned from her mother and her sister stood her in good stead. Her helpful manner and her accent endeared her to the clientele immediately, and her good taste and knowledge of the merchandise enabled her to add the perfect silk scarf to any outfit, standing back to admire the effect while her customer tried it on in the dressing room. Sylvia was so impressed with Ada's new job that she went to the store to buy a skirt from her and left with a skirt and two blouses.

Perhaps the greatest joy Ada's job provided began the Friday she discovered the main library, a few blocks from the store. Every Friday after that, she ate her lunch quickly and rushed to the library where she borrowed three books at a time so she would have a reason to go back the next Friday.

When Ada decided to learn about her new country by reading American authors, Miss Lindler, the librarian, was delighted to suggest titles. "This is Sinclair Lewis's most famous book," she said and handed Ada a copy of *Main Street*. "He's the first American to win the Nobel Prize for literature."

Ada suspected that Miss Lindler recommended *Main Street* because the heroine, Carol, was a librarian, but her suspicion didn't dim her pleasure in the story. Especially once Carol married a doctor and moved with him to his hometown, Gopher Prairie. Ada could appreciate Carol's loneliness when she found herself without friends and adrift in a small town so different from where she had grown up. But she thought Carol lucky to have a house of her own and a husband she saw more than Ada saw Douglas. She couldn't understand why Carol wasn't content or why she tried to reform the whole town. If that was me, Ada thought, I would ignore them all.

Ada read all the Sinclair Lewis titles the library owned and then moved on to Mark Twain, James Fenimore Cooper, and John Dos Passos. She rejected Hemingway because he didn't write about the States, but, with Miss Lindler's guidance, undertook Steinbeck and Fitzgerald. She felt proud when Miss Lindler called her a sophisticated reader.

Though Lillian's reading was confined to books assigned by her teacher and Clara never read anything, Ada tried to talk to them about her favorite stories. When neither of them showed the slightest interest, she decided to read *Caddie Woodlawn* from Lillian's assigned reading list. By the end of the book, Ada was sorry she had wasted her time reading about a child as ridiculous as Caddie, especially since Lillian didn't want to talk about it anyway.

Miss Lindler suggested the first book in the Nancy Drew mystery series as one Lillian might like, and Ada brought it home one Friday afternoon. Lillian did like it, but Ada thought it terribly written and was offended that an unpleasant, arrogant character in the book was named Ada. Lillian read the rest of the series, but Ada didn't.

Even Douglas wouldn't talk about her reading. Whenever Ada brought up books, he complained that he had enough to think about at the hospital, and he didn't want to think when he came home. He was especially uninterested in hearing about *Main Street* and Carol's unhappiness. I should have learned from Carol's example, Ada told herself, and not wasted my time trying to interest this family in literature.

Only Sylvia, though she wasn't interested in reading them herself, enjoyed hearing about the books Ada read. It comforted Ada to hear Sylvia commiserate with Carol and her attempts to make a life in Gopher Prairie.

One sunny Friday, as Ada dashed to the library with three books to return, she heard someone call her name. She turned, expecting to see Douglas, and found herself face-to-face with her father-in-law.

"Ada, my dear, where are you running off to?"

"It's my lunch hour, and I'm going to the library."

"That's the direction I'm going, too. I'll walk along with you, and we'll have time for a little chat." Max took her books and tucked her arm in his. Walking with him reminded Ada of her excursions downtown with Douglas.

"We don't have a chance to get to know each other at home," Max said.

Ada didn't answer that he was rarely home, or that Douglas had warned her not to get to know him. Seeing Max looking so crisp and neatly dressed and smiling at her so warmly made that warning seem silly, anyway.

"It seems we're both busy," Ada answered.

"I can't believe I'm too busy to find time for the delightful little bride of my oldest son," Max said and gave her arm a squeeze. Before she could respond, Ada heard a male voice behind them.

"Hey, Max, old man, who's that you have with you today? Who's the doll?"

Max looked annoyed as he turned, being careful to hold Ada's arm on his. "No need to be rude, Sol."

"I'm not rude. I'm jealous."

"Enough of that. This is Douglas's wife, my daughter-in-law, Ada. Ada, this is an old friend of mine. Sol Pinsky."

"Pleased to meet you, Ada. Sorry, if I sounded rude. Me and Max joke around all the time."

"Don't fret, Mr. Pinsky. It's nice to meet you."

"That's a sweet accent. I bet Douglas never gets tired of hearing you talk. I know I'd never get tired of listening to you."

Ada felt confused. Was this old man flirting with her? She didn't know how to respond and leaned toward Max, grateful that he held her arm.

"Enough, Sol. We are on our way to the library, so we don't have time to stand on the street corner talking to the likes of you."

"The library? That's a new one for you, Max."

"Goodbye, Sol."

"A pleasure to meet you, Ada. I hope this isn't the last time we see each other."

"I hope not," Ada said, more dutifully than sincerely as Sol tipped his hat and walked on ahead of them.

"I'm sorry you had to be subjected to Sol's crudities," Max said quietly. "He's an old friend and he means well, but he never learned how to behave or how to treat a lady. Please don't judge him harshly. He'd never do you any harm." Max patted her hand. "And he's not entirely to blame. You are a pretty little thing, you know. He wasn't wrong there." Max smiled at her and called forth Ada's most charming smile in return.

At the steps of the library, Max looked at the books before returning them to her. "I've always wished I had more time to read Steinbeck," he said. "But now I need to rush to an appointment. How about lunch tomorrow? I'll pick you up outside the store, and lunch will be on me. I want to hear all about your job and what you're reading and how you like America."

Ada saw no reason to say no, so she said yes. Max gave her a paternal hug and rushed away. Ada looked after him. What harm can there be in lunch with my father-in-law, she thought. It will be nice to relax with a man who has time for me and isn't always counting the minutes till he's due back at the hospital.

The next day, Max took Ada to a luncheonette where the corned beef sandwiches were so big they shared one, and he ordered every different kind of pickle so she could taste the differences. Max told her how much he liked her dress and made her laugh with his stories of the people in his office. She told him about work and the ladies who insist on buying dresses that are sizes too small because they've never worn anything larger than a size twelve.

"I tell them that dresses are cut small these days to save fabric and a sixteen is really what a twelve used to be," Ada said, laughing at her trickery.

Max laughed with her. "You tell a great story, Ada. A born storyteller, that's what you are."

"It's easy to tell a story to an appreciative audience."

"That's the truth. At home they don't understand me. It's different with you," Max said. "I work hard, but times are tough, and I hate to come home with nothing to show, so I don't come home at all. It's a sad thing to be misunderstood. But Clara's a good woman, and she stands by me." Max made an obvious effort to smile. "How about dessert?"

"Not for me. I have to go back to the store."

"I thought you might say that, so I brought this along for you to enjoy later." Max took a small bag of chocolates tied with a bright red ribbon from his pocket and gave it to her. Ada was charmed. Here was a man who planned thoughtful gestures ahead of time and had them ready at precisely the right moment.

"Thanks, Dad, that's nice of you, and thanks for lunch."

"Let's skip the 'Dad.' I'm happier if you call me Max like my other friends do. Not at home, of course, but at other times."

Ada was flattered that Max considered her a friend and the one family member he could talk to. There's nothing wrong with this, she assured herself. Maybe Douglas is jealous of him. Sons often misunderstand their fathers.

The next day at work, a delivery boy brought Ada one red rose. The card read, "Thanks for lunch." The other salesladies eagerly speculated about the identity of the sender, until their enthusiasm evaporated when they heard it was her father-in-law. Emma still seemed pensive.

"Does your husband know his father is sending you roses?" she asked.

"One rose, Emma. And don't be silly. It's to cheer me up. He knows it's hard for me to be separated from Douglas so much."

Still, the next time they had lunch, Ada asked Max not to send any more flowers. "The other girls might get the wrong idea," she explained.

"I'm sorry, Ada. It never occurred to me that somebody might misunderstand. Maybe it's a good idea to keep quiet about our little lunches, too."

Ada agreed and wondered if he knew that she had already decided not to tell anybody about them.

Max and Ada lunched together often after that, and Ada found herself looking forward to eating with him. Max was always happy to see her and eager to hear her stories about the other salesladies at the store and their customers. She, in turn, listened sympathetically when he complained about work, praised Clara, told funny stories, and lamented Harold's lazy ways. Once, he asked her advice about how to handle a problem with a client and listened carefully to her suggestions. She was pleased when he said, "You make good sense, Ada. I'm going to try that."

She was even more gratified a few weeks later when Max told her, "I'm a lucky man to have such a sweet daughter-in-law. And such a pretty one to boot. We aren't like the rest of them, Ada. They don't appreciate you the way I do, and nobody understands me better than you."

After lunch one day, Max spent longer than usual sipping his coffee. "We have such a nice time that I don't want it to end too soon. How about we take in a picture show on your next day off? You shouldn't be stuck in the house all the time just because Douglas is stuck at the hospital. I could come from my office and meet you at the theater."

"Sorry, I can't. I always have tea upstairs with Sylvia on my day off. I think she looks forward to it, and so do I."

"I don't know why you bother to visit her."

"I like her, and she's nice to me. Her husband is nice, too."

"That big hulk of a man? He doesn't look nice to me." Max shook his head. "I think you should be very careful around him."

Ada was shocked. "He's always polite to me. Why don't you like them?"

"Sorry if that's how I sounded." Max smiled and reached across the table to pat her hand. "I didn't mean anything by it. I thought a picture show would be fun for you." He dropped the subject until they were standing in front of the store. "Keep that picture show in mind for some week soon," he said before giving Ada a little hug. "I bet you haven't seen *A Day at the Races* yet."

THE NEXT SUNDAY AFTERNOON, ADA WAS PLAYING CARDS with Harold and Max at the dining room table while Lillian stood at her father's elbow and watched, whispering suggestions to him and putting down the card he indicated when it was his turn. Ada was winning, and Max was amused by her delight with her success, though Harold had become sullen and complained repeatedly that Max was letting her win.

When Douglas opened the front door, Ada jumped up to hug him, and Lillian slid into her seat. "Douglas!" Ada said. "I didn't expect you today. What a wonderful surprise!"

Douglas took her in his arms. "I've missed you so much," he said and kissed her right there in front of everybody. Ada was embarrassed and glanced at the table. She blushed when she saw Max watching her intently.

"No need to blush, Ada," Harold said. "It isn't like we don't know what the two of you do together."

Ada hid her face on Douglas's chest.

"Watch how you talk to my wife," Douglas said and took her hand. "C'mon Ada, let's go for a walk."

Douglas went to the kitchen to say hello to his mother while Ada put on her hat and coat. The two of them went out the back door without another word to either Harold or Max. Douglas took her arm as soon as they reached the sidewalk and hurried her away from the house.

"Don't mind Harold. He's a chip off the old block. As crude and lazy as they come. If they're home, you stick with my mother. Don't be around them, Ada, and don't think you have to be nice to my father."

"I can't believe he's as bad as you say. Anyway, I'm your wife. He's not about to be crude to your wife. It's Harold who has no manners."

"Dad might be smoother than Harold, but don't be fooled. Spend your time with my mother and stay away from him."

Spend time with your mother? Ada thought. She's boring. And time with her means listening to a crowd of aunts and cousins all talking at once, comparing abortion stories, gossiping about anyone absent from the table, or cackling over some crude joke. At least your father appreciates me and listens to me and takes me to restaurants. What would you do if you knew that I go to lunch with him? Ada stopped her thoughts right there. Douglas's reaction was too frightening to consider, even for a moment.

"Let's not talk about them anymore," she said. "How are you doing at the hospital? Do you still love me?"

"Everything is fine at the hospital, and I love you more every day." He didn't add anything to that and seemed distracted when Ada talked about the store, and impatient when she said that sometimes she's lonely.

"There's nothing I can do about that. The only thing I have on my mind now is a nap. Are you sleepy, too?"

Fortunately, the house was deserted when they came home from their walk. A cot for Lillian had been set up in her parents' bedroom, and there were fresh sheets on the beds in Lillian's room.

WEEKS LATER, ADA WOKE TO THE SOUND OF SOMEBODY IN the hallway outside her bedroom door. She was frightened until she heard Max's voice say, "Damn" as he bumped into the bathroom door for a second time. Despite the noise, Lillian slept soundly, and Ada didn't hear Clara stir across the hall. Her alarm faded even when she saw her bedroom door open slowly. She assumed Max was just peeking in, until he sat on the edge of her bed and leaned over her. When Ada gasped, he put his hand over her mouth.

"Shhh. Don't wake Lillian. I came to tell you good night," Max whispered.

Ada sat up in bed. "Are you drunk? Get out of here."

"Shhh. No more talking." Max hugged her to him. He smelled of hair oil and cloves, and Ada could feel the rough fabric of his overcoat through her thin nightdress. His lips were cool on her forehead, and then on her cheek.

How could Max be here, in her bed, doing this to her? Ada moved back as quietly as she could until her shoulder bumped the wall. She didn't want to be discovered any more than Max did. Douglas would be so angry he might provoke Max into telling everybody about their lunches. The aunts and the cousins would be thrilled to have that story to pass around. Ada could imagine what pleasure Cousin Vera would take in relating whose head Max had turned this time.

Max leaned forward. "Relax, Ada. I came to say good night." His arm went around her, and he pulled her toward him, kissing her on the lips. "It kills me to think of you and Douglas in here. I'll make you a lot happier than he can. You don't want a little boy, Ada, you want a man."

Ada's breath came in short gasps. What's he talking about? He might do anything.

Max kissed her again, more tenderly and fully than before, and began to pull at her nightdress.

"Get out, Max," she whispered. "Get out of here now."

The bed creaked as Max settled into it. "Just a little more good night, Ada," he said, and his hand found her breast.

"No." Ada managed to pull away and gather the sheets tightly around her.

Max sat up. "Don't be frightened, Ada. I would never hurt you. Maybe I am a little tipsy, and I wandered into the wrong room. It will never happen again." Max got up quietly and left the room, closing the door behind him. Ada heard him say, "Clara, darling, I'm home, and I've been thinking about you."

Ada lay down and tried to sleep. If Douglas was a real husband, he would keep me safe, she thought. He knows I'm unhappy, but he doesn't care. He's left me here with nobody to protect me. Anything could happen, and Douglas would blame me and say it's all my fault.

The next day at work, a delivery boy brought her one red rose with no card, and the day after, a small box of chocolates was delivered. "They're from my husband," Ada told the other salesgirls.

For two weeks, she ate her lunch in the employee lounge, but by the third Friday, Ada had read all her library books twice and needed new ones. Max was waiting for her.

"Hi, Ada. I haven't been home much lately, so we haven't had a chance to chat. I'm glad I ran into you today. Are you on your way to the library?"

"I am."

"Care if I come along?"

"I'd rather go alone."

"Don't be angry, Ada. I don't remember what I do when I'm drunk, but I think I might have frightened you, and if I did, I'm sorry. Can we have lunch together next week?"

"You didn't frighten me. I can take care of myself, but I'm very busy, and we cannot have lunch together."

"Then I'll content myself with carrying your books and walking to the library. I don't want to miss the chance to spend a few minutes with my favorite daughter-in-law."

After that, Max was often waiting to walk her to the library. He carried her books and guided her along the sidewalk with his usual skill. Weeks went by and, eventually, Ada lost her reserve and suspicion. Max seemed genuinely remorseful, and it was so delightful to be appreciated that she agreed to lunch with him now and then.

IT WAS MONTHS BEFORE MAX CAME TO HER ROOM AGAIN. This time, Lillian was away at her first slumber party. The house had been filled with excitement from the moment Lillian was invited to visit her best friend, Dorothy, for the night. Clara rolled a sheet and a blanket together and tied the bundle with string, and Max came home one day with a little cardboard suitcase covered in a paisley fabric.

"Thank you, Daddy," Lillian said, hugging and kissing him. "Nobody's ever given me anything like this before."

Ada bought new slippers for Lillian so she wouldn't be embarrassed by her old torn pair, and helped her pack her clothing, comb, and toothbrush in her new suitcase. Everybody waved goodbye as Dorothy's father drove off with her before dinner.

Late that night, Max came into Ada's bedroom so quietly that she didn't know he was there until he pulled away her covers and lay on top of her. His clothing reeked of cigarette smoke, and Ada could smell whiskey on his breath. She didn't need Clara's sensitive nose to be overwhelmed by his odor.

"It's only me to say good night," he said.

Ada could feel him fumbling with her nightie and was horrified when he managed to pull it to her shoulders without letting her up.

"I love you, Ada," he mumbled as he kissed her breasts. "I'm your friend, and I love you." He kissed her mouth and her neck and stroked her stomach.

Max's belt buckle pressed painfully into her, and his pants were rough against her legs. The shock of his assault and his weight pushing her into the bed left Ada helpless. She couldn't breathe. What if he gets his way? What if I can't stop him?

"I know you didn't say anything about our last little good night," Max whispered, punctuating each phrase with a kiss. "I knew I could trust you. You're the only one who understands me. The only one who has my needs in mind. Don't disappoint me, Ada."

Ada tried to squirm out from under him, but he pressed himself heavily on her.

"Hold still, Ada. You know you're everything to me. And now you're being as quiet as I am, so I know you like this, too."

Ada tried to turn her face aside, but Max grabbed her hair and kissed her deeply on the lips. When she felt his hands on her thighs, Ada whispered, "No, Max. Get off me. Get up now."

"Shhh, Ada. If you wake Clara or the boys, I'll say this was your idea, that Douglas isn't enough for you. Remember, we've had secrets from them for a long time. This isn't my first visit to your bed." Max rubbed himself against her and tugged at his belt. "Don't worry, Ada. I'm a gentle man."

"Max, please. I can't breathe. I'm going to faint."

Max moved aside and Ada sat up, pushing her hands so hard against his chest that he fell backward.

"Now, Ada, you don't want to get rough because then I can get rough, too," Max said, and he slapped her.

Ada stared at him in disbelief and fear. Tears filled her eyes and slipped down her cheeks. Max seemed shocked by the sound of the slap and the look on her face.

"Oh, no. I'm sorry. Forgive me, Ada. I didn't mean to do that. I was just saying good night. You didn't need to get rough. That's not for us."

He didn't move while Ada smoothed down her nightie and retreated to the corner of the bed, too frightened to speak.

In the silence, Max and Ada heard Clara's bedroom door open. Max stepped away from the bed and Ada gathered the covers around her. They heard the click of the hall light switch and the slap, slap of Clara's big slippers cross the hallway. Slowly Ada's bedroom door opened and a sliver of light shone on the bed. Max stepped into the shadow behind the door.

"Ada, darling," Clara said as she sat on the bed and pulled Ada to her. "You must have had a bad dream." Clara took a deep breath and held Ada close, rocking back and forth, and stroking her hair. At first, Ada was stiff in her arms, but Clara rocked and crooned until Ada relaxed against her and began to cry.

"Don't worry about a thing, Ada," she said. "You're a daughter in this family now. You're my daughter and nothing and nobody hurts my daughters. You can count on that. Don't let those bad dreams scare you. Send them across the hall. I can take care of them."

They sat like that until Ada stopped crying. Then Clara tucked her into bed, kissed her forehead, and wished her sweet dreams. When Clara's bedroom door closed, Max crept out of the room without another word, and Ada heard the front door open and close.

THE NEXT MORNING, CLARA DECIDED THAT IT WAS TIME for a major cleaning.

"Ma," Harold complained. "That's Lillian's job."

"You're right. So let's surprise her by doing it ourselves before she comes home from Dorothy's."

The windows were thrown open and everybody was pressed into service. Harold and Ira were ordered into their bedroom and told to stay there until it was neat and clean. The sounds of their arguing filled the house, but neither of them ventured out of the room. Listening to them made Clara laugh and Ada glad she never had a brother. While Clara worked in her own room, Ada cleaned the room she shared with Lillian. She was glad to have so much work to do. It left no time for thought.

After all the linens were changed and the room was thoroughly aired, Ada dusted and swept and rearranged her dresser drawers and closet. She even reorganized Lillian's pile of toys and gathered her coloring books into one stack and her schoolbooks into another. Once the bedrooms were cleaned, Clara seemed to run out of steam and didn't insist that they continue with the rest of the house.

Ada was grateful that Clara made no reference to the night before and relieved that Max didn't reappear at home. Since his absence was not unusual, nobody commented on it. But every time the front door opened, Ada looked up, worried that it might be Max. Her bedroom no longer felt safe, and she took to spending more time in the kitchen with Clara or at the dining room table while Lillian did her homework. She left her bedroom door open at night and was pleased when Clara noticed and, without comment, did the same. Once, Ada was startled by a voice in the boys' bedroom that sounded like Max. Her alarm must have shown on her face because Clara quickly said, "That's Benjy, Harold's friend."

Two weeks later, when Ada came home from work, she was surprised to find Clara and Sylvia having coffee at the dining room table.

"Hello, Ada," Clara said. "Come join us. How was your day at the store?"

Ada sat down and said her day had gone well. She really wanted to ask why Sylvia was downstairs chatting with Clara. She hadn't known them to be neighborly before.

"Sylvia has been telling me that Joe is away many nights, and she's often lonely upstairs by herself. And I was telling her that you have no room down here to unpack your lovely belongings. One thing led to another, and Sylvia suggested that you move into her guest room, the big bedroom off her kitchen. She says nobody uses it, and if she needs it for guests, you'll come back down here for a few nights. You would still live here, but you could read and write letters and sleep upstairs. If you use the back stairs, you won't bother Sylvia at all."

"Even if you use the front door, you won't be a bother," Sylvia said. "But the back stairs will work, too. I'll give you a key to the kitchen door, and you'll be quite independent."

Ada couldn't believe her good luck. A room of her own in a safe place. But after a moment, she wondered if this was good news, after all. What if she was alone there some night, and Max came upstairs? Did he have a key because he's the landlord?

"That's so kind of you," Ada said. "Are you always home, or would I be all alone upstairs sometimes?"

"Joe and I are almost always home."

"And if they go out, you can come down here," Clara said.

"Be sure to lock the kitchen door whenever you come and go," Sylvia said. "And part of the bargain is that you are the only one who can use the room. Except for Douglas, of course, whenever he's off. Nobody else can come upstairs. Do you understand?"

"I do. And I'd not forget to lock up behind me."

"You might hear Joe in the kitchen at night. He's a light sleeper and often makes himself a nighttime snack. I hope that won't bother your sleep."

Joe. Is he really as dangerous as Max said? Ada decided to delay her decision. "I'm sure I wouldn't be disturbed by Joe in the kitchen at night, but before I accept your kind offer, I think I should discuss it with Douglas."

Sylvia and Clara agreed and encouraged her to take whatever time she needed to decide.

As she fell asleep that night, Ada wondered how much Clara knew. She must know Max was in my room, but does she think I encouraged him? Does she think he got what he wanted? That was too horrible a thought to consider. Ada also wondered what Clara had told Sylvia and what Sylvia would tell Joe. She hated the idea of all these people talking about her.

When Ada told Douglas about the new sleeping arrangements, he thought it was a wonderful idea. "You'll be so much more comfortable, and it will be better for everybody," he said. "It's kind of Sylvia to make the offer, and you should accept right away."

There was no way for Ada to bring up her worries about Joe, so she kept them to herself, and the next evening, she moved her things to Sylvia's guest room. Harold and Ira carried her trunk up the back stairs, Ira laughing and Harold grumbling all the way. Lillian was thrilled to have a room with an extra bed and was already planning her first slumber party.

Ada loved her large, sunny bedroom. She hung most of her clothes and Douglas's clothes in the closet. Then she carefully unpacked the wedding gifts she had received from her family and friends. She placed the two beautiful porcelain figures her mother had given her, one dressed in pink and the other in blue, on either side of the dresser mirror. They look like Marie Antoinette must have looked, she thought, elegant and proud in her finery with her curls piled on top of her head in order to show off her long, graceful neck.

A delicate Wedgewood bowl that had been a gift from Rose and the fancy bottle of perfume her friends presented to her on the day she left Edinburgh stood between the porcelain princesses. Ada stepped back to admire the arrangement before she pushed her trunk to the back of the closet.

The peace and quiet of her new bedroom soothed Ada. She could write letters at the little desk and sit in the big chair to read. And if she felt a little sad or lonely, she could cry in private, without fear of being observed.

THE NEXT FRIDAY, ADA DARED A TRIP TO THE LIBRARY AND found Max waiting for her outside the store.

"Don't talk to me, Max."

"You know you don't mean that," Max said as he walked next to her.

"I do, and nothing you say will change my mind."

"Nothing you say will change my mind, either. If I was over the line, I apologize, and it will never happen again." Max tried to take her books, but Ada snatched them away and would not let him take her arm.

"C'mon, Ada. Don't be like that. You know we have a good time together, and I know you've never told anybody what a good time we have. There must be a reason why you keep our little meetings a secret. Have you thought about that?"

Ada frowned and walked more quickly. You know why I can't say anything as well as I do, she thought. Douglas would blame you if he knew, not that you would care. But he'd blame me, too, and I couldn't stand that.

They walked a block in silence before Max continued. "By the way, how do you like having your own room upstairs?"

Ada hadn't seen him at home and wondered how he knew that she had moved upstairs. Max must have read the dismay on her face.

"Surprised I know about that, aren't you? Did you know that Sylvia is getting a little break on the rent for having you as a more or less permanent guest?"

Ada didn't know about the rent arrangement, but she didn't tell Max that. He insisted on walking with her all the way to the library where, with a wave of his hand and a promise to see her again the next week, he left her at the main entrance.

Max continued to meet Ada at the store and walk her to the library every week. Even if she went to the library on a day other than Friday, he was always standing on the sidewalk waiting for her.

"I'm a patient man, Ada," he assured her. "I've already apologized, and now I'll give you all the time you need to get over your bad mood."

Ada didn't speak to him, but she didn't know how to stop him from walking with her. She couldn't risk making him angry because then he might tell everybody about their lunches and accuse her of enticing him to her bed. Even if he was not believed, it would be clear that she had kept secrets. Douglas might never forgive her.

ONE NIGHT, ADA WAS AWAKENED BY THE SOUND OF LITTLE stones tapping on her window. She crept out of bed and peeked through the curtains. The person standing on the lawn below waved. It was Max.

Ada hurried back to bed. Minutes later, she heard soft knocking on Sylvia's kitchen door. When she didn't respond, the knocking grew louder. Ada sat up. I have to make him go away. What if he wakes Sylvia? What if he tells her that I met him for lunch? Or that he was in my room at night?

The knocking grew more insistent. Ada wrapped her robe around her shoulders and pushed her feet into her slippers. I'll whisper through the door that he has to leave. I'll tell him Sylvia doesn't let anybody come upstairs but me.

Suddenly, heavy footsteps crossed the kitchen, and Ada heard the kitchen door pulled open. Then two sets of loud footsteps hurried downstairs and out the back door. Ada looked out the window and saw Max and Joe in the yard. Joe was doing all the talking and a little bit of pushing.

Ada didn't see Max on the sidewalk outside the store again, and nobody seemed worried by his absence from home.

One Sunday morning several weeks later, Ada slipped her bathrobe over her nightie and tied it carefully around her waist. She gathered her toiletries, including her new fragrant shampoo, and peeked into Sylvia's kitchen to make sure the coast was clear. Then she quickly made her way down the stairs to Clara's back door. Douglas was expected home in the early afternoon, and she wanted to greet him looking pretty and smelling nice. Now that she slept upstairs and had more privacy and time to herself, Ada was more relaxed and ready to acknowledge the difficulties of his exhausting life at the hospital. As she became more understanding and forgiving of his moods, he grew more thoughtful and forgiving of hers.

The Thursday night before, Douglas had arrived in her room with a bunch of tiny blue flowers. The bouquet still stood in a vase on her dresser next to the porcelain princess in the blue dress. "Next time I'll bring flowers for the princess in pink," he had promised.

As she came down the stairs, Ada heard Lillian's angry voice.

"You said he would be back soon."

"I said I wasn't sure when he would be back," Clara answered. "I know you miss him, and he misses you, too."

"He was teaching me to play cards. Who's going to teach me now?"

"I'll teach you."

"You play ladies' games. You can't play pinochle."

Clara laughed. "Of course I can. Get the cards."

Ada came into the kitchen to find Lillian sitting at the table dealing out two hands from a deck of cards while Clara slid pans of chicken into the oven.

"Good morning," Clara said. "Do you have time for some early morning pinochle?"

"I've only just learned," Ada said.

"We'll help you. Deal Ada in, Lillian."

Lillian hesitated and then gathered up the cards on the table and dealt three hands.

Clara won the first game. Lillian won the second, and Ada acquitted herself well for a beginner. After Clara won the third game, Ada excused herself to take her bath, and Lillian put the cards back in their box.

Over the running water, Ada heard Clara say, "See, Lillian. We'll be okay."

"Just us by ourselves?"

"Just us. Because that's the kind of women we are, Lillian. We're Kessler women, the kind that will be okay. And Ada, too."

"She's a Kessler woman?"

"That's right."

"Because Douglas married her?"

"I think she was always a Kessler woman."

Ada adjusted the water for her bath and wondered if her mother would be proud to hear she had raised a Kessler woman. She's probably a Kessler woman herself, Ada thought, and Rose, too.

# Emma Finds Love

*1940*

Ada didn't know what to do with herself. A cup of tea sat cooling on the kitchen table next to a sheet of light blue airmail paper while she gazed out the window, her chin resting in her hand, her mother's letter in her lap, and her thoughts far away.

When she was little and her mother said, "You're just like me," or "The apple doesn't fall far from the tree," Ada would cringe and conjure up apples that could fly away into the big, blue sky and never fall anywhere near the tree. She imagined their little golden wings beating against the breeze as they made their escape. Sometimes they traveled in groups, a whole pound of apples rising off the branches at once, but other times, one little apple lifted off alone in the night, careful not to ruffle the leaves and alert the tree.

Ada had thought that moving an ocean away would put her beyond her mother's reach, but now she wondered. As usual, her mother's latest letter was full of news about the Nazi madman in Germany and her mother's fear that German troops would attack Scotland someday soon. But in this letter, Bess also wrote that she had taken in a new boarder whose husband was at the front and Rose had dug up all the flowers Ada had planted because now everybody was part of the Grow More Food campaign and raised vegetables instead. She described the fun she and Rose had making a scarecrow and dressing him up in old clothes to scare away the birds since, although she knew how much Ada loved birds, vegetables were too precious to risk. Ada could imagine the mass of beet greens, carrot tops, and squash vines that had replaced her lovely flowers.

For the first time, the war sounded like an adventure her mother and her sister were sharing, and though her mother never stopped saying she was grateful that Ada was safe, Ada was beginning to think that safety was overrated. Not that she wanted to be under her mother's thumb again, and not that she didn't love Douglas.

Her tea was cold by the time Ada turned back to her task and began her response to her mother's letter. She wrote that the weather was still warm, but the forecast was for another snowy winter. Then she went on to describe the new drapes she ordered for the living room and the new set of guest towels she bought for the downstairs bathroom, and Douglas's delight with the chicken potpie she made for dinner on Friday night. She didn't say that between visiting his patients in the hospital and seeing them in his office, Douglas was home for dinner only on the weekends. Unless there was a baby to deliver. Then he wasn't home at all.

At the end of the letter, she wrote that although she lost the baby, her doctor told her not to worry. Even miscarrying twice was no reason for alarm, especially since both miscarriages occurred so early in the pregnancies. She emphasized how well she felt and her confidence that she and Douglas would be proud parents soon. Ada closed with love to her sister, Rose, and best wishes for the continued success of the shop. Then she wondered how to fill the rest of the day.

Ada hadn't worked since Douglas opened his office. He said it wouldn't do to have his wife selling dresses in a downtown department store now that he was a doctor. Also, they believed that a baby would soon fill her days. But without the anticipated baby, Ada had more time on her hands and less company than she needed. Edith, a friend she met for lunch every so often, was too busy with her own new baby to find time for even a quick cup of coffee, and her weekly teas with Sylvia, her mother-in-law's tenant, had come to an end when Sylvia and her husband were forced to move. Now Harold, Douglas's younger brother, and his wife, Fay, lived in the upstairs apartment, and Ada couldn't imagine tea with Fay.

Douglas's mother, Clara, always welcomed her visits, but Ada didn't like to go there. From early morning to late at night, Clara's kitchen brimmed over with aunts and cousins and in-laws of aunts and cousins, drinking coffee, playing cards, and gossiping. The abundance of Douglas's relatives was still overwhelming, and Ada had never become comfortable with their nosiness, crude humor, and loud voices while they wondered where Thelma's daughter got the money for her expensive clothes, why Minnie didn't put her foot down and stop having children already, or when Ann would finally marry off her son, Nathan, who must be forty if he's a day.

All the gossip swirling around Clara's kitchen was the reason nobody in Douglas's family had been told about the miscarriages. Ada hoped they never learned anything at all about her. She hated the thought of them picking over what she spent on her new drapes or wondering why she didn't shop for discount towels at the five-and-dime like they did. So what if she liked nice things? She was married to a doctor and didn't need to shop at Woolworth's. Still, she was certain that they talked about her when she wasn't at the table since being at the table hadn't protected her from their prying. She'd already been asked what she did with herself all day long and when she was going to make Douglas a father.

A trip to visit Clara also included hearing Fay's latest stories about her pregnancy and invitations to feel the baby move. During her last visit, Ada had been ignored while the conversation centered on Fay and speculation about what Clara's first grandchild would be named. It was more than Ada could bear.

I can't go back to Clara's again so soon, she thought. The weather is lovely and I haven't been downtown in a good while, so this is the perfect day to shop. I'll see if Emma has a cardigan to match my new skirt, and I'll ask if she can come to lunch with me.

Emma had been the assistant manager in the better dresses department when Ada worked there. Now she was the manager and still unmarried. Ada thought she knew why. Emma was a tiny woman with brown eyes, a large nose, and a wide mouth filled with long teeth angled this way and that. Her hair, already graying, was cut short and pushed back from her face. The first day Ada had reported for work, Emma wore a pale gray linen skirt and a matching cashmere cardigan with pearl buttons and a soft collar. A green silk scarf was tied at her neck. Among the other salesladies in simple navy blue dresses, Emma stood out. Of course, everything she wore could be purchased in the store and that was, in fact, the way she made many of her most lucrative sales. Ada admired Emma for always looking good, even though she couldn't be called good-looking.

Emma had appreciated Ada's sales skills, and Ada had appreciated working for such an amiable boss. Their relationship became a friendship when they discovered that they were both avid readers who liked to talk about what they were reading. Discussing books with Emma was a highlight of Ada's lunches with her. Recently, they had had a spirited discussion about *So Big* by Edna Ferber, Emma's favorite author, and had disagreed about whether it ranked with *The Grapes of Wrath*, which had just won the Pulitzer Prize. Lately, Emma had extolled a new novel by Hemingway, but Ada resisted reading it because she wasn't sure he was a nice man.

Ada washed and dried her teacup and returned it to the shelf. She thought about how different her clean, quiet kitchen was from Clara's noisy kitchen. One thought led to another until the chatter about Aunt Ann's son collided with the fact that Emma was still unmarried, and Ada realized they were perfect for each other. Emma will be so grateful if I find her a husband and make her life complete, she thought, and the family will be amazed and thrilled if I find a wife for Nathan. It's a wonder I didn't think of this before.

Ada dressed quickly and called Aunt Ann to make sure that Nathan was interested in meeting someone. Aunt Ann seemed surprised to hear from her but was delighted when Ada explained the reason for her call.

"Of course Nathan is looking to get married, and he'll meet anybody you suggest," Aunt Ann said. "Be sure the girl knows he makes good money and he's a nice man. He's not holding out for a raving beauty, just a girl with a good heart."

Ada was glad to hear that Nathan wasn't holding out for a raving beauty, since he was no beauty himself. But he was a quiet, respectful man, and Ada had enjoyed several pleasant conversations with him at family events. She was confident that he was the sort of man Emma would like.

"I have to check with the lady I have in mind to be certain she also wants to meet someone. So please don't say anything to anyone until I find out if she's available. I'll call you back when I know," Ada said. It was customary to keep dating arrangements quiet until the couple had met once and had decided to meet again. After that, it was up to the couple to make whatever they wanted public. Still, Ada was relieved when Aunt Ann agreed to say nothing for the time being, although Ada didn't know how long such a promise would last in Clara's kitchen.

ADA REACHED THE STORE A LITTLE BEFORE NOON AND HURried to Emma's office. "I'm glad to have caught you before you went out," she said. "I need a new cardigan in a rosy color, and I'm hoping we can have lunch together. There's something I'd like to talk to you about."

"Ada, I'm delighted to see you. I have the perfect cardigan, and I would love to have lunch, but I'm not taking lunch today. Wait right here, and I'll bring something from the back for you to look at." Emma hurried through a curtain leading to the storeroom where one-of-a-kind garments shown to favored customers were kept. She returned with a cashmere cardigan in a pale pink and a mohair cardigan in a deep rose.

"These would suit you," Emma said and draped them gracefully on the counter.

Ada chose the mohair cardigan, and as she was paying for it, Emma said, "I'm sorry about lunch today. It was good idea, and I have a good idea in return. Are you busy for dinner?" Ada looked at her in surprise, and Emma continued, "You told me that your husband isn't home for dinner some evenings. If this is one of them, would you like to come home with me? My mother and my sister would love to meet you, and you can help us celebrate Bernice's promotion."

Ada was tempted. Douglas wouldn't be home until nearly ten o'clock, and she would be happier eating with Emma's family than eating alone.

"Are you sure your family won't mind?"

"It won't be any problem at all. Mother and Bernice will be delighted."

Ada smiled. "In that case, it's kind of you to invite me, and I accept."

They agreed to meet at the bus stop a little before four o'clock and Ada hurried off, pleased to have somewhere to go for dinner. After a quick sandwich, she wandered through several stores, bought herself a new winter scarf, and chose a box of chocolates for Emma's mother. When she arrived at the bus stop, Emma was already there holding a large bouquet. Ada was glad she had chosen chocolates instead of flowers.

During the bus ride, Ada talked about how proud she was of Douglas, and how exciting it was to have her own kitchen to cook in and her own home to decorate. She noticed that Emma listened attentively, and decided to bring up Nathan at dinner, though she was a little worried about Bernice, Emma's older sister. Since Emma was probably in her late thirties and nearly as old as Nathan, Bernice was certainly too old for him. Still, Bernice was the older daughter, so Nathan should be offered to her first.

When Emma opened the front door of her house, Ada was greeted by the aromas of fresh bread and roasting chicken. "Hi, Mama," Emma called out. "Ada and I are here. How can we help?"

As they came into the kitchen, Ada saw a large pot of soup simmering on the stove and a pile of neatly diced vegetables waiting on the cutting board. Fresh rolls cooled on the kitchen table alongside two pies, one cherry and one apple. Emma's mother, Charlotte, stood at the stove.

"Emma, you're home early, and Ada, how nice of you to join us. Emma has told us a lot about you, and I've always wanted to meet the Scottish lass who was such a good saleslady."

Charlotte wiped her hands on her apron to receive the chocolates that Ada gave her. "You didn't need to bring anything, but I must say they look wonderful. Thank you. And thanks for offering to help. The two of you can set the table."

Emma led the way to the dining room. She gave Ada a white linen tablecloth, and while Ada covered the table, Emma took the cut-crystal vase from the mantlepiece, filled it with water, and carefully arranged the flowers she had bought. All the blossoms were yellow or white, and their abundance burst from the vase in a luxurious display.

It didn't take long to set the table for four. When Ada and Emma returned to the kitchen, Charlotte was putting the last touches on the meal. Ada looked around and approved of the well-organized dinner preparations as much as she appreciated the elegance of the table in the dining room. If Bernice was like her mother, she would be a wonderful wife for Nathan.

Soon after Charlotte went upstairs to change, Bernice appeared, calling out "I'm home!" She came into the living room busily smoothing her skirt and tidying her hair. Ada thought she looked like a tall version of Emma.

"This is Ada who worked with me some time ago," Emma said by way of introduction.

"Ada! How nice to meet you. We used to hear about your prowess as a saleslady, and now we hear about your visits with Emma at the store. You must be the reason we're eating in the dining room tonight."

"Bernice, don't be silly," Emma said. "You know why we're eating in the dining room. Ada is here to help celebrate your promotion. You know Mom. Any excuse for a party, and your promotion is a good one."

Dinner was more elaborate than any Ada had experienced before, even in her mother's house. She appreciated the fine cooking but was most impressed by the sprinkling of cilantro floating on each bowl of soup and the braided parsley garnish lining the platter of chicken delicately topped with a ginger sauce.

A lively conversation began as soon as everybody was seated. Bernice enumerated her new obligations at the office. "I'll make appointments for the salesmen, manage the payroll, and supervise the office staff. I don't usually have any problem telling people what to do," she said, and laughed as she added, "but Emma is going to teach me to tell them in the right way."

Ada agreed that Emma would be the perfect mentor, and Emma agreed that, as the little sister, she could attest to Bernice's talent for telling people what to do.

Emma shared stories of her week at the store and the stylish winter items that had come in. There were women in town who never bought anything unless she was there to give her approval, and she had had a busy week helping them choose new outfits.

Ada was pleased to be privy to all this shoptalk. Douglas always refused to discuss his work, sighing and reiterating the importance of patient confidentiality whenever she asked. While Ada had to admit that confidentiality was important, his secrecy made her feel excluded, like a child who could not be trusted with stories about adult life. Now here were these busy women, older than she was, talking about the business world and interested in her reactions.

"Tell us about Scotland. How did you become such a good saleslady, and where did you meet Douglas?" Charlotte asked.

So Ada told them about her mother and her sister, Rose, and their shop, and how Douglas had come to Edinburgh for medical school, boarded with her family, and taken the younger daughter home with him as his wife. She loved Douglas all the more as she told them how much she loved him. They had many questions, and Ada enjoyed the attention. It was lovely to hold their interest and hear her own life sound so complete and purposeful.

The conversation returned, at last, to the reason for the special dinner. "How shall we celebrate your promotion, Bernice?" Emma asked and then answered her own question. "Let's go to New York next month. We could visit the museums and go to the opera. Maybe even see a play. Would you like that?"

Bernice said she would and turned to Ada. "Would you like to join us?"

"I can't," Ada answered. She knew Douglas wouldn't let her run off to New York with two old maids. And she would miss him too much to have a good time, anyway.

After the dinner dishes were cleared and pie and tea served, Ada felt so much at home that, before she had actually made a decision, she found herself saying, "Bernice, I know of a man you might like to meet."

Bernice looked up. For a moment she seemed puzzled, and then both annoyed and amused.

"His name is Nathan Gleason," Ada continued, "and he's a salesman for a big machinery company with headquarters in Detroit. He's been with them for more than fifteen years, and now he's the Eastern Seaboard regional manager. It's a big job, and I'm sure he makes good money." In spite of the chilly silence, Ada rushed on. "He's very nice, but he travels so much he never married. He's Douglas's cousin, and I could find out more about him if you want."

Bernice didn't respond. She was either searching for the right words or had decided not to answer at all. After a long pause, Charlotte said, "That's something to consider, Ada. We'll think about it and let you know."

The awkward moment passed, and the conversation turned to other topics as everybody helped wash and dry the dishes, and return the dining room to its usual appearance, except for the flowers in the center of the table.

Charlotte smiled when Ada gave each of the women a little hug and said, "Thanks for this delicious dinner. Maybe one evening you can come to my house."

Emma walked with Ada to the bus stop and waited with her until the bus came.

"I hope I didn't insult Bernice when I mentioned Nathan," Ada said.

"Don't worry about it. Bernice can be a little prickly."

"He's a nice man. If she doesn't want to meet him, maybe you would like to."

Before Emma could answer, the bus pulled up, and Ada got on. She waved to Emma and settled back for the ride home. Since she hadn't planned to be away so long, Ada hadn't left a light on in the living room like she usually did when she and Douglas went out in the evening. Now she would be letting herself into a dark house. That made her uncomfortable, but she was glad she would arrive home first so Douglas would have no reason to wonder where she was and worry.

EMMA WAVED TO ADA AND WALKED HOME. SHE HAD BEEN as surprised as Bernice when Ada mentioned Nathan. It had been a long time since anybody had tried to play matchmaker for either of them.

At one time, Emma had hoped to marry, but her encounters with men suggested by well-meaning aunts had never come to anything more than a pleasant evening or two. Though there had also been a few unpleasant evenings. Emma chuckled as she recalled the young man who had told her she had too many big ideas for such a short woman. Now marriage seemed very much beside the point. I'm like Edna Ferber, she thought. I believe that I lead a rich and dramatic life, though I may be the only person who thinks so.

As Emma came through the front door, she could hear Charlotte and Bernice in the midst of a conversation.

"Don't judge her harshly, Bernice. She means well."

"Ada is a meddler who doesn't understand that I like my life the way it is. I'm not lacking anything. I'm not interested in marriage, and I'm not going to meet a salesman named Nathan."

"I know. But sleep on it before you make a decision."

"I don't need to sleep on it. I'm not going to meet him." Bernice paused and, as Emma joined them in the living room, added, "I think Emma should meet him."

Emma was surprised at hearing this suggestion for the second time, and even more surprised by her lack of response. Why didn't she refuse immediately?

"We'll talk in the morning," Charlotte said, and went upstairs. Bernice followed.

Emma went to the kitchen for a drink of water. After washing and drying her glass, she folded the dish towel, and turned to hang it on the rack. That's when she noticed the juice glass on the ledge at the back of the stove. It had a golden, sticky residue in the bottom, and, as Emma raised the glass to her nose, a rich, pungent fragrance rose to greet her. It was so distinct and smokey that Emma could almost taste it, smooth in her mouth, fiery in her throat, and warm all the way down. It smelled like the kiss her father gave her at bedtime when she was a little girl.

Emma knew who had used this juice glass. Perhaps this was the way her mother brought him back and made him part of festive dinners like the one tonight. Perhaps keeping him here made each day complete. Her mother often told the story of the evening he came to pick her up for their first date and waited in the foyer. As she came down the stairs, he turned to her, and when she saw his face, her heart leaped up.

"Really, it did," she always insisted when, as children, Emma and Bernice looked at her in disbelief. "When I saw his face, I knew it was the face I wanted to see every day for the rest of my life."

Maybe sipping his favorite Scotch recaptures that moment, Emma thought, and her heart leaps up again.

Upstairs in her bedroom, Emma closed the door and sat on the edge of the bed. The bigger bedroom was Bernice's, as befitted the rights of the older daughter, but Emma had never minded having the smaller room. It was cozy and easily held her bed, a dresser, a small writing desk, a comfy chair, and a tall lamp. Recently, she had added a painting by Lee Brown Coye she found in a downtown gallery. She loved the evening scene with its deep reds and browns and pale crescent moon low in the gray sky. It was a restful painting that matched her mood most nights. But not tonight.

Ada's suggestion of a man for Bernice could be seen as youthful good spirits and a wish to make everyone as happy as she is. Bernice's rejection of the idea was predictable. But the suggestion that she meet Nathan had caught Emma by surprise, and her indecisiveness confused her. She no longer knew if she was genuinely content or merely complacent.

Breakfast was Emma's job. Charlotte volunteered at their neighborhood elementary school and had to be there by eight thirty, and Bernice liked to get to her office by eight o'clock. Emma wasn't expected at the store until nine o'clock, so she let them dress first while she slipped on her robe and slippers and went downstairs to set the kitchen table for three and put out cereal, fruit, muffins, and jam.

This morning, as they ate, it was as if Nathan himself sat at the table with them. Emma put a blueberry muffin on her plate and then replaced it with a bran muffin and a scoop of jam. She poured herself a cup of coffee.

Bernice spoke first. "Emma, I'm sorry I said you should meet Nathan. It wasn't fair of me to push the problem onto you. I'm not going to meet him, but that doesn't mean that you should." She spoke decisively with the calm of someone who knows her own mind.

Emma wished that she felt calm and decisive. Why couldn't she either dismiss the idea of meeting Nathan or feel some enthusiasm for it?

"I'm not sure how I feel about meeting him," she finally admitted.

Her mother and Bernice looked at her and then at each other. After a long silence, Charlotte said, "Think it over. If you aren't sure, it's probably a good idea to meet him. You don't want to miss the opportunity and regret it later."

The bus ride to the store did not provide Emma with a decision. She knew that, at her age, agreeing to meet Nathan meant agreeing to consider marriage. They weren't children and this would not be a fling. Emma frowned. I can't make such a serious decision at work, so I won't think about it now. Her excellent resolution led to a day of trying not to think about Nathan. The hours passed slowly until planning displays for the two windows at the main doors of the store provided a welcome diversion.

By the evening, Emma hadn't so much decided to meet Nathan as she had decided not to say no. She called Ada and told her that Bernice did not want to meet Nathan, but that she was willing to meet him if Ada thought he would like to meet her.

Whatever Emma's decision might have lacked in enthusiasm was more than made up for by Ada's reaction. She was delighted that everything was working out as she had hoped and called Aunt Ann immediately to tell her the good news.

Aunt Ann was equally thrilled. "I'm a happy woman tonight, Ada. You're doing a wonderful thing to help Nathan this way. We're all lucky Douglas brought a girl like you into the family."

"I'm happy to help, Aunt Ann. But remember, don't tell anybody what we're doing." Aunt Ann agreed, and Ada called Emma.

"Nathan would love to meet you, Emma, and he's very pleased that you are willing to meet him. Would you like him to come to your house or meet you someplace else?"

Emma suggested that Nathan pick her up after work on Tuesday for dinner. Ada called Aunt Ann and then Emma again to confirm that he would be outside the store at the Salina Street entrance at six o'clock. Ada said he was tall and that he would be wearing a blue suit and a red tie with a pattern. Emma said she would wear her green coat and scarf.

No sooner had Ada hung up, than her phone rang. It was Aunt Ann.

"So what did she say?" Aunt Ann demanded.

"She said she's glad to be meeting Nathan, and she'll be wearing a green coat and scarf."

"What else? She must have said something else."

Ada had also expected something more from Emma. Even "glad" overstated Emma's willingness to meet Nathan, but Ada didn't tell Aunt Ann that.

"I think we should let them get to know each other. Emma doesn't know much about Nathan, except that he's Douglas's cousin and he has a good job. And you know that Emma is my friend, even though she's older than I am, and she works downtown."

"So what does she look like, and what does her father do?"

"Aunt Ann, I don't mean to be rude, but since they didn't need to know more about each other before they agreed to meet, I don't think any of us needs more information right now, either."

"All right. But I wish I knew more. A meeting is one thing, but then it has to work out."

"Let's not get ahead of ourselves," Ada said, as much to calm herself as to calm Aunt Ann.

Aunt Ann sighed. "Nobody tells me anything, but I see you can't get blood from a stone."

"It's not that I'm trying to keep anything from you, but we need to be patient. And quiet. Remember, we aren't saying anything to anybody yet."

"I remember. You're a good girl, Ada."

It didn't take five minutes for Ada's phone to ring again. This time it was her mother-in-law.

"Ada, darling, it's a wonderful thing you are doing for Aunt Ann."

"Did Aunt Ann call you? She said she wouldn't tell anybody."

"Of course she called me. I'm her sister."

"But they haven't met yet. They might not like each other."

"Why wouldn't they like each other? You say she's a nice lady, and we all know that Nathan's a nice man. They want to get married, so why not to each other?"

"Let's wait to see what happens."

"So far, it's good. And we owe it to you, Ada. I'm so proud of you."

Ada was annoyed that her experiment in matchmaking had not been kept secret. Too much was at stake for Nathan and Emma and for Ada herself to let it play out in public. Too much could go wrong. In particular, Clara's comment that they both want to get married troubled Ada. She hadn't thought about that before, but she gave the matter some thought now. Emma must know that there's nothing better than a husband and children, Ada reassured herself. Even her important job and enough money to dress well and go to New York for the opera can't make up for the lack of a husband. So why isn't she, at least, a little unhappy? Ada searched for an answer. Maybe she's putting on a brave front. That must be it. Nobody wants to grow old as a spinster. Of course, she wants to marry.

The phone kept ringing, and before the evening was over, Aunt Ann's other three sisters and two of her nieces had called to tell Ada she was a wonderful woman and the family was forever grateful that she had found Nathan a bride. Eventually, Ada gave up trying to correct them and allowed herself to be swept into the bosom of the family.

On Tuesday, Emma chose to dress in a stylish but modest blue suit. She liked its sleek lines and the subtle pattern in the weave of the fabric. After some deliberation, she pinned a silver flower on the lapel. Her white silk blouse with ruffles at the neck and cuffs softened the line of the suit jacket, and her navy blue pumps added a tiny bit of stature. "That's as good as it gets," she told her reflection in the mirror, and left for work.

The day dragged on, and Emma was relieved when six o'clock came and she made her way to the Salina Street exit. A tall man in a blue suit waited there, and he smiled when he saw her. She thought he looked pleasant and friendly.

"Emma," he said, "I'm pleased to meet you."

Emma relaxed. She liked the sound of his voice and his calm, relaxed manner. "I'm glad to meet you, too," she answered.

They went to dinner at a small restaurant near the store. Nathan told her about his work and the large machinery he sold up and down the coast, and Emma told him about the sales staff she supervised and the window displays she designed. He spoke of his two nephews and the funny things they did. He had taken the older one to a baseball game recently. She talked about her upcoming trip to New York with her sister. They agreed that Ada was well-meaning, if a little irrepressible.

When Emma returned home, her mother and her sister were too polite to demand a full report. But she wasn't in the house more than ten minutes before the phone rang. Ada had no reticence about asking. She wanted to know all about the evening and if Emma wanted to see him again. Emma said he seemed like a pleasant man and agreed to another date. Ada said that she would tell Nathan he could call.

And so Emma and Nathan began to see each other, and after each date, Emma wondered if they should continue and each time could see no reason not to. They went to the movies and saw the new Kirk Douglas film; they went to a baseball game, and Emma found it more interesting than she thought she would; they visited an art gallery and ate at a new restaurant. They even went to see *Pinocchio* after Nathan had taken his nephews to see it and had decided that it was more than a children's movie, that it was destined to become a great classic. Afterward, they couldn't agree about the benefits of having a Jiminy Cricket following them around, but they concurred that they would enjoy being somebody else's cricket.

Emma was comfortable with Nathan, and he fit nicely into the family. Charlotte and Bernice both liked him, and he was relaxed in their house. If we marry, she thought, I'm sure we'll spend time with my family. It isn't as if I'll never see them. Still, after every date, no matter how pleasant, she looked forward to tea with her mother and Bernice and the quiet of her own room. Emma wondered what would become of this adventure. Ada was already asking if they were "serious." Emma didn't feel serious. She felt confused. If I'm going to change my life, I ought to be sure I'm doing the right thing, she thought. There ought to be a sign.

The first time she visited Clara after Emma started dating Nathan, Ada was received like a hero. "Here's the one who found a girl for my Nathan," Aunt Ann announced, and everybody oohed and aahed and asked for details. Ada was the belle of the ball for weeks, and Fay, growing ever greater with child, no longer held the spotlight if Ada was in the room.

Ada went to the store every week to have tea or lunch with Emma, but the numerous hints she dropped and questions she asked were either ignored or met with a reminder that Emma preferred not to discuss Nathan with Ada.

"It's not that I don't recognize the role you played in my meeting Nathan, but I can't be reporting to you," Emma explained one day as she attached price tags to a stack of new blouses. "It's just that I'm too old to share little secrets with my girlfriends. Let's agree not to talk about Nathan."

It was frustrating for Ada to have no news to share with the aunts and the cousins around Clara's kitchen table. She knew only what Aunt Ann reported: that Nathan and Emma were still dating, that Nathan had talked about marriage and was ready to propose, but that Emma was undecided.

"I don't understand your friend," Aunt Ann said one afternoon. "It's not like my Nathan isn't a good man. So what's her problem?"

"What's there to be undecided about?" Aunt Minnie asked.

Her daughter-in-law, Tessie, nodded in agreement and added, "That's what I'd like to know, too."

"And how come you don't know what she's thinking?" Aunt Florence said.

Ada had no answer and didn't like being challenged in front of everybody to provide one.

"Hush, Florence," Clara said.

"My friend Pearl would love him," Fay piped up. "She's not as old as Emma."

As the weeks went by, Fay added, "And Pearl's ready to get married."

Two weeks later, Ada was visiting her mother-in-law when Aunt Ann burst into Clara's house with big news. "Here's what a man my Nathan is. He's been promoted! He's going to be the director of farm machinery. In charge of everything. The man on top."

"Mazel tov!" Aunt Celia said, and the rest of the table sent up a chorus of congratulations.

Aunt Ann paused before she began to sob. "And for this, my boy has to move to Detroit. So far from home. He has to be there in three months." Aunt Ann looked at Ada. "If that friend of yours won't say yes, he'll have to go alone."

As soon as she got home, Ada called Emma only to find out that Emma knew all about it.

"What are you going to do?" Ada asked.

"Right now, I'm thinking."

Thinking? What is there to think about? Ada took a deep breath to prevent everything she wanted to say from finding expression, and said instead, "I know that moving to Detroit must seem like a huge step, but..."

Emma interrupted her. "Remember, Ada, we don't talk about Nathan. This is something I have to work out for myself."

Ada had no choice but to say, "I understand," and permit Emma to turn the conversation to other topics.

After that phone conversation, Ada decided not to visit Clara for a while.

THE FOLLOWING WEEK, EMMA AND ADA HAD DINNER downtown and then went to Emma's house for dessert. Emma let them in the front door and called out, "We're here."

Her mother and Bernice answered from the kitchen.

"We're in here having tea."

"I made a crumb cake. Come join us."

With Ada right behind her, Emma stopped at the doorway of the kitchen and saw her mother and her sister sitting at the table in a pool of light from the fixture above. Charlotte wore her fuzzy green bathrobe, and Bernice held Hemingway's new novel. They greeted her with smiles and eagerly described a dispute they were having about the book.

"Emma, I'm glad to see you," Bernice said. "You can cast the deciding vote. I say that Pablo was justified in protecting his family, and Robert was morally wrong to threaten them by his actions. What right did he have to meddle in their lives and destroy their sanctuary?"

"But I think Robert did have a moral right to complete his mission," Charlotte said, "and it was Pablo who was wrong to put his small group ahead of the greater good. What do you think?"

Emma couldn't focus on the question. It seemed to her that reality paused for a moment to give her the time she needed to study them, her mother and her sister, to hear their voices and to think. And suddenly she knew, more than that, she was certain, that these were the voices she wanted to hear and these were the faces she wanted to see every day for the rest of her life. And her heart leaped up.

ADA COULDN'T UNDERSTAND WHY EMMA SEEMED SO HAPPY that evening. Her family didn't solve the issue of Robert's culpability, and Emma maintained that that wasn't even the book's best example of Hemingway's genius.

"Did you notice that the first paragraph of the book starts with Robert lying on pine needles in the forest and in the last sentence of the book he feels his heart beat against the pine needles on the floor of the forest?" she asked. "It might look like nothing happened because he ends up in the same position, but that would be completely wrong. He might be in the same position, but everything has changed." She looked around for confirmation of her insight.

"You are exactly right," Bernice said. "Not to mention brilliant. For that you can have another piece of cake," and she served more cake to each of them.

Ada didn't understand the point of Emma's brilliant insight and decided it was because she hadn't read the book. Later, she also failed to understand why Emma stopped seeing Nathan.

"I gave her a chance, and she was too frightened to take it," she told Douglas.

"I guess she made a choice."

"Don't be daft, Douglas. Giving up Nathan was no choice at all. She gave up her last chance at love and marriage. She's a foolish woman who deserves to be an unhappy old maid."

"She doesn't sound unhappy to me," Douglas said. "Maybe her decision not to marry Nathan made her happy."

Ada tried to remember if there had been a moment when she made a decision about marriage. A decision implies a serious consideration of the alternatives, and she'd never done that. Of course, she hadn't. What woman could possibly be happier without a husband and children? Especially a husband as wonderful as Douglas who was handsome and a doctor and who loved her more than anything.

Ada decided that Emma was a fool destined for a bitter life. How sad there was only her mother and her sister to celebrate with her when she was promoted to assistant personnel manager and only her mother to welcome her home when she and Bernice returned from their vacation in the Canadian Rockies.

# A Woman with Ordinary Intelligence

*1943*

EVEN BEFORE THE TWINS WERE BORN, ADA KNEW SHE WAS the perfect mother. Dr. Dafoe spent the opening pages of chapter 1 warning young mothers to disregard the advice of other women and rely solely on their doctors, and Ada always relied solely on hers. She saw him regularly, took her vitamins daily, and spent most of the last three months of her pregnancy resting on the couch while imagining the sweet, smiling babies who would soon fill her days with love. She planned to cook and keep house while they napped so she could focus on them and their development when they were awake. Ada laughed when she found herself planning for their first birthday party and wondered if she wasn't getting a little ahead of herself. But in the next instant, she was thinking about the cheerful, obedient children they would become and saw them playing quietly at her feet in the evenings and asking her to cook their favorite dinner again the next day. She could hear their little friends telling them how lucky they were to have such a wonderful mother.

Ada's obedience to her doctor's orders was rewarded, and the day the twins were born was the happiest day of her life. Except for one tiny disappointment.

When her doctor announced that Baby A was a girl, Ada was thrilled. "That's Melissa," she said, and felt a surge of love for the crying infant she hadn't seen yet. Then she waited for the boy who would be named for her father. A few minutes later, Baby B arrived.

"Another girl," Dr. Atler called out. "Congratulations on your two fine daughters."

For a moment Ada thought there must be some mistake. As if to prompt her, a nurse said, "Do you have a name for this baby?"

"That's Margaret," Ada said.

From her position on the operating table, Ada saw the nurses hug Douglas and watched as they gave him little congratulatory kisses on the cheek. They had seen him suffer through the loss of two previous pregnancies, and each had thought it ironic that the newest obstetrician on staff should experience so much trouble having a child of his own. Now here were these two little girls, healthy and a good size for twins, to confirm his male status and his place among his peers. The delivery room sang with praises of the family and wonder at their great, good fortune, at last.

Douglas received their congratulations like a conquering hero. "I'll need a box of cigars with pink bands," he said. "And I'll have to give everybody two." Then he shook Dr. Atler's hand. "Thanks, Stan, for bringing my daughters safely into the world. I didn't have a moment's worry knowing you were in charge."

"Congratulations," Dr. Atler said. "You've made up for lost time by having two at once."

Douglas laughed, and the two doctors slapped each other on the back.

"You're the luckiest woman in the world," the nurses told Ada. "You have the most wonderful man we know for your husband, and now you have these beautiful twin daughters."

Their voices seemed to bounce off the shiny, silver surfaces, and Ada felt giddy as she laughed and agreed with them.

DOUGLAS DIDN'T HAVE LONG TO SPEND AT THE HOSPITAL before he had to rush off to buy furniture and clothing for the twins and arrange to have everything delivered before they came home from the hospital. Because of Ada's mother, nothing had been purchased before their birth.

Bess lived in Scotland and had had to content herself with sending long letters filled with advice during the pregnancy. Ada knew that Dr. Dafoe did not want her listening to anybody but her doctor, so she felt perfectly safe ignoring her mother until Bess warned against having anything in the house for the babies before they were born. Dr. Dafoe had no opinion about that, but Douglas had voiced his opinion as soon as he heard Bess's advice.

"I won't base my behavior on a silly superstition," he had said.

"It might sound silly, but there's no harm in it."

"It will make everything more hectic after the babies are born. We won't need anything more to think about then, so why not take care of their room now?"

Ada hadn't argued further, nor had she purchased anything. Why tempt fate?

Since her mother hadn't warned against selecting the furniture and clothing, Ada had chosen everything and had given Douglas a detailed list so he would have no difficulty buying the correct items. Before she left for the hospital, Ada taped a map and instructions on the door of the second bedroom, now to be known as the nursery, to show the deliverymen where to place the furniture, and Douglas and his mother, Clara, how to arrange the children's clothing in their new dressers.

After the nursery was ready for the twins, Douglas arranged to have the family's groceries delivered, and hired a girl to wash and boil the babies' diapers and do the laundry three times a week. He also called Miss Benowitz.

When Douglas had suggested hiring a retired maternity ward nurse to live in the house for the first six weeks the twins were home, Ada had insisted on interviewing his choice herself and quizzing her on her approach to the care of babies. Since Miss Benowitz wholeheartedly endorsed scientific child care, Ada convinced Douglas to hire her for twelve weeks. Now Douglas set up her cot in the nursery and set aside space for her belongings in the guest bedroom.

Meanwhile, Ada enjoyed her ten days in the hospital. Although Dr. Dafoe urged mothers to nurse their babies, Ada was relieved when Douglas insisted that nursing twins was out of the question. She protested a little, and then agreed with Douglas that bottle-feeding was best for Melissa and Margaret. Consequently, the babies were in the newborn nursery most of the day, and Ada saw them only if she asked that they be brought to her room. Of course she did not call for the babies when she had company because Dr. Dafoe clearly stated that company must not be allowed to intrude on the babies' routine. Too much company could result in nerve strain, he warned, and one out of eighteen children with nerve strain would spend time in an insane asylum.

So Ada sat in bed alone wearing the new housecoat Clara bought her for the occasion, and greeted her visitors. Clara came for a few minutes every day. She told Ada that the nursery furniture had been delivered and the little undershirts and dresses had all been washed and put away, and she listened to Ada's plans for training the twins to follow an approved schedule.

"Babies are a lot of work. You'll need to go easy on yourself," Clara cautioned one day.

"I know I'll be busy, but I'm not worried. I've only to be organized and think ahead and follow Dr. Dafoe's advice."

Members of Douglas's extended family called on her every afternoon. Aunts and uncles and cousins upon cousins Ada still had trouble keeping straight arrived with flowers for her and gifts for the babies. They stopped by the nursery first, peered at the twins through the window, and then came to her room to tell her how beautiful her daughters looked. Ada happily agreed.

"Two of them!" they exclaimed. "How will you manage?"

"I've been reading *Dr. Dafoe's Guidebook for Mothers*," Ada informed them and held up the book for all to see. "He's the doctor who took care of the Dionne quintuplets, so I'm sure his advice covers twins."

Douglas's brother Harold brought his wife to see the babies. "Oh, Ada, they are so sweet," she gushed. "You're going to be the best mother ever."

Ada smiled and nodded in humble acceptance of the compliment.

"But aren't you a little disappointed that one of them isn't a boy?"

"Don't be absurd," Ada answered. "Of course I'm not disappointed. Nothing could be more wonderful than two beautiful daughters."

Ada's friend Edith came and congratulated her with smiles and hugs. They had a lovely chat about the joys of motherhood and the fulfillment mothers feel as they watch their children grow.

Emma, Ada's former boss, also visited, bringing cookies and best wishes from her mother and her sister. "I baked cookies," she explained, "because my mother says it won't be easy to care for twins, and you have to be sure to care for yourself, as well, and give yourself treats."

"I'm relying on advice from Dr. Dafoe who looked after quintuples, and he says it's simply a matter of being efficient and focused on the welfare of the babies. You remember how I could deal with three demanding customers at once and keep them all happy. It can't be harder to take care of two little babies."

Ada was touched by Emma's thoughtfulness. Dr. Dafoe wrote that women who do not have children can become physically unwell or deranged. So far, Emma showed no signs of the pathological irritability he warned of, and Ada hoped that she would escape the consequences of her spinsterhood.

THE GREAT HOMECOMING ARRIVED AT LAST. AFTER THE babies were tucked safely in their new cribs, Ada unpacked her little suitcase and put her copy of *Dr. Dafoe's Guidebook for Mothers* back on the night table next to her side of the bed. The twins had been fed before leaving the hospital, and the house was quiet and orderly. Ada made a cup of coffee for Douglas and a cup of tea for herself and sat with him at the kitchen table.

"This is the schedule I made while I was in the hospital," she said and handed Douglas a neatly lettered outline of the daily plan for the care of the twins. Douglas read the first page and looked up.

"Is all this detail necessary, Ada?"

"The twins are not going to be raised helter-skelter, hit or miss. We are going to raise them scientifically. Dr. Dafoe says that we must be well-organized, and we will be."

"I can see that," Douglas said and made the mistake of laughing.

"I don't know what's so funny," Ada snapped, grabbing the papers away from him. "Good mothering is as complicated and difficult as good doctoring. I don't laugh at you."

Ada took a sip of tea and looked up to find Douglas quietly focused on her.

"Tell me what I need to know," he said.

"The babies are to be fed every four hours at the same times daily," she began, "and put back to bed immediately after they eat so they learn the routine. They are to drink their bottles in less than twenty minutes. If they haven't finished by then, we are to take the bottles away. That way they'll be hungrier and won't dawdle at the next meal. They are to be bathed at the same time every evening and put to bed right afterward. They are not to be rocked to sleep, and we are not to respond to temperamental demands for attention or they will never learn to fall asleep by themselves. We must never disturb their naps."

Ada paused while Douglas sipped his coffee and resumed when she saw him looking at her again. "The babies are to have their diapers changed frequently and all their bottles and utensils sterilized daily. Their room must be kept clean and well-ventilated, and they are to take their afternoon naps outdoors in their carriages unless it rains."

Ada consulted the outline in her lap and looked up to see that Douglas was still watching her intently. "Everyone who handles the babies must wash their hands first, and nobody is to kiss them. Even we are not to kiss their faces. They are to have a small number of toys so they don't become over-stimulated, and there is to be no play at all between the last feeding of the day and bed."

"Of course, we are to love them and cuddle them sometimes, but we need to be careful not to spoil them," Ada added. She smoothed her papers and put them on the table. "It's 1943, and modern mothers require up-to-date knowledge. We don't listen to old wives' tales or advice from family and friends. We rely on science."

Douglas nodded and sipped his coffee. Ada felt satisfied with herself and pleased that the volume of information and her authoritative delivery had left him at a loss for words.

"You're a smart woman, Ada," Douglas finally said. "And I can see that you intend to be a perfect mother. My daughters will be in the hands of a master."

A master. Ada nodded and smiled. She was delighted to have impressed Douglas and saw no reason to share Dr. Dafoe's assertion that any woman with ordinary intelligence can learn the scientific care of children. She didn't believe it herself. She knew it would take an extraordinary woman to raise children using his system, and she relished Douglas's acknowledgment of her expertise.

A thin cry rose from the nursery, and Ada checked her watch. It was an hour before feeding time. Why was a baby crying now? She couldn't be hungry this soon, and even if she was hungry, she had to wait. What if she cried for an hour? An hour of listening to a baby scream? And what if she wakes the other twin? Then we'll be listening to two of them cry for an hour.

Just as a second cry could be heard, there was a knock on the door. Douglas answered it, and, to Ada's secret relief, Miss Benowitz came into the kitchen followed by Douglas.

"No, you may not take my coat. I'm not here to be waited on. I'll say hello to the little mother and then hang it in the guest room." Miss Benowitz turned to Ada. "I'm glad to see you looking so well, Mrs. Kessler, and I'm happy to be here to help you and Dr. Kessler with your bundles of joy," she said and hurried up the stairs.

Douglas rolled his eyes and looked ready to laugh.

"Hush!" Ada warned him. "She might hear you, and we don't want to insult her. She's going to be a big help till I'm back on my feet."

Miss Benowitz reappeared moments later wearing sensible, white shoes, a crisp white uniform, and a pert white nurse's cap firmly attached to her gray hair with four long bobby pins. She washed her hands at the sink and asked Ada if she would like another cup of tea. "Margaret was fussing a bit, but she's off to sleep again, and I think we have a little while before we'll hear from either of them."

Ada relaxed, accepted another cup of tea, and thought how nice it was to have a competent professional in the house who knew how babies were to be handled.

Douglas excused himself, saying he had better be off to work, and left the two women sipping tea at the kitchen table. An hour later, they woke the twins, changed and fed them, and put them back in their cribs in keeping with the schedule taped on the refrigerator door. Of course I can do this, Ada thought, as each tiny bundle attested to her mother's competence by sleeping quietly in her crib.

No matter how early Ada came downstairs in the morning, Miss Benowitz was in the kitchen, dressed in a fresh uniform, having already brought the milk bottles in from the back stoop and thoroughly shaken them to mix in the cream as Dr. Dafoe instructed. Over the course of the first few weeks, she showed Ada how to draw the twins' bath in the kitchen sink, how to set out everything on the counter, and how to efficiently bathe the babies one at a time while the other one waited in her crib. Miss Benowitz approved of Dr. Dafoe's procedure for preparing the babies' bottles and showed Ada how to use the sterilizer and how to maintain the sterile field until the formula was in the bottles and they were safely sealed and refrigerated.

Ada was tired, but Miss Benowitz was so lavish in her praise of Ada's skill in following the schedule and caring for the twins that she wore her weariness as a badge of honor. The twins smiled and cooed now. They splashed in the bath, and even though she was soaked, Ada let them splash and cleaned up afterward because Dr. Dafoe said she should take pleasure in their playfulness.

On days when the laundry was done and Ada looked out the window to see the lines of sparkling white diapers and tiny nightgowns lifted by the breeze, she was sure that Dr. Dafoe would notice how diligently she took his advice and admire her as much as Miss Benowitz did. And she was confident he would be proud of her in the evening when the sweet-smelling babies were sleeping soundly on their fresh sheets in their clean cribs in the quiet house. It was her favorite time of the day.

Miss Benowitz always fixed herself an early dinner and retired to the guest bedroom for the evening before going to the nursery to sleep. Douglas was busier than ever at the office and gone all night when there was a baby to deliver, but he tried not to miss dinner. Ada looked forward to serving him a well-prepared meal as if to prove that she could mother twins and take care of him, too.

Once, when they heard a baby crying, Douglas left the dinner table and started for the nursery. Ada had to remind him that the twins had been put to bed for the night, and their crying must not become a form of tyranny.

"We don't want to disrupt their schedule or indulge their moods," she said. "The babies must always get themselves to sleep."

"But I never see them awake," Douglas protested.

"That will change when they are older. You need to be patient. Dr. Dafoe is very clear about the importance of keeping to their bedtime routine. We don't want two spoiled daughters because you can't follow the schedule." Ada felt on firm ground because indulgent fathers was one danger Dr. Dafoe warned about in the strongest terms. "But if you don't trust me, you can stay home and take over their care and do it your way," she added.

After that, Ada saw him consult the daily schedule before he left the house in the morning, and sometimes he reappeared at home when he knew the twins would be fed. When that happened, Ada let him feed one baby while she fed the other.

At first, Douglas's aunts and cousins stopped by, but when they realized that they couldn't see the twins if they were napping or pass the babies from hand to hand even if they were awake, the visits stopped. Even Clara knew better than to visit too often, but she did want to see her new granddaughters. So once a week, after she finished cooking for the deli, Clara bathed, dressed, and took the bus to Ada's house. Sometimes she brought a pound of pastrami or a roasted chicken, and sometimes she brought two little dresses or a stuffed animal.

"What do you need with all these rules?" Clara asked one afternoon. "Just feed them when they're hungry, put them in their cribs when they're sleepy, and hug and kiss them when they're awake. That's what I did, and my kids turned out fine."

"You did the best you knew at the time," Ada said. "But now we know better ways. Dr. Dafoe, the doctor for the Dionne quintuplets, wrote the book I'm using, and I'm following his scientific advice. This is the way we do it now."

Clara didn't raise any more questions and followed instructions whenever she was allowed to help with the babies. Ada took pity on her once when Clara visited only to find the twins sleeping for the second week in a row.

"It's weeks since I've seen them," Clara had said and sighed.

With her finger to her lips, Ada had led Clara to the nursery where they tiptoed in and stood watching the babies sleep. Ada could see that Clara was careful to be as quiet as possible.

Edith couldn't visit, of course, because Ada wouldn't permit her toddler in the house, but Emma came by occasionally and praised Ada's skills as a mother and extolled the babies' beautiful faces and dispositions. Sometimes she brought a pot of soup from her mother or a box of chocolates from her sister. Once she also brought a book.

"I haven't much time to read these days," Ada said when the book appeared.

"I'm sure you're busy, but everybody is raving about *A Tree Grows in Brooklyn*, and I thought you would like it."

After Emma left, Ada put *A Tree Grows in Brooklyn* under Dr. Dafoe's book on her night table.

"You haven't read the book, have you?" Emma asked on her next visit, and Ada admitted that she hadn't.

"All I read these days is Dr. Dafoe. Taking care of babies doesn't leave much time for other things." For a moment she felt diminished, and quickly added, "But it's the most important job in the world and completely fulfilling, so reading seems a little beside the point."

“I’m sure that’s true, but one day you’ll have time again. My mother says it’s important for you to get away a little, and a book helps you get away without leaving the house. She thinks I brought you the wrong book, and you might want to start with this.” Emma took a copy of *Fer-de-Lance* out of her bag.

“It’s the first Nero Wolfe mystery. There are quite a few of them, but I knew you would want to start at the beginning.”

Ada didn’t know if she should be insulted that Emma’s mother thought a popular mystery more suited to her now than the latest best seller, but she was sure that Emma meant no harm and added Nero Wolfe to the stack under Dr. Dafoe.

THE DAY THEY FOLDED UP MISS BENOWITZ’S COT AND TOLD her goodbye was a difficult one. Ada knew that Miss Benowitz had another new mother and baby waiting for her and felt a little jealous. She had enjoyed having another adult in the house to witness her success as a mother.

The twins recognized Miss Benowitz’s departure, too. They were already smiling, and they seemed to notice that there was one less person to smile at. Margaret, especially, was more temperamental, and Ada wondered if Margaret didn’t love Miss Benowitz more than she loved her own mother.

“You would be happier if I had been the one to leave,” she told the baby.

Margaret responded by crying, so Ada put her in her crib and fed her second even though it was her turn to be first.

Somehow, Ada survived that first long day on her own and was proud to place the twins in their cribs on time, as usual. She even had a lovely salmon loaf with baked potatoes and green beans ready for dinner when Douglas called to say that a patient had gone into labor and he was driving directly from his office to the hospital. It was a first baby, so he wasn't sure he would be home at all that night.

Ada ate her salmon loaf alone. In the evening, she wrote her mother a long letter acknowledging her mother's observation that it was good to have daughters who couldn't be sent off to war rather than sons who could be sent to fight anywhere, and sharing her mother's relief that Douglas's work as a doctor exempted him from the draft. Then she went on to describe the joys of motherhood and the latest accomplishments of the twins. She told her mother that she was teaching the babies to be good little girls, and that Douglas was proud of her.

Before she left, Miss Benowitz had trained the twins to sleep through the night, so Ada was surprised to be jolted awake by a crying baby. She peered at the clock. A crying baby at three a.m.? The crying didn't stop, and Ada had no choice but to leave her warm bed, fumble around for her slippers, and make her way to the nursery. She turned on the hall light and peeked into the room. Melissa was sleeping where she had been put down, but Margaret had pushed herself to the top of her crib, and her head was pressed against the bumper. Ada pulled the baby back to the center of the crib but didn't pick her up or talk to her. She didn't want Margaret to think she could summon her mother in the middle of the night and be rewarded by being picked up. She took a minute to look at Melissa sleeping quietly and left the room.

Margaret cried for some time, but, eventually, it was quiet. Ada fell back to sleep only to be awakened at four thirty. Douglas was still not home. When Ada saw that the baby had moved to the top of the crib again, she went back to bed. If Margaret was going to scoot around like that, she would have to learn to sleep wherever she ended up.

Ada was shocked at how much her life changed in the weeks that followed. Dr. Dafoe hadn't mentioned that each day would be exactly like the day before or that life would become so tedious she would find herself counting the hours and then the minutes from the time of the first morning feeding to the time the babies went to sleep for the night. Ada knew she was supposed to cuddle them, but cuddling was not on the daily schedule, and there were already enough tasks listed there to occupy her all day long. She knew she was supposed to enjoy the babies' splashing in their baths, but all she could think about was the mess they were making. She wondered if Dr. Dafoe had had to wipe the entire kitchen and change all his clothes after every bath time. For an instant, she doubted that he had ever taken care of babies, day after day, all by himself. And then hastily banished such heresy from her thoughts.

The letters Ada wrote to her mother and the phone conversations she had with her friend Edith were filled with praises of motherhood and stories about how delightful the girls were and how much they changed from day to day. It wasn't true, of course. Every day was so much like the last that Ada longed for a task that could be done once and stay done. She thought the women who told her to cherish every moment because they aren't babies for long were either idiots or lying. The lives of these two little girls stretched out ahead of her forever, and Ada began to hate anyone who told her how lucky she was. Her resentment, fatigue, and boredom became her nasty secret. Above all, no one must ever know.

It seemed to Ada that, as she grew more tired, Douglas grew more robust. His practice was flourishing, and he was busier than ever in his office and at the hospital. He had no time to help at home and, in any case, she had successfully convinced him that she was the expert on babies, that he didn't know how to care for an infant. Now, if he was holding one of the girls and she cried, he handed her back to Ada. The first time that happened, Ada felt superior and competent. But eventually, she grew angry that Douglas always played with the quiet twin, usually Melissa, and she always held the fussy twin, typically Margaret.

In fact, it was especially difficult to be a perfect mother to Margaret. While Melissa was content to be fed every four hours and go down for her nap afterward without a sound, Margaret always woke early and complained. Then she gulped her bottle so quickly that she cried and didn't want to go back in her crib. I'm the same mother, Ada reasoned, so I must be doing a good job if Melissa is happy. It's Margaret who's the problem, and I'll need longer to train her.

Ada worried when she began to sleep every moment she could, always when the twins napped and often when they were awake in their playpen. She was afraid that if she blinked too slowly, she might fall asleep standing at the kitchen stove or changing a diaper. While her need for sleep could be justified, Ada knew this wasn't the way perfect mothers behave.

When she found herself crying several times each day, Ada became alarmed. Once she dropped a milk bottle on the floor and hit her head on the refrigerator as she tried to catch it. After screaming at the bottle for being clumsy and the refrigerator for being in the way, Ada sat in the puddle of milk and cried for fifteen minutes before she found the energy to clean up the mess and change her clothes. It seemed that even the inanimate objects in the house were conspiring against her.

After a day of naps alternating with periods of frustration and boredom, it wasn't easy for Ada to fall asleep at night. One night, while she lay awake in bed, startling thoughts came to her. She was shocked when she couldn't control sudden images of dropping Margaret off the roof or rolling her carriage into traffic. She worried that she was going crazy, that she was the one in danger of becoming deranged, not Emma.

Or maybe she was feeling cooped up. Maybe she was a good mother who had a touch of cabin fever and needed a little time to herself.

The following evening, Ada made Douglas's favorite dinner, steak and French fries. Fortunately, the kitchen appliances and utensils behaved themselves, and the twins cooperated by falling asleep without a problem before he came home. Ada waited until he had finished his meal to broach the topic.

"You are the perfect wife as well as the perfect mother," he said, wiping the last bit of ketchup from his plate with his last French fry. "I don't know how you keep everything under control, but you do. I'm a lucky man."

"And I'm a lucky woman," she said, "to have such a fine, handsome, understanding husband." She smiled at him and took a deep breath. "Now that the twins are older, I think I might need a little time to myself, maybe a couple of afternoons a week." She hesitated, and when he didn't respond, added, "Just to relax. Baby care can be a bit exhausting." Her hands trembled, and Ada hid them in her lap.

"All new mothers experience some fatigue," Douglas said. It sounded to Ada like the beginning of the speech he probably made to his patients when they came in for their six-week check-ups. Her doctor had made such a speech to her. "Try napping when they nap," Douglas continued, "and sipping a little glass of wine to relax yourself. Remember that this will pass as they get older and less demanding. Then you will long for the days when they were little and cuddly."

Ada looked at him in disbelief. How could he talk with such confidence about something he knew nothing about? She couldn't tell him that she already napped when the babies did and sometimes when they didn't. Or that turning to drink was not a helpful suggestion.

"A few hours off a week would give me a chance to shop a little and have lunch downtown. I think I would find that relaxing."

"Who is going to take care of the twins? They are too little to leave with my sister. My mother is too old to look after them, and I won't have them left with strangers."

"Maybe you could be home one afternoon a week, and I could go out," she persisted. "Dr. Dafoe says fathers should help now and again."

"I don't know the first thing about caring for babies, and I can't anticipate when a patient will deliver. You wanted children for so long, I can't believe that after a few months you are looking for a way to get away from them."

"I don't want to get away from them. I just want a bit of time for myself."

"I thought we always put the babies first. You had better consult Dr. Dafoe for his opinion about what's best for them. I'm sure he believes that it's best for babies to be with their mother and that whatever is best for the babies is best for the mother, too."

Ada was angry that Douglas made her seem selfish and uncaring because she wanted a few hours to herself. It was even worse that he used Dr. Dafoe against her. When she stood to clear the table, her napkin fell to the floor, but she didn't trust herself to pick it up without flinging it at him. The dishes rattled as she carried them to the kitchen, and syrup sloshed onto the tablecloth when she put down a bowl of cold, sliced pears for dessert. Ada bit her lip and pretended not to see the stain. She couldn't tell if Douglas noticed.

When Clara telephoned the following day, Ada claimed that she was too busy for visitors. "But I made a pot roast for you this morning, and I'll only stay a minute," Clara said, and was granted a short visit. As soon as she heard the doorbell ring, Ada was overwhelmed by tears.

"It seems I've something in my eye," she said by way of explanation, and was forced to let Clara wash her eye out with water and peer into it, though Ada knew no speck of dirt or eyelash would be found.

After a careful inspection of her eye, Clara said, "There's nothing there, but your eye does look red. Let me make you a cup of tea. I bet nobody is taking care of you these days."

Ada allowed herself to be led to the kitchen table and settled with a cup of hot tea while Clara put the pot roast into the refrigerator and took care of the few dishes left from lunch.

"It's so hard to keep up with everything when the children are tiny. I can remember sleeping every chance I got," Clara said.

Ada nodded but was afraid she would cry if she said anything.

"Nobody can do it all and do it perfectly. It's a good thing that babies turn out fine anyway." Clara made herself a cup of tea and joined Ada at the table.

"I remember once when Douglas was a little thing and I was more tired than I'd ever been in my life, I didn't bother to change his diaper after I fed him one night. By the time we both woke up in the morning, that baby was poopy to his armpits." Clara laughed her big laugh, but Ada was too shocked to laugh. Shocked first, that Clara could do such a thing, second, that she would admit it to anybody, and third, that she thought it was funny.

Clara wiped her eyes. "That story always makes me laugh." She looked closely at Ada. "It should make you laugh, too."

Ada managed a smile. It was a funny story, and it was good to hear Clara admit how tired she'd been. She'd understand if I say I'm tired all the time, too, Ada thought. She wouldn't think I'm a bad mother who doesn't love her babies. Maybe she would help me. Tears filled her eyes as Ada gathered the courage to confess her shortcomings. Before she could speak, Clara continued.

"We can't do it the way the fancy doctor who wrote that book you read says we should. I bet he never took care of a real baby."

Ada blinked back her tears. Clara could be forgiven for believing mothers can't be perfect. And even though Ada had also wondered about how much experience Dr. Dafoe had with real babies, hearing Clara question his credentials was intolerable. If Clara was right, then he was a charlatan and Ada was a fool. That was much worse than failing to be a perfect mother.

"Mothers might not be perfect, but that doesn't make scientific mothering wrong," Ada said, and took her teacup to the sink. "We can't blame him for our failures."

"But how do you have any fun doing it his way?"

"There's satisfaction in knowing you're doing it right."

"I don't mean to criticize," Clara said. "I don't understand this new way of mothering, and I'm not as smart or up-to-date as you are. I've been trying to explain it to the aunts and the cousins, and they are all amazed. They never heard of such a way to raise children. We all agree that it would drive us nuts, and how you can take care of two babies and keep a neat, clean house is more than any of us can understand." Clara looked around the kitchen. "I must admit that I brag about you, since you aren't there to brag for yourself. You're sort of famous, and the aunts can't stop talking about you."

Ada stood at the front window and watched her mother-in-law walk down the sidewalk and turn to go up the block to the bus stop. When she couldn't see Clara's receding back any longer, she returned to the kitchen and sat at the table. It was frightening to recall how close she had come to giving up and confessing how imperfect a mother she really was. And it was terrible to be admired as something she most certainly was not. Ada checked the clock and rested her head on her hands. *I can never admit it's not working without being jeered and exposed as a fraud. Now I'm the charlatan, and they're the fools.*

The next morning, after Ada put the babies in their cribs for their morning naps and returned to the couch for a nap of her own, she heard Margaret crying. When the crying escalated, Ada sat up and began to cry herself. When the baby started to shriek, Ada grabbed a pillow off the couch and ran upstairs.

"What's the problem now?" she yelled as she stormed into the nursery. "No matter what I do, you always make a fuss." She looked down at the baby and saw that Margaret had managed to flip onto her back.

"Dammit," Ada shouted. "If it weren't for you, I'd be the perfect mother." She slammed the pillow down on Margaret's face and held it there. The baby stopped crying.

Ada looked over her shoulder at the other crib. She could see Melissa, her head wobbling as she watched, her eyes wide and her gaze unswerving. Ada pulled back the pillow.

After an instant of silence, Margaret started to cry again. Ada turned her over and looked at Melissa. "I'm lucky you can't talk," she said and rushed to her bedroom, slamming the door and grabbing Dr. Dafoe's book from the stack next to her bed.

"This isn't what you promised," she screamed. "You promised my life would be vitalized and enriched. Liar! Liar!" She tore viciously at the pages and threw the crumpled balls of paper across the room.

"I'm doing everything right. I'm following all the rules. Why isn't it working?" Ada sat on the bed and sobbed. "They're killing me." She dropped the rest of the book and curled up on the bed. Everybody slept.

Ada was the first to wake. She looked with surprise at the mess of crumpled pages on the floor and hurried to pick them up and hide them in her closet. Dr. Dafoe was so mutilated that she hid what was left of the book in the back of the closet, too. If Douglas notices that it's gone, she thought, I'll say that Emma wanted to read it.

As she turned from the closet, Ada caught sight of her reflection in the mirror and was stunned by her disheveled appearance. She grabbed her comb from the top of her dresser and pulled it roughly through her hair. "I'm not a weak woman," she told her reflection, one stroke of the comb for every word. "I don't give in to temper tantrums, my own included. And I'll not be bested by an infant."

Her scalp tingled and her comb was tangled with hair by the time Ada put it back on the dresser. She smoothed her skirt and patted her cheeks. That's enough of that, she admonished herself. I've only to see this through and never speak of what happened today.

Ada peeked in on the sleeping twins, closed their bedroom door, and wandered back to her own room. She sat on the edge of her bed and saw *A Tree Grows in Brooklyn* on top of the books on her night table. She opened it and read the first word. "Serenity." Serenity? It was impossible to read a book that started with the word *serenity*. She picked up the other book from Emma, the mystery, and took it downstairs to the couch. She knew it was the right choice as soon as she met Mr. Wolfe, an imposing man who keeps a rigid schedule and never leaves the house.

# Borrowed Sunshine

*1951*

ADA WOKE WITH A SURGE OF EXCITEMENT AND ANXIETY. If it was sunny, the family would visit Hastings. If not, the outing would be postponed. Each time the breeze lifted the bedroom curtain, she could see a gleam of light catch the edge of the sill and spill onto the floor. Ada willed herself perfectly still so no act of hers would disturb the rising sun and ruin the possibility of a good day. When the room became too warm and stuffy and the suspense became too great, she slipped out of bed and peeked out the window. For an instant, bright sunshine streamed into the room, and she felt a moment of triumph. So much for the newspaper's prediction of stormy weather.

Douglas stirred. Ada hastily dropped the curtain and stood still, hoping he would not wake. She wanted more of this day to herself before she shared it with him.

"Hey, what are you doing up already?"

"Checking the weather. Go back to sleep."

"And how does the weather look?"

"It's sunny," Ada said. "We'll be going to Hastings."

"Not right now," Douglas said, checking the clock on his night table. "Come back to bed, and we'll finish the night."

Ada dawdled at the window a few minutes longer before she crawled under the covers and Douglas drew her to him.

The sun was well up by the time Ada raised the shades in the twins' room. "Rise and shine," she said. "Wash up and come down to breakfast in your nighties."

Margaret threw back her covers and jumped out of bed. "Why nighties?" she asked. "Why today?"

"No questions. Just do as you're told," Ada said and left the room. She could hear Margaret and Melissa calling out to each other.

"I bet we're going to Kitty's house, and we have to eat in our nighties so we don't spill on our clothes," Margaret said.

"You're probably right, but don't bother Mommy with questions," Melissa answered.

"But I want to know. Why can't we know now?"

"Asking won't help so be quiet at breakfast and wait and see."

Margaret sighed. "Why do I have to be quiet all the time?"

At least I have one thoughtful, sensible child, Ada thought. And it helps that she can handle the other one.

The twins ate quickly, and Ada could see that they were careful not to splash milk or drip orange juice on their nighties. Right after breakfast, she announced, "Now go choose a nice outfit because today we are visiting Kitty."

"I knew it!" Margaret cheered and moved as if to hug Ada.

"Not with those sticky hands. Go wash and get dressed. Scoot. Both of you."

Ada was packing the big picnic basket when the twins reappeared. Although they usually objected to dressing alike, they were both wearing their new blue shorts and white shirts with red and blue trim. Even Margaret stood quietly while Ada brushed the tangles out of her hair and pulled her ringlets back with ribbons to match her outfit. Ada had chosen red ribbons for Melissa, but after a little begging from Margaret, agreed to give her blue ribbons so she wouldn't have to spend all day saying, "No, I'm not Melissa. I'm Margaret." Though Ada doubted that anybody who spoke to her for three seconds would mistake her for Melissa.

"Put on your shoes and socks and sit quietly till we are ready to leave," Ada said. This was the usual routine, and the twins hurried to obey. Five minutes later, they were sitting on the couch, pulling on their blue socks and helping each other buckle their new sandals. Now that they were eight years old, Ada would no longer tie or buckle their shoes, and she was pleased to see that even Margaret had stopped asking.

Ada finished packing the basket of food, fresh strawberries she had grown herself in the backyard, a lemon cake, two fruit pies, and, as a special treat for the children, chocolate chip cookies. She added five new coloring books for the girls and a copy of *Curtains for Three*, the latest Nero Wolfe mystery, for Kitty. After checking to be sure the twins were doing as told, she went upstairs to dress. Douglas was sitting on the bed tying his shoes.

"You've coverage for today, haven't you?" she asked. "I don't want to leave early because a patient goes into labor."

"Don't worry. If someone decides to have a baby, Gary will cover for me."

"Good," she said and opened her closet door. She was looking forward to wearing her new green sundress with the sprinkle of little yellow flowers along the hem and strapping sandals on her bare feet. Nobody wore nylons in the country.

Douglas made himself toast and coffee for breakfast while calling out orders to Ada until she felt like one of the children, or the maid. She didn't answer him. I take care of everything all the time, she thought. Let him take care of a few things for a change.

"Hats for everybody," Douglas shouted as he dug out an old canvas hat of his own. "Did you remember the sweaters? Where is my tackle box? Have you seen the worms? I put them in the refrigerator last night." It was quiet for a moment until he announced, "I found them and put the jar in the picnic basket. Now where's the Glenlivet? I've been saving it to share with Nat. It should stir up memories of our days as students," he added, laughing. "Maybe some we can even share out loud."

Ada could hear him sending the girls for their hats and their sweaters and pulling together his fishing gear. Then she heard his deep, rumbly voice singing.

"Without a song, the day would never end. When things go wrong, a man ain't got a friend. Without a song."

Ada could hear the twins giggling and joining in when he came to the chorus. And she heard Margaret say, "You don't sound anything like Perry Como, Daddy." Ada sat on the bed and listened to the three of them laughing. Then she buckled her sandals and pulled on her hat.

At last, everybody was ready, and Douglas carefully backed his new car out of the garage. "The latest model," he had told Ada when he brought it home from the dealer. "A Buick Roadmaster, top of the line. Look at that trim." She had agreed that the polished wood around the door and the windows was quite lovely. Now he always backed out onto the driveway before anybody got in for fear that an open car door might touch the wall of the garage. Ada felt foolish waiting on the lawn with the children, and once the car was in the driveway, she quickly stowed the picnic basket, hurried the twins into the back seat, and sat next to Douglas.

As soon as they left the city neighborhoods and office buildings behind, Douglas said, "Breathe deeply and clear your lungs to get them ready for the good country air." He demonstrated with three big breaths of his own and then insisted that each of them, in turn, take three big breaths, too. Even Ada laughed and complied. Douglas said he wished he could bottle that pure air and bring it home.

"Your mother goes to Hastings for the fresh air," he told the twins.

"Right," Ada agreed. "But I've another reason, as well. I go to see my sister."

"Kitty's not your sister," Margaret objected.

"True enough. She's better than a sister because I picked her myself."

Both Ada and Kitty had grown up in Scotland, married American medical students, and moved to the States as young brides. They hadn't known each other before their husbands, friends from childhood, introduced them years later. Now Douglas was Kitty's doctor, and Ada and Kitty were fast friends, though two more different people could not be imagined. Kitty was like the middle of the afternoon, blond and sunny, and full of smiles and good cheer, while Ada was more like dusk, a landscape of lengthening shadows and sudden dark patches.

"Last time you said we go to Hastings for the sunshine," Margaret said. "Don't you remember?"

There was no answer from the front seat until Douglas said, "I remember, Margaret."

"I still have the bottle of sunshine Kitty gave me that time. It's on the windowsill next to my bed, and every morning I look to see if it's still full of sunshine, and most of the time it is." Margaret poked her twin. "Right, Melissa?"

Melissa nodded her agreement. "Yup. I check it, too, and Margaret's right. It almost always has sunshine in it."

At last, the deep front lawns and white houses of Hastings appeared. The twins bounced in their seats and shouted, "Hurrah!" as Douglas drove through town.

"Too much noise, Margaret," Ada said.

Douglas continued a short way through the countryside and then up a long, gravel driveway to the back of a large farmhouse. Kitty ran out to greet them before Douglas had turned off the engine. She opened the passenger side door and pulled Ada out of the car into an enthusiastic embrace. The twins watched from the car windows. When Douglas opened their door, they rushed to Kitty to hug her and say how happy they were to be visiting. Kitty hugged them and kissed the tops of their heads.

"How are my favorite twins, Little Miss Muffet and Peg o' My Heart?" The girls giggled at the funny nicknames Kitty had given them years before. Even though their mother insisted that they were always to be known by their given names, no nicknames allowed, she had never corrected Kitty.

"You girls are growing so big. I love kissing your bouncing curls, but soon I'll need a ladder to reach them," Kitty said.

Ada watched Nat come out of the house. His condition had worsened since their last visit, and he used two canes for support as he picked his way through the gravel to the car, steadied himself for a moment and shook Douglas's hand. The men's pleasure in seeing each other was evident in Nat's attempt to equal Douglas's boisterous greeting and Douglas's gentle response and steadying hand as he matched Nat's laborious pace back to the house. Ada was struck by the contrast between her robust husband and his thin, weak friend. Nat's pallor seemed accentuated by Douglas's healthy glow.

The men stood talking while Ada and Kitty carried the basket of food and drink through the back door into the brightly lit kitchen. It was a huge room, with a big table under the back windows, a pile of toys and a couch along one wall, and a basket of wool and a spinning wheel near the door. Ada didn't allow toys in her kitchen, and she discouraged the twins from playing in there because, she told them, it was dangerous for cooks to be distracted. She knew that Melissa and Margaret found Kitty's kitchen a wondrous place, and, in fact, so did she.

Laura and Amy were waiting inside. Laura, the oldest, was ten, and Amy was a few months older than the twins. Ada smiled and nodded to the girls saying, "How nice to see you." She was busy unpacking the basket when Kitty's youngest daughter, three-year-old Carrie, ran into the room wearing a flowing red cape over her pinafore and carrying a silver plastic tiara.

"My crown won't stay on my head," she complained.

"Then don't wear it," Laura said. "It'll be in the way and ruin your Little Red Riding Hood costume. She didn't wear a crown."

Carrie looked thoughtful for a moment. "Okay," she said. "I'll put it on my bed for when I'm Cinderella."

Margaret laughed. "It must be fun to have a little sister," she said.

"Sometimes," Laura said, and laughed herself. "She can be funny."

Ada didn't think that Carrie was funny, and she often wondered why she had never warmed to the child. Kitty's pregnancy had surprised her, and, in fact, the twins had once overheard Ada call Carrie "a big surprise." Ada had been afraid that they would repeat the phrase to Kitty or her children, but it had been several years since they heard the remark, and she had stopped worrying about it.

Ada wasn't even sure why she had been so surprised. It must have been Nat's frailty that led her to believe he couldn't father more children. That, and the assumption that if they had been trying to have another baby, Kitty would have told her.

On the night of Carrie's birth, Ada found Douglas sitting at the kitchen table holding his head in his hands. "Douglas," she had said. "It's four in the morning. What's wrong?"

"Kitty had a little girl."

"That's lovely news."

"It was a tricky delivery."

"You must be exhausted. Come up to bed."

"Placenta abruption, hemorrhaging, hypovolemic shock. The baby's premature. They aren't doing well." Douglas rubbed his face with his hands. "We might lose them."

For the next week, Douglas didn't come home. If he wasn't at the office, he was at the hospital with Kitty. He took one break when he went to Hastings to bring Nat to visit his wife and new daughter for a day. Ada had had to go alone to a school presentation by the twins, and she missed a neighborhood party. But she knew these were small sacrifices compared to what Kitty and Nat were going through.

Ada remembered Douglas's relief when it became clear that both Kitty and the baby would survive. At the time, Ada couldn't help blaming Carrie for almost killing Kitty, though she knew how foolish an idea that was. Did she really think Carrie had intended to steal Kitty from her?

Once in the house, the men began their preparations for leaving. Douglas crushed his curls under his hat and retrieved the container of worms from the basket of food. As usual, he said, "I'm glad nobody ate these by accident. They are for the fish!" And everybody laughed, even Ada.

Kitty gave Nat's jacket, hat, and fishing gear to Douglas, and he piled it all in the trunk of the car. Then he returned to the kitchen and helped Nat across the gravel and into the passenger seat. Douglas waved to the women and called out, "We'll see you in a few hours. Plan on fish for dinner."

As soon as the men drove away, Ada said, "All right, girls, outside with you. It's a beautiful day to get some sunshine," and she shooed them out the back door. Laura, Amy, and Carrie gave Kitty a little hug and ran out the door after the twins.

Before they started cooking, each woman took a cup of tea outside and sat on the porch swing watching the children run across the back lawn. Nobody knows how to enjoy a lovely cup of steaming tea like another Scot, Ada thought, and smiled at Kitty, who seemed to know just what she was thinking and smiled back.

As usual, the children stopped at the fence and watched the sheep, most of whom moved to the far corner of the field as soon as the children appeared. Then Laura led the way to the door of the old barn where a big owl was rumored to live in the rafters. The children weren't allowed to play in there, but it was a rite of the day to stand at the doorway and make hooting noises to see if they could provoke the owl into answering them. On the way home after each visit, Margaret always reported that the big owl hadn't answered them again.

Kitty and Ada watched the girls race down the path behind the barn and disappear into the woods.

"It seems the owl failed to respond," Ada said.

"They hoot into the barn to make sure the owl won't answer," Kitty said. "A hoot in response is the last thing they want." Kitty sipped her tea. "I wonder if they'll come back with daisy chains in their hair," she said. "Last time you were here they trooped into the kitchen like a procession of princesses."

"More like a plague of princesses, as I recall," Ada said.

"That's true. They were a bit difficult to get rid of." Kitty laughed and stood up. "It's time we were cooking."

Kitty and Ada were accomplished and inventive cooks who worked well together. Soon the kitchen was filled with the aromas of fresh biscuits and tangy sauces suitable for the fish the men had promised to bring home. As they worked, they shared recipes, knitting patterns, fashion trends, and news of their families. And they laughed, too. It seemed to Ada that she never talked and laughed so much as she did in Hastings.

Kitty asked about the shop that Ada's sister had opened in Sydney and wanted to know if she was happy living in Australia, and Ada wanted to hear about Kitty's sister and her growing family and how her brother, who had been an RAF pilot in the war, was getting along. Of course, there was always news of the royals, speculation about the health of George VI, and conjecture about when Elizabeth would become queen.

"They say he's worse," Ada said, putting another cucumber on the cutting board. "It'll be no time at all till that young girl has all the duties of being queen on her shoulders."

"He may be ailing, but don't think it's the end of him. A sick man can still be strong," Kitty said. "He'll want to protect his daughter as long as he can."

"It's not in his hands, of course," Ada said.

"There's more in his hands than you know. A man who's holding on won't be taken any time soon."

"It's such a shame to see him trying to be king."

"Don't look at the illness. Admire the strength." Kitty lifted a pot from the stove and poured the noodles into a strainer waiting in the sink.

Their talk turned to gardens, sheep, and books. All interesting topics, but Kitty could be talking to anybody. Ada couldn't remember the last time Kitty had spoken about herself in a personal way. She always listened sympathetically to any difficulty or disappointment Ada shared, but all her own stories were cheerful. Could Kitty really be happy all the time? Were her children always helpful and sweet? How did she manage with Nat? Was she more a nurse than a wife? Did she share such confidences with other friends?

Ada pushed these thoughts aside. If Kitty needed to tell lighthearted stories, then Ada was there to listen to them, confident that Kitty knew she would also be there anytime Kitty needed to talk about problems or worries.

THE WOMEN WERE FILLING BOWLS WITH COLESLAW AND potato salad and beginning the sauce for a spicy noodle pudding when they heard the first thunderclap, loud and directly over the house. It silenced them.

"I hadn't noticed it growing so dark," Kitty said.

Ada looked outside and saw black clouds racing across the sky. In the next instant, she heard splats of rain. They confused her. "It never rains when we come to Hastings," she said.

"There's a first time for everything," Kitty said. "I'll ring the bell for the children. I don't understand why they haven't come in before this. Laura, at least, is old enough to know better than to stay in the woods during a storm."

Kitty took a big cowbell from a kitchen shelf and went to the back door with Ada following. Before she could ring the bell, they saw the children racing toward the house. Laura and Amy ran ahead, with Margaret holding Carrie's hand and Melissa behind them. Ada frowned. Why didn't Laura have Carrie's hand? Why wasn't Carrie running with her own sister instead of grabbing on to Margaret?

The children burst into the kitchen before the rain began in earnest, laughing and only a little wet.

"We were almost caught in the rain," Laura said. "But I told everybody to run for the house, and they did."

"It's good you hurried them along," Kitty said, and went for towels to dry the children's hair.

"They didn't want to come," Laura told her mother when Kitty returned. "Margaret kept saying that it doesn't rain in Hastings."

"I didn't think it ever did because it never did before," Margaret said.

"A hasty conclusion," Ada said.

Margaret looked confused.

"You're wrong," Ada explained.

"I guess so. I figured something out though. I figured out that…" Margaret disappeared under a big towel as her mother dried her hair.

"You'll have to tell us another time," Ada said.

Suddenly there was another deafening thunderclap that startled them all and drove Carrie into Kitty's lap. Kitty hugged her and laughed. "Nothing to worry about," she said. "Thunder is a big noise, but it can't hurt you."

After the children had been dried off, and Kitty and Ada had agreed that they weren't wet enough to warrant a change of clothes, they were sent out of the kitchen. They tiptoed through the living room on their way upstairs.

While the kitchen was always bright and busy, the living room was always dark and quiet. The children were not allowed to play there, but after dinner, they would lie on the floor listening to music and coloring while the adults sipped their Scotch and talked. Ada loved that time of quiet conversation and calm music and had been charmed when Melissa said that it was her favorite part of the day, too. "We can color and not worry about anything," Melissa had said, and Ada realized that that was precisely how she herself felt.

All three girls slept in the largest upstairs bedroom. It was so big that each of them had her own bed, dresser, desk, chair, and bookshelf. All their toys were stored there, too. Ada knew her girls were not disappointed to be sent upstairs to play.

"We always play in the big room," Margaret had told her. "There is a yellow guest room and a blue guest room, but we aren't allowed in those rooms because we aren't guests." Ada had nodded in agreement. "It's okay, though," Margaret had reassured her, "because there are no toys in the guest rooms, and there are tons of toys in the big bedroom. If we were guests, we would have to bring our own toys."

As the rain picked up and the wind began to blow, Ada grew worried. "Do you think they are on the lake in the midst of this?" she asked Kitty.

"Don't worry. Nat's a good man with the boat. He'll know what to do. And Douglas knows how to help Nat. As long as they're together, they'll be fine."

Ada worried, nonetheless. She hoped they both wore life vests, especially Nat who would be lost in the water. Who would help Kitty raise her girls if she lost Nat?

"Do you think they're both wearing life vests?" Ada asked.

"Of course. That's one of Nat's rules whenever he takes out the boat. Stop worrying, Ada. There's nothing to worry about."

But Ada saw that Kitty jumped up when the phone rang and rushed to answer it.

"I was right not to worry," she said after she hung up. "That was Nat calling from the marina. They're off the lake, and they'll be home soon."

"As soon as they buy the fish," Ada said.

Kitty nodded and laughed.

When they finally heard the car on the gravel drive, Kitty opened the kitchen door and Ada went to the window to watch Douglas lift Nat's legs out of the car and hand him his canes. Nat leaned heavily on Douglas as they made their way across the slippery gravel to the house. The children also heard the car arrive and rushed downstairs to see the fish.

Douglas and Nat came in, dripping with rain. After Douglas helped Nat to a kitchen chair, he hurried back to the car for Nat's fishing gear and the bucket of fish. Kitty hung the wet jackets in the bathroom, and Ada set out newspaper so Douglas could put the bucket down without dirtying the kitchen floor.

"I'm glad to see you safe and sound," she said. "What happened when it started to rain?"

"The storm tossed the boat around like a cork on the water," Douglas said, picking Carrie up and throwing her once in the air. She giggled and ran to Kitty while Douglas staggered across the kitchen flailing his arms. The other girls squealed and scurried out of his way.

"We rode the waves while our lunch and half the gear disappeared into the lake. When Nat yelled, 'We need to lighten the load,' I knew I would be the next thing overboard. Suddenly, a monstrous wave swept me out to sea. Luckily, Nat thought better of his plan, snagged my jacket with his fishing line, and reeled me back on board." Douglas sat down with a thud in the chair next to Nat. "Then we lashed ourselves to the mast, bailed out the hold, and swabbed the deck."

Kitty laughed.

"It's a little motorboat, Douglas," Ada said. "Nat, what happened?"

"We noticed the clouds, and the wind picking up. It's true that we lost the lunch and one fishing pole, and Douglas did slip off his seat. I had to grab his jacket to keep him from sliding along the deck. But we managed to reach the marina before the rain started. Then we called you and Kitty and were safely inside the car before it really came down." Nat shrugged. "Sorry my story's not as exciting as Douglas's story."

"Your story is quite exciting enough," Ada said.

"I like Daddy's story better," Margaret said, and everybody laughed.

"It was lucky that we had already caught all these fish," Nat said.

"Right," said Kitty. "Now who's telling stories like the ones Douglas tells?"

The children admired the six fish swimming in the bucket, but only Margaret wanted to stand at the counter and watch Douglas prepare the fillets. The others said that the smell of the innards and the sight of the heads on the newspaper made them feel sick.

"Since that's the case, go upstairs and put away the toys," Ada said, as she moved Margaret aside so she wouldn't be in the way and put several layers of newspaper on the kitchen counter. They watched as Douglas laid each fish on the newspaper, cut off its head and tail, opened it, cleaned it, and removed the bones. It took him no time at all to produce twelve fillets.

Ada remembered when this was Nat's job. In the early years, the men had vied for the position, but Nat had insisted that, as the surgeon in the room, he deserved the honor. In those days, Douglas would stand next to him and comment on his technique.

Ada had liked watching Nat's slender hands and thin, tapered fingers handle the fish so gently and confidently that she knew they felt no pain. Douglas's big hands and blunt fingers gave no such assurance. But he was as good with the knife and worked as quickly as Nat used to.

Nat sat near the counter and watched. "Nice job," he told Douglas. "Twelve good fillets with almost no wasted fish."

"I owe it to my years of watching the master," Douglas said.

Ada rolled the newspaper over the mess Douglas left behind, careful that nothing slippery escaped onto the floor. She could hear the bones cracking and feel the lifeless fish heads under her hands as she folded the bundle of paper and forced it to the bottom of the garbage can.

Kitty and Ada fried the fish and finished the salads while the men washed up. After they put the toys away, the children came downstairs and helped carry the food to the big table by the windows. Ada had once overheard Margaret telling Douglas why this was her favorite part of the day.

"At Kitty's house, I put my own food on my plate, and nobody keeps track of what I eat," Margaret had said. "One time, I didn't even have any fish, and nobody cared. And everybody talks at dinner, even the children. We don't have to be silent until spoken to, and we can say anything we want."

Ada had pretended to be engrossed in her book when they came into the living room and noticed her on the couch. Margaret was oblivious to the implied criticism of her mother, but Douglas looked embarrassed. Ada was angry that he had not told Margaret how important it is for growing children to eat a balanced diet and to be respectful when adults are talking to each other. He should have said my rules are good for them, she fumed, and he should recognize that my rules are good for him, too. It's my rules, after all, that allow him to take his children anywhere and know they will be well behaved. He should be grateful. Ada had been too angry to speak about the incident then, and they had never spoken about it since. Now dinnertime at Kitty's was Ada's least favorite part of the day.

It took a bit longer than usual for everybody to be seated. Carrie was worried that it might thunder again and insisted on sitting next to Kitty. That required a rearrangement of all the seating, and Ada found herself at the end of the table between Laura and Amy. She watched as Nat lowered himself into his seat and Kitty placed his legs under the table. Laura took his canes and leaned them against the wall before sitting down herself.

After everybody had helped themselves from the platters and bowls and baskets of food, the men retold the story of their adventure in the boat, and Laura told everybody how the children had run home from the woods. Melissa reported that they had played babies upstairs, and Margaret said, "I figured out why Carrie was a big surprise."

"Eat your food, Margaret," Ada said.

But Kitty laughed and said, "Carrie can be a surprising little girl. Why do you think she's a surprise, Little Peg?"

"She was a surprise because the stork brought her to the wrong house."

"That's stupid," Amy said. "I remember when she was born."

"It is not stupid," Margaret said, frowning at Amy. "Carrie doesn't look anything like you and Laura."

"Margaret, that's enough talk. Pay attention to your food," Ada said.

Margaret took a bite of bread and a mouthful of noodles.

"Sisters don't have to look alike," Amy said. "We aren't twins, you know."

"I know that, but don't you see what I mean?" Margaret pointed across the table at Carrie. "Look at her curls and her blue eyes. When I was running with her in the rain, I looked at her, and it was just like looking at Melissa except that Carrie has yellow hair. That's why I think Carrie is really our sister, not yours, and the stork made a mistake when he brought her to your house. So, of course, she was a big surprise."

The silence in the kitchen was like the silence after a thunderclap. Then Kitty laughed an after-thunder laugh, and said, "Little Peg, you do say the silliest things."

"I think Margaret gets her imagination from me, and her stories make as much sense as mine do," Douglas said.

The children chattered to Kitty and Douglas through the rest of dinner, but Ada and Nat ate silently. Ada stared at Carrie and then at Melissa until she noticed Kitty watching her.

After the dinner dishes were cleared, Ada said, "The ride home will take longer in the rain, so we need an early start. No coloring and listening to records tonight."

"Ada, let's stay long enough to open the Glenlivet and share a bit of it," Douglas said. He put his arm around her shoulders and took the bottle of Scotch from the counter.

"Not tonight, Douglas," she said, moving away. "We have to put these tired children to bed."

Nat said that he was tired, too, and tried to convince Douglas to take the Scotch home with him.

"Please keep it here for next time," Douglas said, holding out the bottle until Kitty took it from him and put it back on the counter.

Ada grabbed the picnic basket and hustled the twins into the car so quickly there was no time for goodbye hugs. Kitty and Carrie stood in the doorway waving as the car pulled away from the house.

"We didn't bring home any sunshine," Margaret said. "Today we're taking the storm home instead."

"And whose fault is that?" Ada said.

"I don't know," Margaret said. "Whose?"

Ada didn't answer. Nobody spoke for a long time. The only sounds were the pounding of the rain on the roof of the car and the swish of the wipers.

"Is everybody asleep back there?" Douglas asked.

Ada turned and saw Melissa and Margaret curled up in a corner of the backseat. Their breathing was slow and regular, and their eyes were closed.

"Yes, they're sleeping."

"Too bad the rain cut short our visit," Douglas said. He paused and then continued. "But it was still worth the drive to see them."

"We never go anywhere, but you always manage to clear a day to go to Hastings."

"I worry about Nat, and I like to check up on him whenever I can. And a trip to Hastings is good for all of us. Don't you agree?"

It was silent in the car for several miles before Douglas took a deep breath and said, "Why are you so quiet?"

"Why do you think?"

"Ada, you can't take a child's silly remark seriously."

"Why do you say it was silly? She knew exactly what she was saying."

"Don't be absurd. She's eight years old, for God's sake."

"As usual, you defend her." Ada wrapped her coat around

herself more tightly and looked out the passenger side window. The rain made it impossible to see beyond the shoulder of the road.

"We don't need to argue, Ada. Let it go." Douglas turned the wipers to their top speed and squinted through the windshield. "This is a lot of rain. I hope the farmers are happy." He glanced at Ada. "I thought Nat looked a little better. Or, at least, no worse. How did he look to you?"

"He looked as upset as I felt. I remember how surprised he was when Kitty got pregnant with Carrie. I thought it had something to do with his illness."

"Of course it had to do with his condition. Obviously her pregnancy wasn't an impossibility, just unlikely. So he was surprised, but he was happy. Better than happy, he was joyous. We all were."

Ada looked at him sharply. "I wasn't joyous, and I didn't know you were joyous, either."

"I was happy for my friend Nat. He has no reason to be upset now, and neither do you."

"Then how do you explain the resemblance? Where do you think Carrie's curls came from?"

"There is no resemblance. When Carrie was born, Kitty said she was pleased to finally have a little girl who looked like her side of the family. She said that she hoped the baby would have curls like her mother. You must remember that."

"I do. And I wondered why Kitty was making such a fuss about curls. I admit I never thought it through the way Margaret did today, but it struck me as odd."

"I don't believe you. I remember you told her that you would teach her how to comb out the tangles. You told her it was something else you could share."

"I never planned on sharing everything with her."

"If that's an accusation, you are way off the mark. If you want to accuse Kitty, okay. Maybe the milkman has curls. But if you're accusing me, I won't stand for it. You have no reason at all to think such a thing. It isn't as if children with curly hair are rare."

Ada rested her head on the car door and watched the rain splatter on the windshield. The wipers could barely keep up with the deluge.

"We've never seen Kitty's mother, or the milkman for that matter. You spend your days surrounded by women, and you're hardly ever home. How do I know what you're doing when I don't see you for days at a time? Sometimes, I think you call me so I won't try to call you."

"We've been through this before, Ada. I'm an obstetrician, so my entire practice is women by definition. And I can't set my schedule in advance because I can't control when my patients will have their babies." Douglas sighed. "This is nuts. I'm not going to try to explain something that is insane on the face of it. No grown person would take Margaret's fairy tale seriously."

"Oh, now I'm a child who shouldn't be taken seriously."

"Don't twist my words, and don't make a problem where there isn't one. I thought you loved going to see Kitty."

"I did, and that's the worst of it. Kitty was somebody I could laugh with." Ada started to cry. "I'm all alone here, Douglas, and now you've stolen my best friend. You have your pick of women. Why Kitty? How could you do this to me?"

"Ada, I already chose the one woman I want and married her and brought her across the ocean to be my wife. How can you believe I would betray you? And how can you believe such a thing of Kitty?"

"Anybody is capable of anything." Ada stared out the window. She imagined herself this morning when the day was full of promise, and she saw herself in that bountiful kitchen warmed by Kitty's energy and enthusiasms. Then she heard the thunder.

"We can never go back there."

Douglas looked at her for a moment. "You can't mean that."

Of course I mean it, Ada thought. Am I expected to crawl back to Hastings and watch my husband and my best friend joke together? Or watch Carrie grow up, looking more and more like my daughters? I don't forgive and forget, and I'll never let myself become an object of their pity or ridicule. There'll be no more trips to Hastings. Ever.

"I do mean it. I have no choice." Her voice was high and tight. "You've stolen all my choices." Covering her face with her hands, Ada gave in to her tears.

Douglas spoke in a soft voice. "Ada, dear, you're tired. Don't make any decisions tonight. Things will look different in the morning."

Ada leaned against the car door and closed her eyes.

THE NEXT AFTERNOON, ADA STOOD AT THE DINING ROOM window and watched the twins get off the camp bus. They walked up the sidewalk holding hands, their heads close together. Margaret was telling Melissa something, and Melissa was laughing. Sisters, Ada thought.

"We had the best day at camp," Margaret shouted as she came through the front door. "Wanna hear a song we learned? It's funny." Margaret tried to pull Melissa to stand next to her, but Melissa was staring at her mother's face and hung back.

"Not now, Margaret," Melissa said. "Maybe after dinner. Let's find our pink balls and go outside."

Margaret stared at Melissa. "I don't want to go outside," she said. "I want to stay in and color, and before you said you want to color, too." Margaret frowned. "And I'm hungry. I want an apple and cheese slices."

"No snack," Ada said.

"No snack? Why not?" Margaret asked.

"It's too close to dinner."

"But we always have a snack after camp."

"Not today." Ada walked into the living room leaving the twins standing in the foyer.

Melissa tugged on Margaret's shirt. "C'mon, we can wait till dinner. Let's go outside."

Margaret shook her head and followed her mother. Melissa trailed behind.

"Then can we have the new coloring books you bought for Kitty's house?" Margaret asked.

"What makes you think I have new coloring books?" Ada sat on the couch and picked up her knitting from the basket on the floor.

"You always have them, and you give them to us after dinner."

"Not yesterday. Your father saw to that, and you helped."

"What did I do?" Margaret asked. She looked at Melissa and then back at her mother. "I'm sorry," she said.

"A bit late for that," Ada said.

"Can we have the coloring books the next time we visit Kitty?"

"We won't be visiting Kitty. So you'll not be getting those or any other coloring books today or any day."

"Not even the next time we visit Kitty?"

"Are you deaf, Margaret? I said we won't be visiting Kitty."

"You mean not ever?"

Ada looked up. "Stop pestering me. Go to your room."

"Why am I being sent to my room?"

Ada threw her knitting in the basket. "Now you've made me lose count."

Melissa stepped forward. "C'mon, Margaret. I'll go with you."

"No," Ada said. "You stay down here with me, Melissa."

"I have to go alone?" Margaret asked in a small, shocked voice. "All alone?"

"And I have to stay down here with you?" Melissa said in the same shocked tone.

"Get out of here," Ada yelled. "Both of you. Now!"

Ada turned away and heard them run up the stairs. Now I'm the one left all alone, she thought, and went upstairs to her own room. She could hear the twins and imagined them sitting on their beds with their matching quilts and pillows that said "Sisters forever."

"Did Mommy really say that we will never have new coloring books and never visit Hastings again in our whole lives?" Margaret said.

"Yes."

"Do you know what I did?"

"No."

"Maybe I shouldn't have said that I liked Daddy's story about when he was in the boat. Or maybe she found out that I didn't put the puzzles back exactly like I found them."

"Maybe."

"Why am I always in trouble and I don't know why? I even said sorry, and I'm still being blamed." There was a long silence before Margaret added, "I bet Daddy knows."

"Don't ask him. Mommy blames him, too, and you don't want to make her madder."

"It's not fair," Margaret said, thumping her pillow. "I wish we lived in Hastings and never visited here."

"Shhh," Melissa cautioned. "Don't talk so loud."

"One day when I'm grown up, I'm going to drive myself to Hastings in my own car and ask Kitty. And she will laugh and say, 'Don't worry about it, Little Peg. I forgive you.' Will you come with me, Melissa?"

"Sure. We'll go together."

Ada could feel her bitterness rise up like a physical presence. The whole family would rather have Kitty, she thought. Every one of them.

THE NEXT MORNING AT BREAKFAST MARGARET ASKED ADA why her bottle of sunshine was missing from the windowsill. Ada told her to eat her Cheerios.

# The Child of Her Old Age

*1952*

Ada's life was awash in sepia tones while the rest of the world went on in technicolor. Melissa and Margaret usually found her napping on the couch when they came home from school, and sometimes they had fish sticks for dinner three evenings in a row.

One night, as she and Douglas were getting ready for bed, he accused her of punishing him even though he had done nothing wrong.

"Nothing wrong?" Ada said, keeping her voice low so she wouldn't wake the twins. "You call having an affair and producing a child with my best friend nothing wrong? Kitty was the only drop of sunshine in my life, and you stole her from me."

"Listen to me. Carrie is not my child. Just because Margaret carried on about how much Carrie looks like Melissa doesn't make it true." His eyes narrowed and his mouth grew tight.

When Ada saw him scowl, her own fury took over. "You've ruined my life. That's what you've done. You took me far from my family and deceived me." Ada gasped for breath. "You're just like your father.

"But I won't be the long-suffering wife your mother was," she warned. "Don't expect me to sit at home while you leave a trail of curly-headed children in your wake."

"I'm finished trying to talk sense to you. Nobody in their right mind would listen to an eight-year-old's silly story and then blow the whole thing out of proportion like this." Douglas looked away and fumbled with his pajama string.

"Nat believed it, and he killed himself."

"Nat knew his illness was terminal, and he took charge of his death rather than wait for the inevitable. Why is that so hard for you to understand?"

"All I know is that he killed himself days after Margaret pointed out that Carrie looks like our children and nothing like her own sisters. His death was your fault, yours and Kitty's. Is that what you hope I'll do? Kill myself so you and Kitty can be free? Is that what you want?"

Douglas looked stunned. He dropped the pajama string and stared across the bed at her. "Addy, you can't—"

"You promised my mother you'd take care of me."

"You can't believe that I wish you—"

"What do you think she would say to you now?"

Douglas sat on the edge of the bed. His back was to her, and he looked down at his hands. "What can I do?"

Ada wasn't sure if he sounded contrite, or if this was the voice he used to calm hysterical patients. "I don't know," she said, and it was the truth. What could either of them do?

Ada lay awake long after Douglas fell asleep beside her. She had known immediately that she could no longer be Kitty's friend, but now she wondered if she could still be Douglas's wife. Maybe her threat to leave hadn't been thrown at Douglas more to wound than to predict. Maybe she had meant it.

Ada had her own bank account where she saved the money left over each month from the household expenses.

After years of saving, she had enough money to travel far away. Now she appreciated the wisdom in her mother's warning never to let her passport expire. She had always assumed it was a silly superstition based on the fears of a woman who had seen the Nazis take over Germany and most of Europe. But now she understood that it was for moments like this, and she was pleased that she had followed her mother's advice. She could leave him. She could leave all of them.

The next morning, Ada hustled the twins off to school and sat at the kitchen table to look over her bank statement and think through her plans. There was enough money for a plane ticket, she was sure of that. Her friend Milly had recently returned from London and had told her all about buying the ticket and packing for the trip. I don't think my steamer trunk can go, she thought, but I can afford new luggage, the kind they carry on airplanes these days. Or maybe I can take the trunk. I'll bring it downstairs to see how much it holds and think about what I'll pack.

Getting to the attic was more trouble than Ada had anticipated. The stairs from the second floor hallway were steep, and she wished she had taken time to put on proper shoes instead of wearing her slippers. The attic was a cluttered, dusty place with a low ceiling and one dim bulb hanging from a rafter. A precarious stack of folding chairs and old sleds leaned into one corner, and boxes upon boxes loomed along the walls. One good shake and everything threatened to tumble down. This room could use a thorough cleaning, she thought. But why should I worry about the mess? It will be Douglas's problem soon enough.

Picking her way past mounds of old baby dolls, roller skates and small, forgotten toys, stepping over rolled up rugs and around two high chairs, and pushing aside two white, wicker basinets filled with baby clothes, Ada reached her trunk. This was the trunk that had carried all her possessions, including her treasured porcelain figurines, her beautiful Wedgewood bowl, and her first fancy bottle of perfume, across the ocean nearly fifteen years before.

Ada brushed off the dust as best she could, dragged the trunk to the top of the stairs, and holding on to the thick, leather strap at the back, let it slide down to the second floor. Then she pulled it into her bedroom and raised the top. The contents were surprisingly fresh. Her wedding dress was on top, and Ada took a moment to admire the lace her sister, Rose, had so carefully sewn around the collar and along the bodice, and the seed pearls Rose had added with stitches so tiny they couldn't be seen. Nestled under the dress, Ada found the white cape with a blue satin lining Rose had made to protect her and the dress on the ride to the synagogue. She found the hat she had given Douglas before they were engaged, and the scarf Rose had given him when he first became their boarder. Ada had never dared to throw it away, but when he asked for it winter after winter, she always claimed she couldn't find it. She hadn't wanted any memory of Rose to keep him warm.

There were also several books in the trunk, including *The Treasure Book of Fairy Tales* with all of Ada's scraps pressed between the pages to keep them from becoming wrinkled and worn. In Scotland, all little girls had a collection of the colorful, shiny pictures that could be bought by the page, cut out, and traded or saved. On Ada's eighth birthday, Rose's gift had been her entire collection of scraps so that, overnight, Ada had a larger collection than any of her friends. After that, Rose always bought her the latest scraps as soon as they came out until Ada's collection was the envy of the neighborhood, and every little girl wished she had an older sister like Rose.

Ada carried the book to the kitchen table and made herself a cup of tea before she opened it. When she came to the end of the scraps, she saw that something else had been inserted in the pages. She took out a square of drawing paper she didn't recognize, looked at it carefully, and continued to pull out squares until she had a small stack of them on the table.

Each one showed two portraits beautifully drawn by Rose in ink and colored pencils. They were all there, the sisters from the books that she and Rose had read together so many years before: Laura, dressed in white and looking frail, and Marian, not ugly as Ada remembered her described, but with a strong, bold expression; Elinor, sensible and a bit stern, and Marianne, laughing with excitement and about to jump off the page; Miss Jenkins, dressed in black and looking most proper alongside sweet, kind Miss Matty; beautiful Dorothea and amiable Celia; Margaret, looking capable, and Helen, great with child; Olive in a severe dark dress without any ornament and Adeline in a dress that barely covered her ample bosom, her hair in ringlets. Ada would have recognized each of them even if they had not been labeled.

The last page showed two young girls, Snow White and Rose Red, with a bear in the background. Snow White looked much like Ada, and Rose Red looked like Rose. Ada laughed when she saw that the bear looked like Douglas. She could remember cuddling up to Rose on the sofa and listening to this story night after night when she was little. At the end of the tale, the bear turns into the king's son and marries Snow White, while Rose Red marries his brother. Rose always said the story was about them because they were also sisters who loved each other, but, she would add, that didn't mean that their story would end the same way.

At the bottom of her picture, Rose had written, "Not every Rose Red wants to marry, and if she doesn't want to, she is not forced because the story should have a happy ending for everybody. And ours does. Love, Rose."

Rose had made a big fuss about her taking her scraps with her to the States. At that time, Ada had felt threatened by Douglas's friendship with Rose and had buried the book in her trunk. Now she wondered if her sister had been waiting all these years for her to acknowledge the pictures hidden among the scraps. Ada looked slowly through the stack of pictures again. I'll go to Rose, she thought. I'll say it's a visit to make up for not being there when Mama died. And I'll say that I want to meet her little girl because it's not right to have a niece I've never seen. And Rose will gather me into a big hug and kiss my cheek and laugh. She'll make a cup of tea for each of us, and we'll have a long chat and tell each other everything. I'll go, and maybe I'll never come back.

Ada drank the last of her tea and hurried back upstairs. She had nearly finished unpacking the trunk when she heard Douglas come in.

"Ada!" he called and bounded up the stairs. "I need to talk to you." He stopped at the bedroom door and stared at her sitting on the floor beside the open trunk, its contents spread across the room. "What are you doing?"

"What does it look like I'm doing? I'm taking my things out of my trunk."

"Why?"

"I'm going to visit Rose."

Douglas looked away. When he looked back, Ada had never seen him so stricken. Not when he heard about her mother's death, though she knew he had loved her mother. Not when she lost the babies before the twins were born. Never. She hadn't known he could cry, but she knew it now.

"Don't go, Addy, please don't go. Give me a chance to change your mind." Douglas sat next to her on the floor and took her hands in his. "I love you, Addy, with all my heart. There's nobody else I love or need, and it's my fault you don't know that."

Ada was unprepared for his reaction. She was surprised that he realized immediately what she was planning, that he didn't argue with her, that he didn't bring up Carrie or defend himself, that he cared about her and loved her and needed her. When he moved closer and wrapped his arms around her and held her, she relaxed against his chest. They sat like that on the floor without speaking for a long time.

Douglas kissed her. "I need to leave for the office." And after a few minutes, he did.

Ada carried her belongings by the handful to the guest room and left them on the bed and the dresser. Then she dragged the empty trunk to the middle of the guest room floor and closed the door.

The next morning, after the twins left for school, Douglas sat at the kitchen table to drink his morning coffee. "Let's both have lunch here today. Are you free?"

Ada nodded.

"I'll call before I leave the hospital, and you can let me know if there's anything you'd like me to pick up. Maybe sandwiches from the deli if that sounds good to you."

They did have deli sandwiches that day, but on other days when Douglas called to say he was on his way home, Ada told him she was making a big salad or cooking omelets for the two of them. Sometimes he called from the office to say hello or to tell her a funny thing his nurse had said or to recount the latest hospital gossip.

The time he took in the morning to talk about their plans for the day and their quiet lunches together soothed her, and his attentiveness comforted her. They didn't talk about Kitty again, and Douglas never admitted any wrongdoing. But he seemed at pains to make Ada feel loved and secure, and it was working. Once, it had seemed like that difficult time would never end, but slowly, miraculously, things were changing.

"Can you believe it, Ada?" he crowed one day. "It's going to be another set of triplets for Mrs. Downing. You're the first to know, so don't tell anybody, though it won't be a secret for long." Douglas laughed. "With a few more patients like Mrs. Downing, I might deliver more than two hundred babies this year."

That day, Ada served little glasses of wine with lunch and lemon tarts for dessert.

SEVERAL WEEKS LATER, ADA CAME INTO THE KITCHEN WITH a bag from the supermarket and regretted, yet again, that the kitchen was not yellow. Pale blue is not a kitchen color, she thought as she unpacked the groceries. It's barely a color at all. What kind of fool paints a kitchen pale blue? And what kind of fool lives with a pale blue kitchen for years and years and does nothing about it? She placed the loaf of bread in the bread box and opened the refrigerator to put the apples in the bin and the cheese in the cheese drawer. I'll redo the kitchen. She stood and thought a moment. No, I'll redo the house, the whole house. Without ever having entertained that thought before, Ada felt the idea arrive fully formed. She knew what she wanted to do in every room, starting with a lovely, yellow kitchen. When she told Douglas her plan, he was delighted and gave her a generous budget.

Ada had the house repainted, a sunny yellow for the kitchen, a quiet beige and aqua for the living room, and a deep, restful blue for the master bedroom. She bought new furniture for the breakfast nook and hung new curtains in every window. For the dining room, she ordered white wainscoting below a white chair rail with white crown molding to match. Then she selected a boldly patterned black wallpaper for the walls. The effect was dramatic beyond her expectations. She also bought a piano, brown to match the woodwork in the living room, and a beautiful tall floor lamp to stand next to it. For the twins' room she chose pink wallpaper with huge plumes and blossoms. She even put a cuckoo clock in their room, until, after its ticking kept both of them awake all night, it was relegated to its box in the attic.

There was one room left, the guest room. It hadn't needed painting or new furniture, so Ada hadn't paid it any attention. Now she stood in the doorway and looked at her old trunk in the middle of the floor and her belongings covering the bed and the dresser. Had she really intended to leave? Setting aside the book of fairy tales, Ada slowly repacked until only the cape and her wedding dress remained on the bed. She folded the cape carefully, placed it in the trunk, and added her wedding dress on top, smoothing the lace and admiring Rose's skill. When he came home that evening, Douglas carried the trunk upstairs and stowed it in its corner of the attic.

With the house finished, Ada announced that she wanted to learn to drive. Douglas seemed alarmed and worried aloud that she was doing too much and would tire herself, but Ada assured him that every new project increased her energy. She called the Anderson Driving School and, in a few weeks, had her license. Mr. Anderson said she was the best pupil he had ever had, and Douglas surprised her with a brand-new car, a silver Buick sedan with a fancy grille.

Ada joined a women's volleyball league and the chorus at the community center where she also signed up to learn to play bridge. She rejoined the library book discussion group, and, after all these years, decided to become a citizen, though it meant giving up her allegiance to the queen. Despite Douglas's warning that her change of citizenship threatened the stability of the empire since Queen Elizabeth might not be able to go on without her, Ada persisted. She went to the classes and amazed her family by reciting the names of all forty-eight states and their capitals. Douglas brought the twins to her naturalization ceremony and insisted on dinner at a fancy restaurant afterward.

One afternoon, Ada showed her scraps to Melissa and Margaret. They delighted in the shiny pictures and the story of how their Aunt Rose, a person they had never met and had barely heard about, gave them to Mommy when she was a little girl.

"Can we play with them?" Melissa asked.

"If you are careful. They are old, and I don't want them to be torn," Ada replied.

"I'll be very, very careful," Margaret assured her. "Really, I'll be super careful." And then, in her most adult voice, "I promise to be extremely careful."

Ada watched as they huddled under the piano to keep the scraps safe from being stepped on. They arranged a parade of children carrying baskets of fruit to medieval lords and ladies inside a border of large blossoms and hearts filled with flowers, all the while telling each other elaborate stories about the scenes they created. Ducklings wearing jaunty blue caps swam along the bottom of the display. Their stories took an alarming turn when they discovered pictures of lions and tigers prowling through the jungle.

Ada began to answer Rose's letters promptly, rather than waiting weeks as she sometimes had in the past. Her letters were longer, and, in addition to news of the family, included book recommendations. After she wrote that she had discovered James Fenimore Cooper's *The Last of the Mohicans*, she received a package in the mail containing little portraits of Cora and Alice.

ADA AND DOUGLAS RARELY ENTERTAINED. BUT NOW, PROUD of her newly decorated house and with their fifteenth wedding anniversary approaching, Ada wanted to show off her home and celebrate her position as Douglas's wife. She wanted a party.

"Just a few couples, Douglas," she said one Sunday morning at breakfast after the children had finished their cereal and been sent to clean their room. "We owe a lot of invitations, and this would give us a chance to pay back some of them."

"Okay, Ada. Have a party if you want. It's fine with me," Douglas answered from behind his newspaper.

"Douglas, this is important. We miss a lot of things because some patient decides to have a baby, but you can't miss your own party. You need to make arrangements."

Douglas put down the paper. "I'll ask Dr. Gordon to cover for me till the next morning, and I'll buy the wine and liquor. But don't count on me for anything else."

Ada hadn't expected him to help and was happy to take on the party preparations alone. She asked Mrs. Schuyler, her cleaning lady, to come on the morning of the party and hired a girl to serve and to clean the kitchen after dinner. But with her reputation as a gourmet cook to protect, Ada planned to do all the cooking herself.

For the entire week before the party, Ada was busy in the kitchen. When Margaret saw miniature cakes and little tarts cooling on the kitchen counter, she asked for a tart to share with Melissa.

"Get along with you," Ada said.

"Can I have one tart to taste while I get along?" Margaret begged.

"No, you can't. These are for the guests, not for the people who live here."

"I wish I was a guest instead of a person who lives here," Margaret said.

"A guest? If you didn't live here, don't be so sure you would be invited." Ada turned back to the oven.

Early on the day of the party, Mrs. Schuyler came to clean the first floor, and the children were told to play upstairs and stay out of the way. Ada spent the day preparing the ingredients and sliding the bouillabaisse into the oven, organizing the items for the Caesar salad, and arranging the desserts on several silver platters. She knew that nothing like this had ever been served at anybody else's house and looked forward to the dismay of the ladies at the table when the girl brought out the main course.

Douglas came home early to set out the liquor and the glasses. Margaret left Melissa reading on her bed and snuck downstairs to watch him. She saw him put short, squat glasses in one group and tall, thin glasses in another. Douglas laughed when she said the short glasses looked like ladies and the tall ones like men, and then confused her when he said that the short glasses were actually for the men, and the ladies used the tall, thin ones. They were both laughing when Ada came into the living room and shooed Margaret back upstairs.

The children were given a quick dinner in the breakfast nook and sent to bed. There was no point in complaining about the early bedtime, but Margaret complained anyway, pointing out that it was still the afternoon.

"I've no time to argue with you, Margaret, so if you don't want this same bedtime for all of next week, I suggest that you go to your room," Ada said.

The hired girl set the dining room table with the best silver and china while Ada and Douglas dressed. Douglas chose his favorite suit and the new tie clip and cuff links Ada had given him. Ada wore a long dress in a rich russet tone with a wide, white collar, and the crystal earrings and matching necklace she had bought as Douglas's anniversary gift to her. Mr. Gilman, the owner of the jewelry story, had helped her choose the set, and she was confident that it complemented her new dress perfectly. She didn't plan to tell anybody that she had chosen the jewels herself, of course, but she did plan to let everybody know that they were Douglas's anniversary gift.

As they were leaving their bedroom, Douglas stopped Ada at the door. "You never had an engagement ring, Ada. Let me rectify that tonight," he said and slipped a sparkling diamond ring on her finger. "I love you. No man has a better wife."

Ada was speechless as she held her hand up to the light. The large emerald cut diamond in the center and the intricate triangular diamonds on either side sparkled with a lovely intensity, and the band matched her wedding ring perfectly. Mr. Gilman's knowledge of her taste had certainly played a part in the choice. Ada could picture him placing a tray of rings on the counter and patiently guiding Douglas's decision. She almost said as much, and then thought better of it. Douglas deserved all the credit.

"It's beautiful, Douglas," she said, smiling up at him. "And unexpected." Ada smoothed his collar and kissed him. "I love you, too."

The children watched them go downstairs, leaving behind the lingering fragrance of Ada's fanciest Guerlain perfume, a scent that made Melissa think of lords and ladies and Margaret think of tiny tarts in the kitchen that weren't for her.

ADA SCRUTINIZED THE BEAUTIFULLY SET TABLE IN HER dramatically redecorated dining room and was proud. For a moment she wished that Kitty could admire the effect with her. Kitty? Why had she come to mind now? Ada moved the wineglasses closer to the water glasses, and refolded the napkins, positioning them perfectly under their forks. Lotty was sure to notice if they weren't.

The first guests to arrive were Edith and Arthur. He and Douglas had grown up together and loved to tell funny stories of their childhood, apparently spent playing cards, setting small fires in trash cans, and brewing wine, when they weren't stealing apples and selling newspapers. Now that Douglas was a doctor and Arthur was a pharmacist, their childhood pranks could be made to seem amusing. Arthur also liked to talk politics and strut his knowledge and opinions about workers' rights and what he called "bold progressive programs." But lately he avoided such talk, and there seemed to be a new caution in him and a new deference to his wife. She was the woman who had encouraged Ada to join the community center chorus.

Milly and Bernie arrived next. Ada had met Milly at the library book discussion group. They were older by more than ten years, and Bernie, who owned an appliance store, was the only man in the group who had not been to college. He was loud and sometimes his joking went too far, but they were fun to have at a party. Two doctors from the hospital, Perry and Mack, and their wives, Lotty and Norma, completed the group. Margaret and Melissa leaned over the bannister, watching the guests arrive and listening to the sounds of laughter, clinking glasses, and conversation. Their peeking was cut short when Ada came through the foyer below and, looking up, caught sight of them. She frowned and shook her fist, and they scampered back to bed.

The conversation in the living room before dinner never lagged, and Ada received numerous compliments on the beautiful decor and her skill as an interior decorator.

"I'll have to have you over to help me," Norma said. "I'm so stupid about these things that I never know what goes together and what doesn't."

Ada smiled and accepted the compliment graciously, knowing that she had no intention of helping Norma redecorate her drab living room.

Ada also had the opportunity to display her new dress and jewelry. The women were impressed by the crystal earrings and necklace, but it was the new ring that drew the most attention.

"Bernie, come look at this," Milly called out when she first saw Ada's ring. "How come you didn't give me a ring on our fifteenth anniversary?" Everybody laughed, and all the women took the opportunity to admire the ring.

"Picked it himself?" Edith asked, shaking her head in wonder. "How nice to have a husband with such good taste."

One political discussion arose, but Douglas cut it short by reminding everybody that this was an anniversary party, and they wouldn't be able to settle the issue of communists in the government, anyway. Ada was grateful to him. She liked a serious discussion as much as the next person, but not in this group where there was sure to be a disagreeable difference of opinion. Arthur looked relieved and quickly turned to tell Perry about a new drug he had stocked.

Dinner did not disappoint Ada's expectations. The group found the food exotic and delicious, and Ada's prowess in the kitchen was extolled again and again. There were many toasts to the next fifteen years, and a few mildly ribald suggestions about how to celebrate an anniversary once the guests left. The ladies pretended to blush, and then showed themselves to be so modern and such good sports that they laughed along with the men. Everybody extolled the tasty desserts, and Ada was praised yet again as a marvelous cook and Douglas as a lucky man. All the women wanted the recipe for the bouillabaisse, and Ada promised to copy it out for them.

"I tried your baked ziti recipe," Lotty said, "but it didn't come out as good as yours. What's the magic?"

Ada looked mystified and shrugged. She wondered what made Lotty think that she would share a complete recipe. Ada never gave anybody the recipe exactly as it was. She couldn't have everybody matching her expertise in the kitchen. If they wanted to be known as great cooks, they would need to find or create their own recipes, just as she did. She certainly wasn't going to let them use her to build their reputations.

The guests lingered over coffee in the living room while the girl washed and dried the dishes and cleaned the kitchen before she left. Edith and Arthur helped clear the cups and saucers and were the last to leave.

"Don't worry about these few things," Ada said as she went for their coats. With hugs and little kisses on the cheek, she sent them on their way and began emptying ashtrays and collecting the glasses that had been overlooked.

Douglas came up behind her. "This was a wonderful party, and you were the perfect hostess. They couldn't get over how good the food was and what a wonderful cook you are. You're something special, Ada." He kissed her and added, "And beautiful besides. You must be exhausted. Let's go upstairs."

"You go up. I want to set this room to rights before I go to bed."

Douglas put his arm around her waist and kissed the back of her neck. "There's something else that wants to be set to rights. Let the cleaning wait."

"Douglas," Ada protested and then giggled because his kisses were tickling her. He turned her to face him and kissed her. "I think you are a little drunk," she said.

"Not too drunk. And I think you are a little tipsy yourself."

"You may be right about that. Maybe I should go to bed and sleep it off."

Ada moved to the stairs and tripped on the first step. Laughing, she sat down, and Douglas had to help her up. He pushed her, giggling, up the stairs ahead of him. They went into their bedroom and closed the door, ignoring their usual nighttime routines.

WHEN ADA BEGAN TO FEEL TIRED, SHE BLAMED THE ACTIVity of the past several months and looked forward to a quiet winter of reading, knitting, and crossword puzzles. A few weeks later, she noticed that her body was changing in ways she regarded with suspicion, and the nausea she felt first thing every morning reminded her of mornings in the past. Ada was not pleased. This is what I get for behaving like a schoolgirl with my husband, she thought. And who will pay? His life won't change, but mine will never be the same.

Ada imagined the months and months she would be trapped in the house, the endless tedium of infant care, all the things she would have to give up. I'm too old for this. I won't do it again. I'll make Douglas get rid of it.

Day after day, she railed against her fate when Douglas was not home and grew quiet when he was. Though she knew she should tell him before it was too late to be easily freed from her predicament, keeping the news to herself felt like a small revenge for his carelessness the night of their anniversary party. As long as she said nothing, this baby was hers alone, and all decisions were hers to make. Eventually, she found herself admitting a grudging admiration for the little person who insisted on being there no matter how unwelcome, and then she knew she would not consult Douglas. She would have the baby.

Though she was certain, Ada went to see Dr. Atler to confirm the pregnancy, and coyly told him that she wanted to share the news with Douglas in her own time. She left the office assured that he would respect her wishes.

Ada took pleasure in having a secret. She liked being in the midst of a family oblivious to the coming change in their lives. When Clara stopped by one afternoon, Ada was pleased to let her prattle on about Ira's new job while hiding news much bigger than that. She enjoyed having a secret from her friends, too, but there she felt less superior. She didn't look forward to Milly's pity or Lotty's amusement or Norma's commiseration and secret scorn. One person might have understood and could have been counted on to say the right thing. But telling Kitty was impossible, of course. So, for the time being, Ada said nothing and waited for the right moment to share her little secret on her own terms.

When sweet, elderly Miss Lindler retired from the library, a new, young librarian, Miss Enderbrook, took her place. Not everybody in the first-Wednesday-morning-of-the-month book group was pleased. While Miss Enderbrook was impressed by how many recently published novels they had read, she was appalled at what she called their "ignorance of the classics," and set about to rectify the situation. Ada had been looking forward to the group's discussion of *Howards End*, but she found herself lost in her own thoughts during most of the conversation. After the meeting, Ada and Milly walked to Schrafft's, as usual.

"I don't know why Miss Enderbrook thinks we need to read such long, old books," Milly complained after they were seated and had placed their usual order, tea for Ada, coffee for Milly, and a double order of toast to share. "Aren't there any new, short classics?"

Ada laughed. "It seems she's trying to stretch our minds," she said, pouring a drop of cream into her tea. "Tell me about your children. Does David still like his job? And what is Julie up to?"

"They're fine, but I'm a little worried about you. You were unusually quiet at the library today, and you look a bit under the weather, Ada. Are you well?"

"I'm fine. No need to worry about me."

"I thought you looked upset when that new lady went on and on about Helen's 'unfortunate pregnancy' as she put it, and Corrine complained that authors are always doing things like that to women. I thought you would have something to say, too."

Before Ada could bring herself under control, her eyes filled with tears, and she knew her nose was turning red.

"Ada, dear, what is it? Is somebody sick?"

Ada shook her head and reached for another piece of toast. When she looked up, Milly was watching her closely. Nobody had looked at her like that for years. It had been the look on Douglas's face when she came out of the anesthetic after her second miscarriage, and it had been the look on Margaret's face when she climbed out of her crib one afternoon and found Ada crying in the living room. Now Milly was looking at her with the same concern. It was too much to resist and undid the last of Ada's reserve. She began to cry and was immediately furious with herself for showing such weakness.

"I'm pregnant, Milly. Can you believe it? I'm going to have another baby. The twins are ten, and I'm going to start all over with another one." Ada wiped her eyes with her napkin and took a tissue from her purse to dab at her nose.

"This must have been unexpected," Milly said. "How did Douglas react?"

"He doesn't know yet."

Milly's surprise was evident, and the look on her face made Ada laugh in the midst of her tears. "I think that surprises you more than my news did," she said. "I wanted to become comfortable with the idea myself before sharing it with anyone else."

"Are you becoming comfortable with the idea?"

"Not as quickly as I would like," Ada admitted.

"Well, I think it's wonderful news," Milly said, heaping strawberry preserves on her toast. "Second babies are easier, and even though you have two girls, you've never really had a second baby." Milly took a bite of toast and a sip of coffee before continuing. "You won't take every little thing so seriously this time around, and Melissa and Margaret will want to help, so you won't have to do everything yourself." Milly chuckled. "Once they recover from their surprise, everybody's going to be jealous that you have a little one to snuggle and love. I know I'll be coming over for my turn to hold the baby."

Milly's reaction cast a new light on the pregnancy. Ada had assumed that everybody would treat her with either excessive sympathy or derision, but Milly made her feel lucky. Maybe Milly was right about second children. Maybe she would bounce back more quickly than she thought and be out and about in no time at all.

Ada's new attitude lasted half the ride home, and by the time she pulled into her driveway, she was again thinking about all the long days she would spend at home with an infant instead of rehearsing with the chorus, or playing volleyball, or perfecting her bridge game, or going downtown to shop whenever she felt like it. Would she even have the time and energy to read?

That night Ada served lasagna, a family favorite, for dinner. Douglas didn't have a delivery, so he was at the table, too. Ada waited until everybody was served and she was seated.

"I have some news," she said.

"Tell us," Margaret said.

"There's going to be a new baby in this house soon."

Melissa and Margaret looked confused. Douglas looked astonished.

"You're pregnant?" he said.

"That's right."

"A new baby?" Margaret said.

Ada nodded.

Melissa clapped her hands, and Margaret sprang from her chair and ran around the table to her mother, peppering her with questions. "Is it a boy or a girl? When will it be here? Where will it sleep? What will its name be? Can I hold it?"

"Sit down Margaret and be still. The baby will be here in the spring," Ada said.

Douglas looked even more surprised.

"Isn't this so exciting, Daddy?" Margaret said, bouncing in her seat. "Isn't it the best news ever?"

When Douglas came home from his evening office hours, Ada made him a cup of tea and sat with him at the kitchen table. He asked her why she had taken so long to tell him.

"After I saw Dr. Atler, I needed time to get used to the idea myself," she said.

"You've seen Stan already?" Douglas sat back in his chair and looked at her. "If you had told me first, before you told anybody else, I could have helped you, if that's what we wanted." Douglas waited for Ada to respond, and when she simply looked back at him, he said, "But it seems you knew what you wanted."

"I'm fine, Douglas."

Douglas reached across the table and took her hand. "It must have been the night of our anniversary party. I hope you aren't sorry we weren't more careful."

"I could have said something, and I didn't. The blame's not all yours."

Douglas relaxed and smiled. "Another baby sounds good to me," he said, and then laughed. "This will certainly surprise our friends, but so what? A new baby will keep us young."

Douglas sipped his tea and after a long pause, he said, "The baby isn't the only surprise, Ada. I'm also surprised you're so good at keeping secrets."

But my secret involved no deception, no deceit, no betrayal, and no baby delivered to the wrong house, she thought. Ada cleared the dishes from the table while Douglas went upstairs to shower. Let it go, she told herself as she set out bowls and boxes of cereal for breakfast. It's not part of the present, so let it become the past.

Over the course of the next week, Ada shared the news with Douglas's family and with her friends, and her apparent pleasure did not falter. She couldn't control what people said behind her back, but nobody was going to pity her to her face.

Ada did what she could to maintain her busy schedule, and the new baby cooperated. Carrying one baby was a breeze after carrying twins, and Ada was amazed at how well she felt. Nothing else about the pregnancy surprised her, and the months passed without incident.

The guest bedroom was renamed the nursery and painted a lovely shade of pale yellow. Ada chose the new baby's furniture and clothing and arranged to have everything delivered after the birth. She also hired a baby nurse to stay in the house for the first three weeks the baby was home. One week before Ada's due date, Lillian, Douglas's sister, arrived each evening to spend the night. She said she didn't mind and wanted to be the one to tell the twins about their new brother or sister.

THE NIGHT SHE WENT INTO LABOR, ADA TOOK A CAB TO the hospital. Douglas was already there monitoring a patient. He spent as much time as he could with Ada, but the other delivery was complicated, and he wasn't with her when his own new baby was born. It was a girl. She came into the world without a sound, as if she was uncertain of her welcome.

"Why isn't she crying?" Ada asked. "Is she well?"

"Don't worry, Mrs. Kessler," Dr. Atler said. "She's fine. Her breathing is good, and her eyes are wide open. She's just a quiet little thing."

The baby did cry then, as if to reassure her mother. She had already had her first bath and was sleeping in the nursery when Douglas came into Ada's room and apologized for missing the birth. He sat in the chair by her bed and took her hand in his.

"She's a lovely baby, Ada. I have a great-aunt I'd like to name her for."

"You named both the twins after your great-aunts."

"We have a big family."

"I know that, but I don't think you should name this baby. You named the first two."

"But you don't have a big family, and your sister already named a baby after your parents. In my family, we have lots of names waiting to be given to new babies."

Ada looked at him. They were both tired from a night spent delivering babies, and she didn't want to argue with him. But she wasn't going to let him name this little girl. I claim her, Ada thought. I make her mine right now. I name her.

"All that may be true," she said. "But this is my last chance to name a baby, and I'm naming her."

Ada hadn't known she felt so strongly, and, in fact, had not been thinking about the baby's name. It was the twins who had been suggesting names for months and months until she had refused to hear another one. She didn't want a Steven or a Dennis or a Linda or a Barbara. She didn't want a baby with a common name. And Douglas was wrong. She did have an aunt. Her mother had left an older sister behind in Russia when she emigrated to Scotland. One day when Ada was still a child, her mother told her and Rose that their Aunt Faigel had died. She had been matter-of-fact, stern even, when she made the announcement, so Ada hadn't thought much about it at the time. Weeks later, she found her mother crying in the kitchen.

"What's wrong?" Ada had asked.

"My sister's dead. That's what's wrong. My only other relative. And you didn't even cry."

Ada had resented being made to feel hard-hearted. She had wanted to say, "I didn't know a thing about her, and you didn't cry, either." But she didn't say anything. Now she wondered if it would have made her mother happy to hear that this little baby was to be named for her sister.

"We'll talk later when we're both rested," Douglas said and patted her hand.

"I did have an aunt," Ada said. "I'm going to name her after my aunt."

"What was her name?"

"Faigel."

"I guess that will be Frances or Florence on her birth certificate," he said, but he didn't sound enthusiastic. "Or maybe Frederica," he added.

"I'm still thinking," Ada said. She didn't want to admit that none of those names appealed to her.

"Or we could translate the name and call her Birdie." When Ada didn't respond, he smoothed her hair back from her forehead. "I'm sorry I wasn't there with you. You're a strong woman, Ada, and I'm a lucky man to have you. You've given me another beautiful daughter." He kissed the top of her head. "Now get some sleep."

"You, too, Douglas."

Ada tried to follow Douglas's advice, but the hospital is not the place for a good night's sleep. At five o'clock, she asked for the baby, and then insisted when the nurse said it would be better if she rested now because, once she was home, there would be no choice about getting up before dawn.

The baby arrived wrapped tightly in a blanket and sleeping. Ada hadn't had a good look at her in the delivery room and was surprised by the bundle the nurse rested carefully in her arms. She had expected somebody who looked like the twins when they were newborns. But this baby looked different.

"Who are you?" Ada said and peered closely into the little face. She took off the baby's cap expecting thick dark curls, but this baby had wispy, light colored hair. When the baby stirred and opened her eyes, Ada had another surprise. They were not light blue eyes. This baby had dark eyes. And her face was more round than long.

"You don't look like your sisters or your father," Ada said. "You look like me." The baby didn't respond. "I take your reaction to that news to be favorable," Ada said and laughed. She kissed the baby's cheek and the top of her head and held her close.

"Now what shall I call you?" The baby had no comment. "I'm naming you Faigel for my aunt. That will anchor you and give you a little bit of history. The name means a little bird, but I'm not going to call you Birdie. That was one of your father's ideas. And I don't like the other names he mentioned, either." Ada leaned back against the pillows. The baby seemed content to let her take her time.

"I want your name to come from me, so I'd best name you before everybody shows up with suggestions."

When the nurse came in, she scolded Ada for falling asleep holding the baby.

"I'm not sleeping. I'm thinking," Ada said, and suddenly she knew the baby's name although she hadn't been able to think of one until that moment.

Douglas came to see her after he visited his patients so he could spend the rest of the morning with her. "I hope you managed to get a little sleep," he said.

"I hope you did, as well."

"The twins were all excited this morning and hurried off to school full of news about their new baby sister. Lillian said to tell you she is thrilled, and she'll come with my mother to see you this afternoon. Everybody wants to know her name, so shall we talk about it?"

"No need. I named her this morning."

Douglas seemed disappointed as he put the paper he had taken out back into his pocket. For a moment, Ada felt a little sorry for him, but not sorry enough to let him have a say in the baby's name.

"Well? Don't make me wait any longer. What's my new daughter to be called?"

"Her name is Phoebe," Ada announced.

Douglas grinned. "That's a great name. I hadn't even thought of that one," he said. "It's perfect."

Ada hadn't thought about how Douglas might respond, but now she was pleased by his enthusiasm.

The afternoon brought a parade of visitors who admired the baby through the nursery's window and then came to Ada's room to congratulate her on the birth of such a beautiful infant. Douglas's mother and Lillian were the first.

"She's lovely, even though she doesn't look anything like any of my babies or the twins," Clara said. "She must favor your side of the family. And I think her name is very pretty."

"Thank you," Ada said. "How are the twins doing?"

"They're fine," Lillian said. "I couldn't braid their hair the way you do, so I let them wear it down with a hair band, and they were pleased as punch. They couldn't be more excited about their new little sister."

Ada hoped it wouldn't take long to reassert the usual morning routine, but she didn't say anything about that to Clara or Lillian. Colleagues of Douglas poked their heads into the room all day long to congratulate her, and Milly visited, bringing a sweet little dress for the baby. In the early evening,

Emma, Ada's friend who still lived at home with her sister and her mother, came by.

"Phoebe is a wonderful name," she said. "It's a name that soars."

Ada had thought of it as a quiet name, but now she agreed with Emma. It did soar.

"I have a gift for you," Emma said, holding out a small wrapped package. "My mother's busy crocheting as we speak, so I'll let her give you our gift for the baby. This is for you."

"Maintaining tradition, I see," Ada said as she unwrapped the latest Nero Wolfe mystery, *The Golden Spiders*. Emma had given her a mystery when the twins were born, and that book had turned her into a devoted Nero Wolfe fan. "Thank you so much, Emma. This is the perfect gift."

That night, Ada opened her new book, expecting to find her favorite detective happily following his rigid daily schedule and solving mysteries without leaving the house. To her surprise, his schedule was interrupted in the very first chapter by a child. Ada knew that Nero Wolfe didn't like children and was astonished when he permitted this one into his house. "Unexpected children are more common than I thought," Ada said to herself. "Both Mr. Wolfe and I have recently welcomed one into our lives."

ADA'S HOMECOMING WENT SMOOTHLY, AND WHEN THE twins came home from school, she allowed them to tiptoe into the nursery to admire Phoebe. The afternoon sunlight streamed through the curtains, lighting up the room and falling across the crib.

Margaret gasped. "She looks like she's shining," she said, creeping closer to the crib and peering down at Phoebe.

"We're lucky to have this baby. She's like a little bit of sunshine we can keep."

Phoebe obliged them by waking up and crying. Then Melissa and Margaret were permitted to sit on the couch and hold her in turn. After Phoebe was fed and back in her crib and Douglas had come home from his office, the family sat down to dinner.

"How did you girls manage while I was in the hospital?" Ada asked.

"We were fine," Melissa answered. "Aunt Lillian and Grandma took good care of us, but Aunt Lillian couldn't braid our hair, so we wore it down every day."

"Can we still do that?" Margaret said. "We really like wearing our hair down, and all the kids say it looks great."

"No more wearing it down. I'm home now, and I'll braid it for you as usual. Tomorrow morning will be like all the mornings before we had a new baby."

Margaret sighed, and then brightened up. "Did you know that Daddy can cook?"

Ada said she didn't know that and looked at Douglas in mock amazement.

"He's a great cook," Margaret continued. "He doesn't make everyday things like spaghetti and meatballs and eggplant Parmesan. He makes steak! That's the hardest thing of all to cook, isn't it?"

Ada nodded.

"One night, Daddy made steak for dinner all by himself. We watched him cook it," Margaret said.

"What did you have with it?" Ada asked.

Margaret looked confused. "Nothing," she said. "We didn't need anything else. We just ate up all the steak."

Ada smiled. "I had no idea you were such a good cook, Douglas. I'll have to give you more opportunities to prove yourself in the kitchen."

Douglas laughed, but Margaret frowned. It wasn't clear that her mother really appreciated her father's expertise in the kitchen, and she seemed worried that she had somehow diminished rather than enhanced his reputation as a cook.

Ada slept soundly that night, while the baby nurse cared for Phoebe. In the morning, Ada helped the twins get ready for school and sent them on their way before Phoebe woke.

The nursery was bright with sunlight when Ada opened the door. "Good morning, you sweet thing," she said to the baby and picked her up from the crib. "Margaret's right. You are a drop of sunshine."

After Phoebe was fed, Ada continued to sit in the rocker and hold her.

"Now, Mrs. Kessler," the baby nurse warned, "don't let her fall asleep while you rock her. You don't want her to expect to be rocked to sleep all the time."

"I know the danger, Miss Lockland. Thank you. Here's the bottle to rinse."

Ada rocked and patted the baby's back. She could feel Phoebe relax and then reward her with a little burp. Ada smiled. "Everything about you is quiet," she said. "You aren't like anybody I've met before."

Ada held the baby close and looked out the window. The garden was coming into bloom. "We'll make hollyhock princesses," she promised and wondered why she had never made them with the twins. "And you'll think I'm the one who's fun, and you'll like my cooking best." Ada could feel tears fill her eyes. "You're the best thing that's ever happened to me, and I'm going to be the best thing that ever happened to you." When the tears spilled down her cheeks, Ada blamed those pesky hormones that unbalance a woman after childbirth, and then thought better of that explanation.

"It's you, Phoebe. You soar, and you're flying away with me so quickly that I hardly know myself. Look at me, doing and saying things my mother never did or said. I'm becoming quite silly in my old age."

# PART TWO

# The Promised Land

*1955*

MARGARET HAD BEEN THINKING ABOUT MIRACLES SINCE December when Mary Katherine McKenzie whispered to her all through social studies class about the Christmas miracle. Sixth grade social studies was so boring that Margaret had been glad for the distraction, even though she knew the Christmas story and didn't think it was a miracle. But she did think it might have been a miracle that they weren't caught and made to stand in the hallway.

All winter Margaret talked about miracles. She asked everybody she knew if they had ever seen a miracle, if miracles happened only to Christian people or could they happen to anybody, if miracles were always good things or could bad things be miracles, too.

When her father was home, Margaret had to compete with her two sisters and the newspaper for his attention, so she had few opportunities to ask him about miracles. But she did ask him if he thought it was a miracle that Hurricane Hazel hadn't blown the house down. She remembered how the windows had rattled, and she was sure her bed had been blown closer to Melissa's bed in the night. He put aside his newspaper and thought for a moment before responding.

"I know the hurricane was frightening, but we didn't need a miracle to be safe. This is a strong house, and there was nothing to worry about." He picked up his paper before adding, "And a real miracle wouldn't have left three inches of water in the basement."

Margaret's little sister, Phoebe, was a baby, so she didn't have an opinion about miracles, and Margaret's twin sister, Melissa, usually had her face in a book. Even though she said she was listening, she wasn't really paying attention, and Margaret knew there was no sense in talking to her about miracles.

Margaret's mother became impatient immediately, saying, "It's a miracle I haven't sent you to your room, Margaret. I don't want to hear one more word. Now get out of the kitchen before you run out of miracles."

Margaret didn't point out that nobody yelled when Phoebe toddled into the kitchen and got underfoot. And she left with an added concern. Could you run out of miracles?

After dinner at their house the following week, Aunt Lillian sat in the breakfast nook while Margaret washed the dishes and Melissa dried them. Margaret took the opportunity to ask her aunt about miracles.

"Let's say that Mrs. Tolley woke up one morning and decided to walk down the hill to the store," Margaret said as she stacked a wet plate in the dish rack.

"Margaret, Mrs. Tolley is very old and hasn't been out of her wheelchair in years," Aunt Lillian said.

"So if she decided to walk to the store, that would be a miracle. Right?"

Aunt Lillian agreed that if Mrs. Tolley walked to the store, it would probably qualify as a miracle.

"And what if Mr. Tolley decided to drive to his doctor's appointment by himself on the very same morning?"

"Mr. Tolley is blind."

"I know. So if he drove to his appointment, that would be a miracle. Right?" Margaret turned to Aunt Lillian, and Melissa shrieked.

"Margaret, you're getting suds all over my shoes!"

"Sorry," Margaret said turning back to the sink. "Aunt Lillian, are you still listening?"

"I am."

"Okay. Now let's say that Mrs. Tolley didn't tell Mr. Tolley that she was planning to walk down the hill to the store, because, you know, she really can't talk anymore." Margaret kept her hands in the sink and turned her head to be sure that Aunt Lillian was still listening. She was. "After Mr. Tolley left and drove to the doctor himself, Mrs. Tolley put on her coat and walked down the hill. And on her way back from the store, Mr. Tolley didn't see her crossing the street, and he ran her over and she died." Margaret didn't like the fact that she heard a little sound that might have been Aunt Lillian trying not to laugh.

"You're listening, aren't you?"

"Yes, Margaret, I am listening, and you have told an extremely complicated story."

"But the question is, when Mr. Tolley hits Mrs. Tolley with the car, would that be another miracle, or would they have run out of miracles?"

"That question is too difficult for me," Aunt Lillian said, and Margaret had to be satisfied that, at least, Aunt Lillian had listened.

Miracles were still on Margaret's mind in the spring. By then she was wondering if miracles were always a surprise or if you could make them happen. For weeks she tried to force ice cream to appear for dessert after dinner. Her lack of success convinced her that she had no power to bring about that particular miracle.

SPRINGTIME BROUGHT THE ONE JEWISH HOLIDAY MARGARET's whole family celebrated, Passover. Other holidays were marked by her father going to synagogue, but nobody went with him. He lit candles the nights he was home during Chanukah, but Chanukah gifts were always things like socks and underwear and, consequently, no cause for celebration. Passover was different. There was a big family dinner called a *seder*, and matzah to eat all week. Margaret liked matzah, especially spread with sweet butter.

Since their mother insisted on taking care of everything herself, the twins were not part of the planning or preparation for the seder. But Margaret overheard enough telephone conversations to know that her grandmother and her Aunt Lillian would be there, though her father's brothers were not coming this year.

One Sunday morning, Margaret heard her mother tell her father, "It's insulting, that's what it is."

"But Ada, you always say you have to do all the work on Passover, and nobody else does anything but show up. And you know that as soon as my brothers arrive, there's an argument. You complain about that every year."

"I can see why Harold has to go to Fay's family. She's his wife, but why does Ira have to go with them?"

"Maybe Ira likes Fay's family."

"I'm sure it's because they agreed to invite some girl Ira has his eye on. Fay would love to play matchmaker and marry off her husband's little brother."

"We don't know anything of the sort."

"And why isn't Lillian bringing her new boyfriend?"

"I didn't know she had a new boyfriend."

"Your mother told me, but she said that Lillian doesn't want to talk about him. I wonder if Lillian made him up to stop people from suggesting their fat cousins to her."

"I don't think Lillian has imaginary friends."

"Then why is he such a secret?"

"I have no idea. You'll have to ask her."

"She's not a bad looking girl and she's smart enough, but she's not getting any younger. Sometimes I think it'll be a miracle if she ever marries."

"Now you sound like Margaret." There was the sound of a newspaper page being turned before he continued. "Relax, Ada, and enjoy the fact that you only have to cook for my mother and my sister."

"Your mother is sure to bring that tin seder plate again."

"It's silver, as you know, and she's used it every year since she was married. We'll use your mother's cup of Elijah, and we'll use my mother's seder plate. I don't know why you make yourself so unhappy about everything."

"My mother gave me a seder plate, too, and we've never used it."

Margaret heard the newspaper crinkle as her father put it aside and knew that was a bad sign.

"As I recall, you couldn't wait to escape your mother's house and put an ocean between the two of you, so I don't know why you are yearning for reminders of her now."

Her father's paper rustled, and Margaret assumed he had picked it up again.

"You arranged for coverage, didn't you?" her mother asked. Her father must have nodded because she continued, "Good. I'm not going to have you running out of the house during the seder to deliver a baby."

Margaret heard her mother begin to clear the breakfast dishes and hurried back to the bedroom she was supposed to be cleaning. Melissa had already cleaned her half of the room and was reading.

"What are you reading?" Margaret asked. Melissa held up the book so that Margaret could read the title on the cover, *The Swiss Family Robinson.* "That's a fat book. Is it good?"

Melissa nodded.

"Did you know that Aunt Lillian has a new boyfriend?"

"No."

"What do you suppose he's like?"

"Dunno."

"Would you like beetles and ants for lunch?"

"Okay."

"That's what I thought," Margaret said and turned her attention to the bedroom. She didn't mind cleaning her half of the room. There was often a pleasant surprise like the time she found her charm bracelet before she knew it was missing. And there was the orderly room when she finished. Margaret liked her sheets and blanket tucked in smooth and tight, her pillow under the center of the headboard of her bed, her schoolbooks stacked neatly on her desk, and her pencils lined up next to them. Which was why she did her best to keep Phoebe out.

It was different when Melissa and Margaret cleaned Phoebe's room. Then it didn't matter if Phoebe helped even though it took them twice as long, partly because she undid their work as they went along, and partly because they took time to play dolls with her or to have a tea party where she was the honored guest.

This morning Phoebe was downstairs, and their work was quickly done. They put away her toys and dusted the family photographs on the shelf over the changing table. Whenever Margaret dusted the photographs, she was surprised at how little Phoebe looked like her. She and Melissa had dark, curly hair and blue eyes like their father, but Phoebe had brown eyes like their mother and wispy, light brown hair. The twins liked to smooth it down with their hands and then blow on her to see it fly around her head like a dandelion in bloom.

Whenever Phoebe spilled her cereal and needed a complete change of clothes right after breakfast, or rubbed maple syrup in her hair at lunch and needed a bath, she was picked up and carried off to her bedroom with hugs and kisses. The twins had discussed whether or not their mother had been as nice to them when they were babies and had decided probably not. Margaret didn't understand Phoebe's immunity to her mother's moods. Sweet, sunny, oblivious Phoebe went about her baby business and, like Daniel in the lions' den, emerged at the end of each day, unscathed. In fact, she seemed to improve her mother's mood, so Margaret liked to have Phoebe around.

Margaret always took as long as possible cleaning Phoebe's room in order to delay her next Sunday morning chore, folding the laundry. She had to take the clothes off the lines in the basement and fold them into the laundry baskets left there, one for each family member. Down in the basement all by herself, Margaret could hear the family walking overhead and she could hear their voices, though she couldn't understand what they were saying. Folding the laundry was a sad, lonely business, and Margaret hated it.

While she was folding the laundry, Melissa was dusting the living room, a job Margaret would have preferred. Even though Melissa said she would trade with her every other week, their mother would not allow it. The laundry was Margaret's job and the dusting was Melissa's, and that was that. Margaret even asked her father to intervene, but he told her that decisions about managing the house were up to her mother.

"She must have her reasons, Margaret," he had said.

"Why won't she tell me what they are?"

"She must have her reasons for that, too."

Margaret thought he was lucky to be a doctor who delivered babies and wasn't home much.

ON THE WEDNESDAY OF THE SEDER, THE TWINS HURRIED home right after school. The table was already set, and Margaret was pleased to see that Phoebe's high chair had been pulled into the dining room.

"Why aren't we using the company dishes?" Margaret asked her mother.

"Always a question, Margaret. We don't need the company dishes because we aren't having company."

"Aren't Grandma and Aunt Lillian coming?"

"They aren't company. They're family."

"I'm going to put on a party dress and my dress-up shoes," Margaret said, heading for the stairs with Melissa right behind her.

"No, you're not. There's no need to make extra laundry. Your school clothes will do."

"But I want to wear a party dress."

"That's enough, Margaret. Take your books upstairs and do your homework in your bedroom. And be very quiet because I put Phoebe down for a late nap so she won't fall asleep at the seder."

"But I didn't get a snack."

"Then you'll have a good appetite for dinner."

"But it's forever till we eat."

"No more complaints. And don't scuff your shoes on your way upstairs."

Margaret went upstairs, and Melissa followed her.

"At least wearing our school clothes is better than wearing our pajamas," Melissa said. "Remember how we had to wear our pajamas when we were little so we could go to bed as soon as everybody left after the seder? This year Phoebe will have to wear her pajamas."

"Do you think we'll be sent to bed right afterward because it's a school night, or will we have to stay up because it's our job to wash and dry the dishes?" Margaret asked.

Melissa shrugged.

As the twins tiptoed down the hallway, they could hear Phoebe talking to herself in her crib. Slowly, Margaret opened Phoebe's bedroom door and saw her lying down with her blanket over her head. Margaret's laugh brought Phoebe out from under her blanket, and she laughed, too. Margaret went into the room, and Melissa followed, closing the door behind her. They signaled Phoebe to be quiet and hid under her crib, appearing suddenly and making her laugh. Then they danced for her and made funny faces and laughed themselves when she made faces back.

Finally, Melissa said, "We better do our homework or we won't be finished before Aunt Lillian and Grandma get here."

Margaret reluctantly agreed, and they tiptoed out of Phoebe's room and closed her bedroom door. Left alone, she complained loudly, and the twins could hear their mother coming up the back stairs as they hurried into their own bedroom and closed the door.

"Here I come, Phoebe," their mother called out. "You've had quite a nice little nap and that should hold you for the seder." She opened the twins' door as she went past. "Why do you two have your door closed? What's going on in there?"

Melissa looked up from her notebook and said, "We thought Phoebe might hear us talking about our homework and wake up."

"That's thoughtful of you, Melissa. Are you both doing a good job?"

"Oh, yes," Margaret said. "The homework isn't hard tonight." And she went back to labeling the graph in her arithmetic workbook.

"Do your best, but work quickly. The seder starts at five o'clock," her mother said and opened Phoebe's door. "I hope you slept well, Phoebe. Now let's feed you so you'll be good company tonight."

"I'll feed her, if you're busy," Margaret called out.

"No, you won't. I know what you're up to. Any excuse to get out of homework. You'll stay in your room till your schoolwork is finished."

When their mother was safely downstairs, Margaret said, "Do you think that was a miracle? I mean that we weren't caught, and we even had time to get our stuff out before Mommy opened our door."

"No, I don't think that was a miracle."

Margaret was disappointed, but she had to agree. A miracle would have to be something bigger. Their homework didn't take the twins long, and by the time their mother came back upstairs, they were finished.

"Wash your faces, but don't change your clothes," she told them. "I'm going to dress Phoebe."

Margaret and Melissa washed their faces, smoothed their hair, and went downstairs. They found their father at the kitchen table with a bottle of wine, a bag of apples, a handful of walnuts, a cutting board, and a bowl in front of him.

"We want to help you make the *charoset*," Margaret said.

"Find the cinnamon," he responded.

By the time Margaret found the jar of cinnamon on the spice shelf and placed it on the table, her father had peeled two apples.

"Stay out of the way," he warned. "I just sharpened this knife."

"Can you make some extra so we can have a taste now?" Margaret asked, and her father added another apple to his pile. He chopped the apples and the walnuts and added a bit of wine and a pinch of cinnamon.

"I need some tasters," he said, and handed each of the girls a teaspoon. They helped themselves to generous portions.

"Hey! Leave some for the seder," he said, laughing.

"We didn't have any snack, so we're hungry," Margaret explained.

Her father handed each twin an apple and took the bowl of charoset to the dining room. Margaret and Melissa were finishing their apples when they heard their father answer the doorbell.

"Lillian, good to see you. Mom, thanks for bringing your world-famous sponge cake and your seder plate."

The twins tossed their apple cores into the garbage and ran to greet their grandmother and aunt with hugs and kisses while their father went to the kitchen to find the items needed for the seder plate. "Ada put them in the refrigerator for us, but we have to figure out where they go. I don't know why we can't remember how to do this from year to year," he said.

While the three adults studied the Hebrew words embossed in the indentations on the seder plate, the twins put a little blue booklet at each person's place.

"Look who's ready for a party!" Aunt Lillian suddenly called out.

The twins looked up to see their mother coming down the stairs carrying Phoebe, who was wearing a new party dress. It was pale blue with smocking on the bodice and frills everywhere else. Phoebe smiled and held out her foot so everybody could see her shiny white party shoes.

"Phoebe looks beautiful. Doesn't she, Margaret?" Melissa said, squeezing Margaret's hand.

"She sure does," Margaret said, and whispered to Melissa, "but she'd look a lot better to me in her pajamas."

"Margaret, bring me the blue bib from her dresser," her mother said and tucked Phoebe into her high chair.

By the time Margaret returned, everybody was seated, and the candles had been lit. She handed her mother the bib, slipped into her seat, and watched her father pour little goblets of wine for the adults and grape juice for the twins.

Margaret listened to her father intone a prayer over the wine before they all drank. Then everybody ate a piece of parsley from the seder plate. Margaret could not understand what her father was saying, but she liked the rumble of his deep voice and the fact that he knew how to make the seder happen. He broke a piece of matzah, wrapped the bigger half in a napkin, and handed it to her mother. Margaret knew that some of her classmates hid the piece of matzah and held it for a ransom the adults were willing to pay because they needed it to complete the seder. But when she suggested to her mother that she and Melissa could do the same, her mother had said, "No, you can't. Children do not trick their parents in this house."

Her father read a bit more in the booklet and then said it was the twins' turn. After everybody found page five, the twins read together aloud in English, "Wherefore is this night distinguished from all other nights?" Then they took turns reading the rest of the questions. When they finished, their father read on in a steady drone, and nobody at the table listened to him.

"This night is different because Phoebe isn't wearing her pajamas," Margaret whispered. Melissa suppressed a laugh and read ahead in her booklet.

"Look here, Margaret," she whispered. "See the part about the four sons? In the book I'm reading, the family lives on a desert island, and they also have four sons."

"Are they like these four sons?"

"Sort of. One of them is smart and another one is lazy, so I suppose you could call him evil, but he's really not. And there is one so little that he can't ask. The other one isn't stupid, but he doesn't like to read. Can you imagine a family with four sons?"

Margaret couldn't. Based on what she saw at recess, she assumed there would be nothing but pushing and shoving and what her mother called "carrying on" all the time.

Margaret heard her grandmother say, "The table looks lovely, Ada," and saw her mother smile before answering.

"I was surprised that Harold and Ira made other plans this year," she said.

"Fay's family has been complaining that Fay and Harold and the children never go to them for Passover, so Harold thought they better go there this year. Ira decided to tag along. It makes less work for you, Ada, and it's a change of pace for them."

"And what about your new boyfriend, Lillian? He knows he was invited, doesn't he?"

"I did share your invitation with him, but he had plans already."

"When will we have a chance to meet him?"

Clara looked up at Ada and then over to Lillian. "We're all..."

Lillian smiled and interrupted her mother. "When the time is right, Ada."

"I hope it's soon."

Margaret looked at the little pictures in her booklet until the adult conversation caught her attention again when her mother said, "I've no difficulty cooking for everybody." That's not true, Margaret thought. I hear you complain about the extra work every year.

"I never minded the cooking, either," her grandmother said. "It's the extra cleaning that's so hard. My mother used to work for months getting everything clean enough. Then she would bring huge bushel baskets full of dishes and pots and pans up from the basement and take boxes of dishes downstairs for the week. It was a lot of work, but it was exciting, too. Was Passover an exciting time in your house when you were a girl, Ada?"

"It's been some time since I've thought about Passover in Edinburgh. My mother had the shop to worry about, so Passover was an added strain. I can't say I remember the extra cleaning and the cooking as exciting."

Their conversation was suddenly interrupted by a loud announcement from the head of the table. "Time for the plagues. I think I have a plague of talkative females this year!"

Margaret watched her father pour more wine or grape juice for everybody and dipped a pinky finger into her grape juice and dabbed it on her little plate as her father called out each plague. At the end of the list, everybody wiped their fingers with paper napkins, and her mother took the little plates and the napkins off the table.

"Do you know what the plagues mean?" Margaret asked Melissa.

"Everything except murrain. What's that?" Melissa whispered.

"I don't know that one, either. Did the family in your book have plagues?"

"Not really. Nobody even caught a cold."

"That sounds like a miracle. Did they cry out like the Jews and ask to be saved?"

"No, they seemed happy, and at the end not all of them went home."

"If I'd been in Egypt, I would have cried out right away instead of waiting hundreds of years."

"Crying out doesn't always help. You cry out all the time, and it doesn't do you any good."

Margaret thought about that while her father continued to mumble and turn the pages in his booklet and the ladies chatted. Then the family sang a song about how God did more than the Jews really needed and any one of the miracles He performed for them would have been enough. It was the only song in the seder, and Margaret thought one song was not enough. Aunt Lillian had told her that Moses was shown the land, but he wasn't allowed to go in, even though he always did what he was told with just a tiny bit of arguing. Margaret wondered if that made Moses mad or if it was enough.

Her father gave out a bit of this and a bit of that to eat. When it came time for the horseradish, all the ladies insisted on tiny portions.

"Who will join me in doing this right?" her father asked.

Margaret quickly volunteered, but her mother refused to let her eat the portion he heaped on her piece of matzah.

"I see I'm on my own," he said.

"Don't be silly, Douglas," Ada said. "Without your brothers here, you have nothing to prove." But he went ahead and ate it in one bite and then coughed and sneezed and blew his nose and wiped his eyes while Ada shook her head and everybody else laughed.

"You run the seder like my father taught you," Clara said. "Including the foolishness with the horseradish."

"I'll take that as a compliment," Douglas said and put his booklet aside. "Now it's time for the festive meal." He looked over at the high chair and laughed. "Phoebe is the only one who didn't talk all the way through the seder, and now I see why."

Everybody turned to look at Phoebe fast asleep with her head on the tray of her high chair. Ada frowned. "I was sure the extra nap would be enough to keep her awake," she said. "Maybe she'll wake up and join us for some dinner."

Gefilte fish was the first course. Each small circle of fish had a little round of cooked carrot on top. The adults helped themselves, but the twins declined, and Margaret was relieved that her mother didn't insist that she taste everything. After the dishes and forks were cleared, her mother filled bowls with chicken broth and fluffy matzah balls. Aunt Lillian carried them, one by one, to the table.

"This is my favorite part of dinner at the seder," Margaret said.

"I like the soup best, too," her grandmother agreed. "I think I could be happy with the soup and nothing else." She took another sip of broth and a mouthful of matzah ball. "Ada, I think you make the best matzah balls in the family. Every year they are light and fluffy. I hate little matzah balls that are chewy like rubber."

The adults laughed because they knew whose matzah balls she meant.

"Aunt Rae always claimed she wanted them to come out like that. She said that's how Uncle Manny liked them," Aunt Lillian said.

"Don't you believe it for a minute. She cried every year when she saw those little blobs sink to the bottom of the soup kettle and stay there. Ada, try to wake Phoebe so she can taste a matzah ball." But Phoebe was sleeping so soundly she could not be roused.

After the soup, the family shared platters of brisket and green beans and potato kugel.

"Delicious, as usual, Ada," Aunt Lillian said. "Don't you agree, Douglas?"

"I do agree, and her reward is another cup of wine."

As he poured, Margaret realized that the grown-ups had almost finished the bottle of wine, and the faces of the women looked rosy and their eyes looked bright. She wondered if it was the way the candlelight flickered and shone on them.

"Careful, Douglas," her mother said. "You need to save enough wine for Elijah."

"He'll have his share," her father answered. "But we need our share, too. After all, we're about to walk through the sea and across the desert."

Margaret was pleased when her mother cut especially generous portions of sponge cake for dessert and passed around a bowl of strawberries for those who wanted a topping. Her grandmother's sponge cake was light and luscious. It seemed to spring back when Margaret tried to chew it before suddenly dissolving in her mouth. Aunt Lillian said that was because the egg whites were whipped until they stood stiff with fear that the beating would never end. Anybody in the house when the sponge cake was being made had to take a turn, until everybody's arms hurt so much they worried they wouldn't be able to get their forks to their mouths the next day. Margaret always ate hers plain, and Melissa always covered hers with strawberries.

"They may look alike, but they are as different as can be, and here's yet more evidence," her mother said, indicating the twins' dessert plates.

Margaret had a moment of worry before she saw that her mother was laughing along with everyone else, and she knew she hadn't done anything wrong.

When everybody agreed they couldn't eat another morsel, her mother brought out the piece of matzah that had been wrapped in a napkin, and everybody ate a little piece of it. Then her father opened his booklet and started to read.

"Douglas, put out Elijah's cup," her mother said.

He nodded, placed a beautiful silver goblet on a small plate in the center of the table, and filled it to the brim with wine.

"Every year I marvel at how lovely that cup is," her grandmother said.

"It is, isn't it," her mother agreed. "My mother knew I would think of her at every seder."

Margaret watched her grandmother pat her mother's hand and was surprised to see her mother smile and pat her grandmother's hand in return.

"Okay, we're ready here," her father said, and her mother went to open the front door. The twins watched the cup while her father read the prayer inviting Elijah the Prophet to come in and drink some wine. At least that's what the twins had been told the prayer meant. As her father finished reading and sat down, the wine in the cup moved and a little spilled onto the plate.

"See?" Aunt Lillian said. "He was here, and he sipped the wine."

"He didn't drink much," Melissa said.

"He takes a little sip at each house or he'd be too drunk to visit everyone," her grandmother answered.

"I think Daddy bumped the table when he sat down," Margaret said.

"I did not. I was very careful because I remember being accused of that very thing last year."

Her father opened his booklet, but when her mother came back to the table she said, "Enough, Douglas. Skip to the end."

Everybody turned to the back of the book, and, in unison, read "The following year grant us to be in Jerusalem."

The twins watched their mother lift Phoebe out of the high chair. "I'll take the baby upstairs," she said. "She's not going to remember anything about the seder, but we'll remember she was here. Margaret and Melissa, you start on the dishes."

Margaret went to the kitchen and filled the dishpan with sudsy water. She felt tired and overwhelmed by the number of dishes to be washed, but she was sure her mother wouldn't want them left until morning. Melissa took a clean dish towel, and everybody else helped clear the table and return the extra chairs to their usual places.

As the dishes accumulated on the counter, Aunt Lillian took the extra sponge and nudged Margaret aside. "There's room here for both of us to wash," she said and called to her mother. "Hey, Mom. Come in here and help Melissa dry. With four of us, we'll finish these in no time."

When her mother returned from putting Phoebe to bed, Margaret looked up in alarm. "This wasn't my idea."

"That's right," Aunt Lillian quickly interjected. "It was my idea."

"And a good idea it was," her mother said.

Margaret looked at her in disbelief and went back to washing the dishes so as not to break the spell. Her mother began returning the clean dishes to the cupboards, and as she worked, she began to sing.

Margaret had never heard this song before. In fact, she couldn't remember hearing her mother sing anything but lullabies to Phoebe. At first Margaret thought it was a beautiful, slow song about a deer, but then she realized that the words were in Hebrew, so she didn't know what it was about.

The adults must have heard it before because after the first line they all joined in. Margaret could hear her father's deep voice from the dining room adding harmony at the bottom and her aunt's light soprano adding harmony at the top. Aunt Lillian nudged her and said, "Join in," and Margaret noticed that the verses repeated and she could sing the "a deer who" phrase and the "bim hay rah" phrase when they came around. Her mother smiled at her when she joined the chorus, and Margaret's heart sang along with her voice.

Margaret listened carefully to the next song. It was another one she couldn't understand, and it seemed to be a race. Everybody sang as fast as they could, and the song went by so quickly that Margaret had a hard time joining in. By the end, the women were flushed and laughing. Her father came into the kitchen, and first he and then Aunt Lillian sang the longest verse alone to see who could finish it on one breath. After they both failed, her mother insisted on a turn.

"Okay, but you'll never manage," her father said.

Her mother took three deep breaths and began. To the amazement and cheers of all, she did it.

Margaret had never seen her mother look so happy. "This is a miracle," she whispered to Melissa. "Don't you think this is a miracle?"

Before Melissa could answer, her father gathered her up and danced her once around the kitchen and then did the same with Margaret. Then her grandmother danced with each of them while her father danced with her mother and Aunt Lillian. Margaret thought their kitchen had never seen or heard such happiness.

Melissa and Margaret kissed everybody before going up to bed. As she kissed her cheek, Margaret whispered into Aunt Lillian's ear, "If there can be one miracle, there can be more. You'll get your miracle, too."

Aunt Lillian looked confused but gave Margaret a hug and wished her good night.

"Yes," Melissa said as they were falling asleep.

Margaret thought she must have missed most of whatever Melissa had said. "What?"

"Yes."

"What are you talking about?"

"You asked me if what happened in the kitchen was a miracle, and my answer is yes. I'm not sure I believe in miracles, but if there is such a thing, that was one."

"I guess that means that miracles are a surprise."

"Maybe."

"I hope they last."

THE NEXT MORNING WAS A TYPICAL SCHOOL DAY MORNING. After being rushed through breakfast, scolded for not standing still while her hair was braided, and accused of dawdling when it was time to gather her schoolbooks, Margaret found herself walking to school with Melissa.

"Last night I found out that miracles are a surprise, and this morning I found out they don't last," she said.

"But at least you had a peek at what things would be like if a miracle happened every minute. I think that's enough, don't you?" Melissa said.

"No," Margaret said and scuffed her shoes along the pavement all the way to school.

# Lillian and Anshel

*1956*

Lillian stopped at the "No Admittance" sign on the door. Although she had been working at the Schottenstein Ink Company for over five years, she had never been in the factory. It was understood that women did not venture into the area where the ink was mixed and the men who mixed it did not come into the office. But when a salesman had a question, even one she could answer, Lillian went looking for Mr. Schottenstein. She was, after all, a mere secretary, and he was the owner.

Mr. Schottenstein wasn't in his office. He wasn't in the back office, and he wasn't in the coffee room; the door to the bathroom was open, so she was confident he wasn't in there, and there was no chance he was sitting in the rain at one of the picnic tables in the yard. The last place to look was the large area at the back of the building that Mr. Schottenstein called the formulation lab. Lillian thought of it as the factory.

Lillian pictured the factory as a filthy place, with cobwebs hanging from the ceiling, splotches of color covering the floor, and long, sticky ribbons of ink dripping down the walls. In her imagination, steam rose from dark, mysterious liquids bubbling in vast cauldrons stirred by huge men who looked more like trolls than humans. Earlier this morning, she had been glad that she wore her new yellow dress and matching silk scarf. Her mother said she looked like a buttercup when she left the house, and Mr. Schottenstein told her she was a welcome ray of sunshine on an otherwise rainy day. Now she hoped she wasn't going to get dirty. As she hesitated at the door, Lillian laughed out loud. "Grow up," she told herself. "This isn't a fairy tale."

Lillian stepped inside and looked around in surprise at how right she had been about the factory. Large vats and huge rollers filled a space stained with splashed ink. Along one wall, packages of powders rested on shelves, and drums of liquid lined the wall opposite. The only things missing were the cobwebs and the trolls.

At first, Lillian thought the room was empty. Then she saw a man standing among the vats. He had ginger-colored hair and wore spectacles and an ink-splattered coverall that was as much camouflage as protection for his clothing. He appeared to take up no space at all.

"Have you seen Mr. Schottenstein?" Lillian called out from the doorway. She saw the man inhale sharply and rub his hand once across his cheek, leaving a smudge of yellow behind. Then he looked down and answered in a quiet voice with such a heavy accent that she didn't understand what he said. Since he sounded exactly like her Uncle Shlomo, Lillian, without thinking, did what she always did with her uncle and repeated herself louder in Yiddish.

"*Vu iz* Mr. Schottenstein?" The man stared at her in dismay and confusion, and Lillian took pity on him for the shock he must have suffered seeing a woman walk into the factory and speak to him at all, much less in Yiddish.

"*Heysn*, Lillian," she said, introducing herself in a soft voice. "*Vi hayst ir*?"

"Anshel," he answered.

"*Shalom Aleichem*, Anshel." Lillian said and then repeated her question. "*Vu iz* Mr. Schottenstein?"

"*Er iz nischt do*."

Lillian could see for herself that Mr. Schottenstein was not in the factory, but she didn't think it would be kind to prolong this conversation by asking again if Anshel knew where he was. So she decided to thank him and retreat.

"*A sheynem dank*, Anshel."

"*Nishta far vos*."

"*Zayt gezunt*," she said, turning to leave.

"*Zayt gezunt*," he responded.

Lillian went back to her desk, took a message from the salesman, and left it next to Mr. Schottenstein's phone.

At five o'clock, Lillian cleared her desk, put on her coat and hat, and gathered up her purse and gloves. The evening was still misty. Grateful, yet again, that her brother Ira let her use his car on weekdays, Lillian drove carefully down the alley. As she pulled onto the street, she noticed the same tall, lanky figure she saw almost every evening walking close to the buildings. Now she recognized the figure as Anshel. Lillian pulled up next to him, but by the time she rolled down the window to offer him a ride, he had turned the corner. Though he must have been aware of the car, he did not glance in her direction before he was gone. Lillian felt peeved; she was used to welcoming smiles and eager conversation when she took an interest in a man, and she didn't like being ignored.

Clara, Lillian's mother, put great store by a hot meal, especially on a rainy day, and dinner was on the table as soon as Lillian took off her hat and coat. As the two women ate, Lillian told her mother about work and about the strange man she had seen in the factory.

"Maybe he came over right after the war, Lillian. I bet he's a refugee."

"Could be, Mom."

"If he's a refugee, he had a sponsor."

"He didn't look like a person who has anybody."

"If you see him again, ask him to dinner. We don't want him to be lonely."

That's just like you, Lillian thought. You would feed the world if you could. Still, she couldn't dispute the fact that a hot meal might be precisely what Anshel needed. Then Lillian had another thought and looked closely at her mother.

"If he ever comes here for a meal, promise me there won't be any matchmaking."

"Don't worry, Lillian. He sounds like a lonely foreigner, and that doesn't seem like the boy for you. Though I hope you'll find that lucky boy sometime soon."

"In my own time, Mom." The way Anshel didn't notice her forced Lillian to agree that he was unlikely to be the lucky boy her mother had in mind. Worse yet, he would probably think himself lucky if she didn't notice him, either.

"That's what you always say, but time has its own way of running by. Last week Mrs. Alpert's daughter got engaged, and she's younger than you are."

"Congratulations to Mrs. Alpert. When I meet the right man, I'll get engaged, too."

"Just let it be in my lifetime."

This was an old discussion, and neither woman chose to pursue it now. Lillian knew she wanted a husband eventually, but, even though most girls her age were already married, she felt no urgency to change her marital status. She didn't see herself as old. Most of the time. You're only as old as you feel, she reassured herself, and twenty-five isn't old at all. So what's the hurry?

The marriages Lillian knew most about provided little encouragement. Her own father left home when she was a little girl. Her oldest brother hated him, and Lillian had had to look up "philanderer" in the dictionary after Douglas once scolded her for saying she missed him. She hadn't had to look up "bum." But Lillian remembered his goodnight hugs and kisses, and the fragrance of his aftershave, and sitting next to him on Sunday afternoons while he taught her to play pinochle, and the time he bought her a little suitcase to take on her first overnight at a friend's house. She assumed he lived in another city and never understood why he didn't visit or try to see her.

Lillian's sister-in-law Ada was a formal, aloof woman who had been born and raised in Scotland. While Clara never complained about Ada, Lillian knew that Ada's stiff reserve and lack of affection saddened her mother and made it impossible to bring Ada into the extended family in the way Clara would have liked. Though Ada lent Lillian books, they never shared confidences, and Lillian didn't know if Ada was happily married. Her other sister-in-law, Fay, hadn't finished high school when Harold married her a few months before the birth of their first child. She was pleasant, and Lillian had no trouble adopting Clara's attitude that Fay made Harold happy in spite of the quarrels that could be heard coming from the upstairs apartment where they lived. So Lillian's immediate family provided no examples of women made obviously happier and more fulfilled by marriage.

Lillian had no shortage of dates when she wanted them. Her friends were constantly suggesting their cousins or brothers-in-law or somebody from work. They were usually nice men, secure in their careers and pleasant companions, but, eventually, their interests struck her as narrow, and their conversation became predictable and uninteresting. How much could be said about cars and basketball and neighborhood baseball teams? For now, she was happy to enjoy her job and help her mother with the household expenses. I value my independence, she told herself, like every modern woman.

The one person Lillian felt sorry for was Mr. Schottenstein. In the thirty years that he had owned the ink company, Mr. Schottenstein had earned a reputation as a matchmaker. Every secretary he hired had married one of his salesmen within three years of joining the company. It wasn't his fault that the end of the war brought less turnover in his sales team, or that all his current salesmen were married. Still, Lillian worried that he saw her as his first failure and hoped he wasn't feeling guilty about her unmarried state. So she was careful to be very kind to him in the office, and she noticed that he was very kind to her, too. Clara was also kind to Mr. Schottenstein and sometimes sent him a corned beef sandwich for lunch.

The next day, Lillian wore her plaid, pleated skirt and a new blue sweater that brought out the blue in her eyes. She was disappointed when no excuse to visit the factory materialized. Mr. Schottenstein was at his desk all day and even read the monthly sales reports while he ate a sandwich that Lillian picked up for him at the corner store. Every time a call came in, he was available. Lillian realized that sometimes Mr. Schottenstein's work ethic annoyed her.

All that week and the next, Lillian had no reason to go into the factory. This shouldn't have surprised her. She hadn't had a reason to visit the factory but that once in all the five years she had worked at the company. Maybe she wouldn't have another excuse for another five years. It was more surprising and irritating that she didn't catch sight of Anshel walking home again, either. It was as if he had disappeared.

NEARLY A MONTH LATER, AS LILLIAN RETURNED FROM taking the mail to the post office, she saw Anshel smoking at a picnic table under the tree at the side of the building. There were several picnic tables on the lawn, and sometimes Lillian or the salesmen ate their lunches there. Other times, the men who mixed the ink had lunch or smoked at the tables. The two groups didn't typically notice each other, but on this day, Lillian noticed Anshel.

It was a little early for lunch, but Lillian knew the family stories about how her sister-in-law Ada had secretly left lunches in Douglas's room when he boarded with her family. It was the beginning of their courtship. Lillian decided to try Ada's strategy. She took her sandwich, the sandwich that her mother had sent for Mr. Schottenstein, and two bottles of Coke from the refrigerator in the coffee room. Then she grabbed a handful of napkins from the counter, slipped the bottle opener into her skirt pocket, and hurried out to the picnic table. Anshel didn't see her coming.

"*Shalom Aleichem*, Anshel," Lillian said, and sat opposite him. Anshel inhaled sharply and brought his hand to his cheek. For an instant, she thought he might flee, but a moment later, he was calm and composed, and Lillian wondered if she had imagined his first reaction.

He ground his cigarette under his shoe. "We are in America now. We should speak English," he said.

Lillian thought that her Yiddish was probably better than his English, but she nodded in agreement. Speaking slowly and clearly, she said, "I have an extra sandwich today, and it would make me happy to give it to you."

Anshel seemed about to refuse, but then thought better of it. "America is a surprising place," he said. "Thank you very much. Why do you have two?"

Lillian opened both sandwiches and both bottles of Coke before she took a bite of her sandwich. Only then did Anshel take a bite of his. "This is very good," he said and took another bite. "But I ask again, why do you have two?"

"Sometimes my mother gives me two."

"Thank your mother for me."

"I will. I told her I met you, and she said you should come for dinner sometime." Anshel made no response. "Have you been working here for long?"

"Since the winter."

"Where are you from?"

"I came here from Chicago."

Lillian almost said something about Chicago accents before she saw that he had not intended any joke. Instead, she nodded slowly and asked, "Did you like Chicago? I've never been there."

"It's very cold there, and I didn't like it. So I came here."

"Do you like it here?"

"Yes." Anshel stood and brushed the crumbs from his lap onto the grass. "Now I must go back to work. Thank you for the sandwich and the Coke. You are a nice lady."

Lillian watched him walk to the back of the building. Nice lady? She couldn't tell if that was excessive politeness or if he saw her as old enough to be his aunt or his schoolteacher. It was impossible for Lillian to guess his age, but she doubted that many years separated them. He certainly didn't treat me like an eligible woman, she thought, or like a woman at all.

Now he'll probably avoid the picnic table the same way he avoids the street where I used to see him.

As if to prove her right, Anshel was not to be seen at a picnic table for the next two weeks. Of course, Lillian had never seen him at the picnic tables before the day she gave him Mr. Schottenstein's sandwich. Maybe that was the only time he had ever been out there. Maybe he wouldn't venture out there again for years.

In spite of herself, Lillian thought more and more often about the mysterious Anshel. Her experience growing up with three older brothers had convinced her that she understood men, that she could get her way with them. But here was a man of a different breed, whose Yiddish was from Poland, whose eyes always looked down, who seemed both fearful and defiant at the same time. What sort of man was he? And why was she thinking about him?

LILLIAN HAD MIXED FEELINGS ABOUT THE PARTY AT DOTTY'S house. Her date was Dotty's sister-in-law's cousin, and Lillian had met him originally as a favor to Dotty. When she found that Jack was an amusing companion and a good dancer, she accepted subsequent dates and had been seeing him regularly for several weeks. Jack worked in an insurance office and told her repeatedly about the good living he made and his plans to make some lucky girl happy. He had even hinted that she might be that lucky girl.

Dotty usually invited three or four couples. They chatted and laughed, and then turned on the radio and danced. The station they liked best played the latest tunes, and Lillian looked forward to "Rock Around the Clock" and that new song, "Love is a Many Splendored Thing." Jack was a flamboyant and dramatic dancer, throwing himself into the fast tunes with flair and gracefully executing the slow ones. Lillian particularly liked the confident pressure of his hand on her back as he led her through the romantic dances. Though she wasn't sure that translated into romantic feelings toward Jack himself.

This weekend, Lillian had reluctantly agreed to see a movie with Jack on Sunday. When a boy spent money on a date, it was a mark of special favor that she didn't want to encourage. And two dates in one weekend might be similarly misunderstood.

Lillian chose her pink dress with intricate stitching and frills on the bodice. She hadn't worn it yet on a date with Jack.

Clara smiled when she saw her and straightened Lillian's collar a bit. "I love this dress on you," she said. "Jack seems like a nice boy."

"No need to hint and fish for information, Mom. Ask what you want to know."

"Are you serious about him?"

Lillian shrugged. "I can't say that I feel serious."

"So what's wrong with him?"

"Nothing is wrong with him. He's handsome and amusing, but I'm not going to force myself to love him."

"At least you're giving him a chance." Clara paused a moment. "It's good to be careful, but I'm afraid you might be getting too picky."

"I'm waiting for someone who isn't boring after a few evenings together. Someone who thinks about more than saving money for a car."

"Not all good men are deep thinkers, Lillian. I hope you're not waiting for the perfect man because, if that's the case, you'll wait forever."

Jack came by a few minutes later, and he and Lillian walked the three blocks to Dotty's house.

"Sorry we're walking again tonight. I've saved almost enough, and it won't be long before I'll be able to drive everywhere we go."

"I don't mind walking. It's a lovely evening to be outside," Lillian said.

"You look very pretty tonight. That's a nice dress, and I like how your pink shoes match. They look new."

"Thank you." Lillian made a point of looking him over, and Jack enjoyed her scrutiny. "You're quite smart, yourself. And it looks like you have new shoes, too. Quite stylish with their snappy bows."

Jack accepted her compliment with a nod. "I'll pass that along to my youngest brother who considers me nearly hopeless. He approved the shoes and actually lent me his favorite tie when he saw the one I planned to wear. He said he hopes I marry a woman with good taste so he can stop worrying about me."

Lillian laughed. She appreciated his effort to amuse her, but she didn't believe a word of it. She knew that Jack always dressed well and had probably bought his brother the tie he was wearing tonight. He might even be encouraging his brother to think he needs help, and she liked him for that, too.

Meanwhile, Jack had launched into a story about the new salesman in his office. "You should see this guy's briefcase. Leather and brand-new, but we all know it's empty. He'd be better off with less briefcase and more orders."

Conversation never lagged with Jack. Usually Lillian enjoyed the torrent of words, but tonight she found it a little exhausting.

Lillian knew that Jack helped support his mother and three brothers. It was understood that when the next brother in line earned enough to help the family, Jack would be free to think about a family of his own. Since the next oldest brother was a junior in high school, Jack's freedom was more than a year in the future, and he was in no position to pressure her for a commitment. At the same time, Lillian knew she couldn't keep him around as a boyfriend for too long before a tacit agreement would be assumed. A few weeks isn't too long, she told herself, but why keep him around at all? Just because he tells funny stories and knows the latest dance steps? That doesn't sound like a formula for a successful marriage, though it does make for a pleasant evening. Maybe we'll settle into a pattern of pleasant evenings with no strings attached, Lillian thought, though she knew that was the least likely scenario.

The next day, Jack took her to see *Marty*, and after the movie, they went for ice cream. Jack bought her a cup of vanilla and settled her at a little table by the window.

"Are you sure you don't want chocolate sauce?" he asked. "Vanilla ice cream is too plain without chocolate sauce."

"I'm fine."

"Okay," he said and went back to the counter for his own ice cream topped with sauce that dripped over the lip of the cup.

"That Marty was some shlub," Jack said, licking a drop of chocolate from his spoon. "He's lucky anybody liked him. And that girl was lucky she met him because who else would look at her?"

Lillian didn't answer right away, and the usual pace of their repartee broke down.

"Hey, Lil, are you okay?"

"I was thinking about how he was the perfect man for her, and how lucky it was that she waited for him and he came to find her."

"I guess they were both sort of waiting. Not that they intended to."

As he left her at her door, Lillian thanked him for a lovely afternoon, and Jack said he hoped Dotty would have another party the next weekend. Lillian nodded in agreement but hoped Dotty had other plans. She doubted that cheerful, confident Jack was the man she was waiting for, and she knew it would be cruel to let him think otherwise or spend any more money on her. Maybe she had become too picky, after all.

If she hadn't bought shoes that were the latest thing and worn her new shoes to work, Lillian might never have had another encounter with Anshel. The shoes were white, with little leather straps that ran crisscross over her foot and looked very smart. Unfortunately, they also pinched when she walked.

Mr. Schottenstein noticed her hobbling around the office. "Lillian, what's with your feet? Do they hurt? Or maybe you twisted your ankle?"

"I did twist my ankle a little," she said, grateful he had suggested a reason that sounded better than admitting her shoes were too tight.

"I'll have a man drive you home. You need to get off your feet, and we can manage the rest of the day without you," he said. "Who's in the office?"

As it turned out, no salesmen were there, and, though Lillian assured him that she could drive herself home, he would not hear of it. "I would take you myself, but Gordon is calling from Detroit, and I need to be here to talk to him. Would you mind if a man from the back drove?"

"Mr. Schottenstein, this is very kind of you, but completely unnecessary. I do appreciate your concern, and it will be good to get off my feet, but I'm sure I can drive."

"If you're sure. But I insist on calling for somebody to help you to your car."

While Lillian put on her hat and coat and gathered her purse and gloves, she could hear Mr. Schottenstein on the phone asking that a man wash up and report to the front. Shortly afterward, the phone rang and Lillian put the call from Mr. Gordon through. Though she closed his office door so he would not be disturbed while they talked, she could hear Mr. Schottenstein scolding Mr. Gordon for the mix-up in an order the previous week.

Several minutes later, Lillian looked up to see Anshel standing in the doorway of her little office. He had taken off his coveralls and was wearing an old shirt and faded pants. His hands looked freshly scrubbed. He stood very still, frowning and rubbing his cheek. Lillian realized that this was probably the first time he had been in any part of the building except the factory.

"I'm sent to carry something heavy to your car."

"That would be me." Lillian laughed, but then became serious when she saw how dismayed Anshel looked. "I don't need to be carried," she assured him. "I twisted my ankle a little, and Mr. Schottenstein thinks I need help getting to my car."

Lillian saw that even the prospect of taking her arm alarmed Anshel and realized that he must have grown up in a community where physical contact was allowed only between husband and wife. She was charmed. It made her feel special to be off-limits, like a princess.

"Don't worry. I'm sure I can cure my ankle and sneak out without anybody seeing. And I won't need any help at all."

Anshel looked down at her feet. He must understand, she thought. My ankle isn't swollen and the tops of my feet are red and puffy. He must see that this sprained ankle is nothing more than simple vanity. For an instant she was embarrassed and then relieved when he smiled and shook his head.

Lillian slipped off her shoes and, with Anshel following behind, walked through the building to the back door. She stopped when confronted with the gravel yard. She and Anshel looked at it. Though it was no distance at all to her car, the gravel looked menacing.

"Now I return the favor of the sandwich," Anshel said. "Wait here." It didn't take but a minute for him to return with several large, empty bags. He brushed the ink powder off them and laid them end to end across the gravel.

"I'll have to call you 'Sir Walter Raleigh' from now on," Lillian said, as she walked on the bags to her car. Anshel looked confused and she added, "He was a gallant Englishman long ago. You are also gallant, so I'm sure you won't tell the secret of my sprained ankle."

"I can keep a secret," he said.

Lillian watched him gather the empty bags and return to the building before she pulled out of her parking space and drove down the alley.

THE NEXT DAY, LILLIAN WOUND A BANDAGE LOOSELY around her ankle, wore her most sensible shoes, and returned to work. She had three sandwiches with her.

"Lillian, my dear," Mr. Schottenstein greeted her. "You're walking much better today."

"I am. Thank you for letting me go home early yesterday. I rested in the afternoon and that made all the difference."

Mr. Schottenstein smiled and nodded.

"My mother is grateful, too. She sent you this sandwich for lunch, and she sent a sandwich for the man who helped me to my car."

"Who did Rusty send?"

"I think he said his name was Anshel."

"He sent the new man? I don't know him so well. But if Rusty sent him, I'm sure he was polite and helpful."

"He was very polite and helpful. How shall I give him the sandwich from my mother?"

"I'll ask Rusty to send him to the office when he can be spared for a minute."

Lillian knew that Mr. Schottenstein was careful to treat his foreman with courtesy and to make requests in a way that acknowledged Rusty's dominion over the ink-mixing component of the business. So when she waited most of the morning to see Anshel, she was not surprised. In fact, she was pleased that it was almost lunchtime before he appeared at her office door, looking worried. When she smiled at him, he did not smile in return. And when she invited him to come into her office, he took one step through the doorway.

"Thank you for helping me yesterday."

"You are welcome. Did I do something wrong?"

"No, not at all. But my mother said to tell you that she is also grateful to you for helping me, and she sent you this sandwich for lunch." Lillian put his sandwich on her desk, and he came forward to take it.

"Tell your mother thank you from me."

"I have a sandwich, too. Are you going to eat outside?"

They both looked out the window and saw the ink-mixing crew gathering at the tables with their lunch boxes.

"No," Anshel said and looked down at the floor.

"It does look crowded," Lillian said. She couldn't think of another idea. We can't sit at my desk right outside Mr. Schottenstein's office. We can't walk around with our sandwiches in our hands. If he wants to have lunch with me, he'll have to figure it out for himself. The first time I saw him, it was happenstance. The second time, I admit I managed it. But the third time was a coincidence. I managed it again this time, but I can't do more. And why would I want to?

After a long pause while Anshel seemed lost in his own thoughts, Lillian decided that even if he wasn't interested in having lunch with her, Anshel still looked like a lonely refugee who could use one of her mother's dinners. "My mother would like you to come to dinner so she can thank you in person," she said.

For the first time, Anshel looked directly at her. She hadn't noticed before that his eyes were a deep, shiny brown. Living in a family that prized its blue eyes, Lillian had never appreciated how beautiful brown eyes could be. He looked at her intently, as if taking an accounting of her merits. It gave their encounter an unexpected intensity.

"I have another idea for eating outside," he said, and put his sandwich back into the paper bag on her desk. "Is it time for your lunch?"

"Yes, I can go anytime, but I only have a half hour."

"Good. I also have a short time."

"I'll tell Mr. Schottenstein that I'm leaving."

By the time Lillian cleared her desk and told Mr. Schottenstein that she would be having lunch out today, Anshel had returned to her office. He was holding a thermos and two cups in one hand, and he picked up the bag of sandwiches with the other.

"We go out the back," he said.

The two of them walked a few steps down the alley before turning on a tiny street and walking to a small grassy patch and two wooden benches. Anshel sat at the end of one of them and indicated that Lillian should sit at the other end. He tore the bag open to make a place mat between them and set their sandwiches on it.

"You like tea?" he asked.

"Yes," Lillian said, and he poured them each a cup of steaming tea from the thermos.

"All the men in the back use the cups, but I washed them very much, and they are clean."

They ate their sandwiches in silence for several minutes.

"I never knew this little street was here," Lillian said.

"It's always quiet here, so I bring my tea to this bench." Again, Anshel seemed lost in thought. Then he took a deep breath, put his cup on the bench, and looked directly at Lillian.

"I am twenty-seven years old, and I am in this country four years. First, I live with my uncle in Chicago, and now I send him money to pay back what he spent helping me and having me in his house. Soon that will be paid, and all my salary will be mine."

This rush of information surprised Lillian with its seriousness and intimacy. She was used to lighthearted, flirtatious conversations about things like basketball, movies, and dance steps. Talking to Anshel wasn't like talking to any boy she'd met before.

"I am US citizen already," Anshel continued. "My uncle made this happen quickly in Chicago."

"Why did you leave Chicago?"

"It wasn't good for me to stay longer there. How old are you?"

So sudden and direct a question caught Lillian off guard. Didn't he know how indelicate it was to ask a woman her age? But after his revelations, she felt compelled to answer honestly without the coy tactics she typically used to deflect the question whenever anybody was rude enough to ask.

"I am twenty-five."

"Do you live with your family?"

"I live with my mother and Ira, one of my older brothers, but he isn't home much. My other brothers are married. Harold lives upstairs from us with his family, and Douglas, my oldest brother, lives a few blocks away. He married a girl from Scotland, and they have three little daughters. Where does your family live?"

"My family is no more."

Well, thought Lillian, that's one thoughtless question each.

After several minutes of eating in silence, Anshel said, "I'm not so religious. I don't pray every day or keep so kosher. But I don't eat *trafe*, and I go to *shul* sometimes. I was never married."

Lillian had no idea how to respond.

Anshel finished his sandwich and wiped his hands on the wrapper. Lillian also brushed the crumbs from her hands and finished her cup of tea.

"Thank you for the tea."

"Thank you for the sandwich." Anshel looked away, and then added, "I bring my tea to this bench at lunchtime, if it's not raining."

"It's a lovely spot for lunch," Lillian said and wondered if that was an invitation.

At dinner that night, Lillian told her mother about her lunch with Anshel. "He's not like anybody I've met before. I thought he was much older than I am, but we are about the same age. I think he thought I was younger," she added and laughed. "But he didn't seem distressed by my advanced years."

"This boy worries me," Clara said.

"You think he's not honorable?"

"That's possible, of course, but I'm more worried that he's too solemn. This is not the boy for you. You like to laugh and have fun. This boy is too different. He might not even know how to have fun." Clara helped herself to more stew and put another generous spoonful on Lillian's plate before continuing. "Remember, he was in the war and had experiences we can't even imagine. Like that refugee Shirley almost married before she found out that he hides food all over the house and doesn't sleep a night without screaming."

"That doesn't sound like Anshel. He's just quiet and reserved."

But then there were his revelations about himself. He doesn't say anything, and then he suddenly tells her things about himself she still doesn't know about boys she's talked to for years. What about that? Her mother also had a theory there.

"You need to be careful for another reason, too, Lilly. I think he was telling you things a matchmaker would have told you when she suggested his name and tried to arrange a *shidduch*."

Lillian was stunned. "A matchmaker? We don't use matchmakers." Then the import of her mother's words sank in. "You mean he's thinking of marrying me after one lunch on a park bench?"

"I do. He's from the old country. In that world, young people didn't date for months and months. They met once or twice, decided if they liked each other, and then either went their separate ways or got married." Clara leaned across the table to emphasize her words. "This boy's trying to find his way in a strange, new country all by himself. You can't treat him like a casual date. You have to be as serious as he is or make it clear to him that you're not." Clara sat back in her chair. "It amazes me that he took a chance on you."

When Lillian frowned, Clara quickly added, "Not because you aren't worth it, God forbid. But because, if you're right, he's been avoiding you till now. So why was he so open with you today?"

My very question, thought Lillian. Why today? She had no answer.

Lillian heeded her mother's warning and ignored Anshel's invitation, if, in fact, his comment had been an invitation. Suddenly, joining someone on a park bench for another cup of tea became a momentous step, something that meeting a boy or going on a date had never been before.

Though she decided not to see Anshel, Lillian wondered about him endlessly. Was she ready for somebody so serious, so different? Maybe her mother was right, and this was not the boy for her. But the thought of seeing Jack or boys like him, and all boys were like him, bored her.

And Anshel's eyes were lovely. On the park bench, he had looked at her as though he was looking right into her and was pleased with what he saw. It wasn't that he was deciding she was pretty; Lillian knew boys thought she was pretty. It was as if he was deciding she was good.

"What's going on, Lillian?" Jack asked one evening on the phone. "I thought we were getting along fine."

"I've been busy, Jack."

"What's keeping you so busy? Are you mad at me?"

"No, I'm not angry."

"Do you think I'm too young for you?" Lillian's silence must have transmitted her shock, and he explained. "I asked Dotty if she knew why you don't want to go out with me anymore, and she told me you are older than I am. Is that it?"

"It isn't anything like that, Jack. I just need a rest."

"A rest from everybody or from me?"

"Just a rest."

"Okay, I'll give you a rest. Dotty says you do this a lot, and I shouldn't take it personally. When you're rested, I hope you'll tell Dotty to let me know."

Lillian was sorry to hear that she had a reputation for doing this a lot, but she wasn't sorry enough to change her mind about seeing Jack again. It wasn't like they had ever had a serious conversation.

When she wouldn't have dinner with Mrs. Steinberg's nephew who was visiting from Boston, Clara became concerned enough to ask her why.

"It sounds boring, and I don't feel like meeting another boring boy," Lillian said.

"You haven't gone anywhere for weeks. And this boy owns his own moving business. He's very successful."

"I'm happy for him, but I'm not going to dinner with him, and he better not show up for dinner here, either."

"This isn't like you at all, Lillian. I've never known you to be secretive, but I have to ask if you're seeing somebody you haven't told me about. It would be dreadful to keep something like that from your mother."

"Calm down, Mom. I'm not seeing anybody, and I don't feel like seeing anybody."

"Are you thinking too much about somebody?"

Exactly right, Lillian thought. She's on to me as usual. Lillian looked at her mother, and her eyes fill with tears she didn't understand.

"Lilly, baby, what's wrong?" Clara sat next to Lillian on the couch. "It's that refugee, isn't it?"

"I know you said he's not for me, so I haven't seen him again," Lillian said. "But I keep thinking about him. He's so much on my mind it's like we're dating without him even being there."

"You're a sweet girl and you're smart. Maybe you're thinking about him because he's so different that he seems mysterious." Clara frowned. "But it wouldn't be good if he was too sad or too different. Your Aunt Thelma married a man who was too different. He never sat with the family for a meal. Said all the tumult gave him a headache. At least he had the good sense to run off after a year, and, by then, even Thelma was relieved to see him go." Clara took Lillian's hand. "You like to laugh, Lillian. I wouldn't want anybody to change that about you."

Clara sat for a long moment without speaking before she sighed and looked up. "Maybe you should see him and solve the mystery. But remember that he's a serious boy and be careful not to lead him on. When the mystery is solved, you'll be able to decide about him, and he'll be able to decide about you." Clara smiled. "That's enough advice. There must be a reason why he's on your mind, so do whatever you choose to do, and I know it will be the right thing."

Even with Clara's permission and her vote of confidence, however hedged and qualified, Lillian hesitated. Meeting Anshel for tea seemed tantamount to marrying him, or, at least, to thinking about marrying him.

FOR THE NEXT THREE DAYS, LILLIAN ATE LUNCH IN THE coffee room and read the bestseller Ada had lent her. By day four, she had had enough of Marjorie Morningstar, a self-centered social climber, and Marjorie's endlessly pontificating boyfriends. Lillian could see the men from the back gathering at the picnic tables for lunch, but Anshel was not among them. She ate her lunch quickly at her desk and told Mr. Schottenstein she was going out for a walk.

"Take your time, my dear. We'll be fine here," he said.

Lillian slipped on her sweater and walked through the building before hesitating at the back door. This can't be the hasty decision of an idle moment, she reminded herself. If I want a date, this is not the boy. If I want a husband, he might be. He might be somebody whose stories interest me, and who will listen to my stories, too. But a husband has to be more than interesting. A husband has to be somebody you can love. Am I ready to say that about Anshel? Am I ready to say that about anybody?

Lillian stood for a moment without reaching a decision before she walked out the door, crossed the gravel parking lot, and entered the alley. She walked down the alley and turned on the little street. I can't say I understand myself, she thought, but apparently, I am going to walk all the way to that little park and see if, three weeks later, he's on the bench. Halfway to the park, she stood for a moment and squinted into the sunlight.

Anshel was sitting on the bench. He stood when he saw her and watched her walk toward him. Suddenly every step she took seemed filled with significance. As she came closer, Lillian saw that he had his thermos and two cups set out on the bench along with a little bag from the kosher bakery. He must have set this up every day for three weeks and waited.

Anshel smiled when she sat down. "I am glad to see you. You are wearing the same dress you wore the first time I saw you." Lillian realized that this was true and was surprised that Anshel remembered.

"I like this yellow dress. It makes me feel happy," she said.

"It's not yellow. It's process yellow. That's a better color. Very pure and goes well with other colors to make new shades," he said.

Lillian liked her dress even better.

Anshel opened the bag. "I hope you like rugelach. It goes with tea," he said and poured her a cup.

"I love rugelach, and the ones from this bakery are especially good," Lillian said, though she knew that Clara's rugelach were better. "And tea would be nice, thank you."

"I bought the ones with raisins and cinnamon and sugar. They are my favorite. I hope you like them, too."

"I also like these best," Lillian said, pleased that it was true.

They ate quietly for several minutes. Lillian was used to boys who talked and talked, and if they didn't, she did. Now she didn't know what to say; she didn't know how to amuse him. She didn't even know if he wanted to be amused. The silence felt awkward until she looked at Anshel. He seemed content to be sipping tea and eating rugelach. Lillian relaxed. Don't be in such a hurry, she warned herself. Finally, she asked, "Do you like working for Mr. Schottenstein?"

"I don't like his big voice, but he seems like a nice man. Really, I work for Rusty, and if you are careful with each order, he is a good boss. Do you like working here?"

"I do. The work is interesting, and Mr. Schottenstein is a good boss, too, even though he does have a big voice. He was understanding last month when there was a mix-up in an order and we received enough red ink powder to last fifty years."

"I heard about that," Anshel said. "Rusty said that Mr. Schottenstein must be planning to make another Red Sea right here. He said that Mr. Schottenstein would probably be able to split it by yelling. He wouldn't need a stick."

Lillian laughed. She hadn't realized that Anshel could tell a funny story, or that the men were so lighthearted in their talk about Mr. Schottenstein.

Anshel smiled broadly when she laughed. "Now I must go back to work," he said. "I like looking at paintings at the art museum. Maybe we can go there on Saturday and see the pictures together."

"I would like that," Lillian said.

They decided to meet at the museum at two o'clock, and their first date was arranged.

THAT EVENING, LILLIAN TOLD HER MOTHER THAT SHE HAD had tea with Anshel. "He suggested we go to the art museum on Saturday. I wonder if he knows I've never looked at paintings on a date before." Lillian glanced down at her hands and was surprised to see a smudge of ink. She rubbed the spot and wondered where she had picked it up until she remembered her difficulty replacing her typewriter ribbon.

Lillian looked back at her mother. "You're right that he is serious. And you're right that getting to know him won't be easy. He's very quiet, and I imagine there are things he doesn't want to talk about. But even though I've only spoken to him a few times, and I hardly know anything about him, he seems as important in my life as people I've known forever. It doesn't make sense, and it scares me a little."

"You're a good girl, Lilly," Clara said, "and you'll do the right thing."

"Oh, I almost forgot. You will be happy to hear that he told a funny story that made me laugh."

Clara smiled. "I'm glad to hear that. A little laughter goes a long way. That's what my mother always said. Just don't make any decisions till you're sure they're the right ones."

"Don't worry. The decision I've made is to go to the museum."

"No, you've made a bigger decision than that."

After a moment, Lillian said, "That's true. I have."

Lillian took a long time dressing on Saturday. Not because this was her first date at a museum, but because her mother was right. This wasn't any date. This was a serious date. She finally settled on a plaid skirt and a soft, gray sweater that matched the gray in the plaid. And sensible shoes.

The bus left her off a few blocks from the museum, and Lillian walked the rest of the way along wide sidewalks lined with tall trees. The houses were set back on broad lawns. This wasn't the sort of neighborhood Lillian was used to, and she felt intimidated by the grandeur. One home had three gardeners working out front, one trimming bushes with huge shears, and the other two on their knees setting rows of flowers in the soil along the walkway to the house. Except for the snip of the garden shears, the neighborhood was silent. There should be more noise than this on a Saturday afternoon, Lillian thought. Where are all the children?

Lillian looked for a large building with the address she had memorized until she realized that the museum must be in one of the mansions. Then she saw Anshel standing at the curb waiting for her. He was facing the wrong direction. As she approached, she clattered her shoes on the pavement as much as possible so she wouldn't come up on him unawares and startle him. He must have heard her because he turned and smiled.

"I thought you would be coming the other way."

"Maybe I got off one stop too soon. I wasn't sure which was the closer stop, and I didn't want to go right past the museum."

"Have you seen the paintings before?"

Lillian shook her head, hoping that her ignorance wouldn't disappoint him.

"Good," he said. "It makes me happy to be the first person to show them to you."

The afternoon went by quickly. Anshel was an able guide, and Lillian was an eager pupil. They walked from painting to painting while he talked about the colors the artists used, and Lillian talked about the people in the pictures. She found his comments interesting, and he listened carefully to hers. She especially liked a painting called *The Black Teapot.*

"It's interesting that the lovely little teapot gets the title," she said. "I think the artist wants to be sure we notice it in the midst of the beautiful flowers and bright colors."

Anshel took a notebook out of his coat pocket and showed Lillian sketches of some of his favorite pictures. *The Black Teapot* was one of them. Lillian was impressed.

"You not only draw the objects and the people right, but you show the feelings the artists have toward them as well," she said.

Anshel smiled and seemed pleased. They promised each other that they would spend more time looking at the ceramics on their next visit.

Anshel walked her to her bus stop and waited with her until the bus came. "Maybe you will have tea one day next week? Maybe Wednesday?"

"Yes," she answered.

On the way home, Lillian looked out the bus window and thought about her afternoon. I've always assumed I would fall for a boy who is like the men in our family, funny and outgoing with big personalities. Anshel couldn't be more different, but I like being with him. He's kind and interesting and thoughtful. How can it be that the least likely man I could imagine is sweeping me off my feet in record time?

Lillian met Anshel for tea several times; they returned to the museum twice, and they took walks. They especially liked to walk to Thornden Park and sit on a bench watching the people go by and the children play in the grass. They talked about the ink company and art and colors and Lillian's family. But they didn't talk about the war or Anshel's childhood or his experiences in Chicago. Lillian was shy about asking, though she wished he would tell her something about his life before they met.

One day, when they were having tea, she did find the courage to ask him why he had decided to have lunch with her that first time.

"You want to know what I was thinking then?"

"Yes. I thought you were avoiding me, and then suddenly you showed me this little street and the park at the end of it." There was a long pause, and Lillian worried that she had gone too far.

"That was the day I talked to you for the fourth time. Three times before I talked to you, and now it was the fourth time." Lillian's blank stare told Anshel that the significance of this was lost on her. He seemed reluctant to explain further, but after a moment, he continued.

"I am alone here, and sometimes I wonder if I will ever find a wife. I don't know a matchmaker, and I have no money for one anyway. Then I talked to you three times. There is a teaching that if you do something three times, it is an obligation for you. When I saw you the fourth time, I knew that God had put you in my path. He is the matchmaker, and I should try to know you even if I don't know how to talk to you."

Lillian didn't spend much time thinking about God, and it alarmed her to learn that God spent any time at all thinking about her. She saw herself as a person in charge of her own destiny, and the thought of intrusive supernatural forces made her feel rebellious. Until she looked at Anshel's worried face. Then Lillian understood the risk he'd taken in having tea with her that first time, and the chance he'd taken in telling her why. She might not have felt a comparable risk before, but she felt the full weight of it now. She smiled, and Anshel smiled back.

One evening, Dotty called. "Where have you been hiding, Lillian? The girls and I haven't seen you in weeks. Are you okay?"

"I'm fine, Dotty. Just busy."

"I know you aren't seeing Jack anymore, and really, Lil, you can't keep throwing boys away, one after the next. What's keeping you busy now? Or should I say, who?"

"Just busy."

"That sounds mysterious. What's his name?"

"No point in quizzing me, Dotty. I'm just busy, that's all."

"There's a basketball game this weekend, and a dance afterward. A bunch of us are going. Why don't you bring Mr. Just Busy and meet us there?"

Lillian could picture Anshel sitting in the stands at a basketball game, silent and confused while everybody around him screamed and cheered. And what would he do at a dance? Stand as far from the couples as possible, trying to hide his discomfort with what he saw? As Lillian thought about it, neither place sounded inviting to her, either.

"Thanks anyway, Dotty, but I have plans."

"Okay. Let me know when we'll catch a glimpse of you again."

Lillian was surprised at her reluctance to share news of Anshel with Dotty, and even more surprised when that reluctance extended to include her mother. Clara heard little about the time she and Anshel spent together and knew only that

Lillian found him easy to be with and, best of all, interesting to talk to. Why do I hesitate to talk about him? she asked herself. Am I embarrassed by my interest in him? Or am I protecting our relationship until it becomes stronger? Or has he made me secretive?

One evening at dinner, Clara brought him up herself. "Has Anshel told you anything about his childhood or his time in the war?" she asked.

"No," Lillian admitted. "He hasn't even talked about his uncle or living in Chicago."

"That worries me," Clara said. "And it worries Aunt Ann."

"You told Aunt Ann about Anshel?"

"Of course. She's the oldest sister. We tell her everything."

Lillian knew that, as the oldest sister, Aunt Ann's opinion was to be taken seriously. But she didn't need Aunt Ann to warn her about Anshel's silence. His silence worried her, too.

Maybe his war experiences had been benign, though how that was possible, she couldn't imagine. More likely, they had been overwhelming. In the face of his silence, Lillian didn't know how to ask about the war or his family. He knew a lot about her mother and her brothers and their families, but not because he had asked. She had offered stories about them. Except about her father. Anshel knew nothing about her father.

LILLIAN HAD BEEN MEETING ANSHEL FOR WALKS ON THE weekends and tea once a week for over a month when they had a surprise encounter on their way back to work one Wednesday. As they stood at the end of the street, Mr. Schottenstein drove by. He didn't usually use the alley to leave the building, so Lillian was unprepared to see him. But her reaction didn't come close to matching his. He was shocked.

When he came back to work, Mr. Schottenstein breezed past Lillian's desk and told her that he was not to be disturbed. Lillian went to the back office for a box of paper clips, and when she returned to her desk, she could hear Mr. Schottenstein on the phone with his wife, his side of the conversation reaching her easily through his closed office door.

"I'm telling you, Ida, he's done for here. I won't have it." … "I know she's not a child, but she has nobody to look out for her." … "Say what you want, I'm going to fire him." … "Okay, you're right there. I'll have Rusty fire him." With that, he hung up the phone and opened his door.

"Lillian, call Rusty and tell him I need to see him."

Rusty came to the office some time later looking confused. "The boss wants to see me?"

"I do," Mr. Schottenstein said, rushing out of his office to usher Rusty in and close the door behind them.

For once, Lillian could not hear the conversation. Mr. Schottenstein seemed to be whispering, and Rusty always spoke quietly. After several minutes, she was startled to hear Rusty's words carry through the closed door.

"I won't do it. He's the best man I have for mixing colors. As far as I'm concerned, his personal life is his own business. I'm not going to talk to him or anybody else about it. And what's so terrible about spending time with a 'man from the back,' as you call him? You want him fired, you do it yourself." Mr. Schottenstein's door burst open and Rusty hurried past Lillian's desk without looking at her, his face as red as his hair.

Lillian waited for Mr. Schottenstein to tell her to send Anshel to the office, but he never did. Instead, he came out of his office with several orders for her to take to the post office right away, and since it was close to the end of the day, he told her to go home from there. She knew there was no rush for the orders and wondered what he planned to do in her absence.

If Anshel was fired, how would she find him again? She didn't know where he lived. In fact, she knew very little about him, distressingly little now that she thought about it. From the payroll records, she knew his last name was Szymanski and that he was paid in cash; she also knew he could draw; she knew he loved paintings; she knew she felt calm and content when she was with him.

As soon as she arrived home, Lillian learned what Mr. Schottenstein had done with the rest of his afternoon.

"Lillian," her mother called out from the kitchen, "you'll never guess who phoned me this afternoon."

Lillian needed one guess.

"He had shocking news for me. He said he saw you with a 'man from the back.'" Clara laughed. "Then I told him the even more shocking news that I know all about it."

Now Lillian laughed, too.

"I also told him that I would look into this man and make sure it's a good idea for you to be 'going around with him' in Mr. Schottenstein's words."

"Poor Mr. Schottenstein," Lillian said. "He had quite an afternoon. I guess he's given up his plan to fire Anshel now that he's made my behavior your responsibility."

"Since I assured him that I would look into it, maybe I'd better."

"How are you going to do that? I don't know anybody you could call and ask about him."

"You've known him for a couple of months already. And you haven't had a date with anybody else in that time, have you?"

"No."

"This sounds serious to me. If you are going to continue to see him, I think it's time he came here for dinner."

Lillian convinced her mother that lunch would be less intimidating than dinner and a quiet lunch for the three of them would be less stressful than a meal for the whole family. Clara suggested they keep the menu simple and choose foods that are served cold so nobody would be left cooking in the kitchen while Anshel is in the house. She also said that it would be better to eat right away and let the food help them through any awkward moments at the beginning of his visit. They decided to start the meal with borscht and then serve lox and cream cheese on bagels and tea and cookies for dessert.

The next day, Mr. Schottenstein called Lillian into his office as soon as he arrived in the morning. "Lillian, you should know that I saw you walking with the new man from the back yesterday. My wife tried to calm me down in the afternoon, and when I got home, she calmed me down in no uncertain terms. And she said I need to tell you that I called your mother, and I need to apologize if I was meddling."

"Don't worry, Mr. Schottenstein. My mother was not sorry you called, and we both know you called because you are concerned."

"That's right. My wife said you would forgive me. Now it's up to your mother, not me. And Ida says it was always up to your mother, not me. She's a smart woman, my Ida."

THAT DAY AT LUNCHTIME, LILLIAN WALKED TO THE LITTLE park. She and Anshel hadn't seen each other on consecutive days before, and he looked up in surprise as she approached.

"I didn't expect you, but I'm glad to see you," he said and moved over to make room for her on the bench.

Lillian sat down. Either he's unaware of his near brush with unemployment, she thought, or he chooses to ignore it. "I come with an invitation from my mother to lunch on Sunday. She wants to meet you."

Anshel nodded, but he didn't say anything.

"I hope you'll be able to come."

Still Anshel didn't respond.

"Look at it this way, Anshel, God may be your matchmaker, but my mother is mine. Your matchmaker knows all about me, but my matchmaker never met you." Lillian started to laugh and so did he.

"I see that I gave you that argument," he said, "so now I have no choice. Tell your mother I'll come to lunch on Sunday. Will your father be there?"

"No, he won't."

Lillian gave Anshel her address, and they agreed that he would be there at noon.

"Sometimes people bring something to the house when they are invited for a meal, but my mother told me to make it clear to you that you are not to bring anything at all." Clara and Lillian had spoken about this and had agreed that they didn't want him worrying about what to bring, or learning too late that a gift was expected.

"Your mother is very kind. I hope she will like me." He stood and walked away leaving Lillian sitting on the bench wondering why he had left her there. Anshel himself must have realized that his behavior might seem rude, and he turned and walked back to her.

"You should go first so I can watch you and be sure you are safe. Until your mother says she likes me, we shouldn't walk together. Maybe I was wrong to meet you before I talked to her."

"She doesn't think that. And I don't think that. But now she says it's time to meet you."

"She is right. I should say now that very much I like you, but if your mother doesn't like me and says no, I won't bother you."

Lillian was stunned. She hadn't anticipated the possibility that her mother might not like Anshel or would consider preventing her from seeing him again. Why did he think it could come to that?

"I also like you, and I think my mother will like you, too."

Anshel stood aside, and Lillian walked in front of him to the building. She assumed he followed at a distance, but she did not look back.

BY THE TIME ANSHEL KNOCKED ON THE DOOR AT NOON on Sunday, the table was set and the food was prepared. When Lillian opened the door, she hardly recognized him. He was wearing a limp, brown suit she had never seen before, a white dress shirt, and a blue tie. His hair was freshly cut and slicked back, and his shoes were newly polished. She was surprised by a surge of tenderness for him and his attempt to make a good first impression.

"Come in," she said. "We're ready for lunch."

Clara came out of the kitchen, wiping her hands on a dish towel. "Welcome," she said. "I'm Lillian's mother, and I'm glad to meet you." Anshel seemed relieved that she made no move to shake hands.

In no time, they were seated at the table and Clara had served each of them a bowl of borscht.

"This is very good," Anshel said.

"Thank you," Clara said. "I cook for a deli near here, and this is one of my recipes the customers like best. I'm glad you like it, too."

Lillian talked about two paintings she particularly admired at the museum. Then Anshel talked about color and paint and ink and the art of mixing. Lillian was pleased that her mother asked many questions and was interested in his answers.

"Lillian told me you also draw."

"I like to draw, and I make sketches at the museum." Anshel smiled. "I try to understand the paintings in my drawings, but Lillian is good at understanding them in words. She sees the heart of a picture."

Lillian hadn't known that Anshel valued her for the way she talked about paintings, and she was touched that he wanted her mother to know how much he admired her.

"You also like to walk in Thornden Park."

"It's a pretty park, and we walk and watch the people."

Their conversation was interrupted by the sound of heavy footsteps from the apartment above. Clara laughed and so did Lillian. Anshel looked confused.

"That's probably Bobby," Lillian explained. "Running around like he's not supposed to."

"My son lives upstairs with his family and Bobby is his youngest child," Clara said. "My youngest son lives here, and my oldest son lives near us with his wife and his children. I'm sure Lillian told you about our family."

"Yes, she did," Anshel said.

"Did your family live in Poland?" Clara asked.

"Yes, they did. But they are gone."

"Did you have brothers and sisters?"

Anshel didn't answer, and Lillian worried that her mother had been too inquisitive.

Finally, he said, "They are gone."

Clara turned the conversation to other topics and discovered that Anshel liked to read, but had few books. "My brother-in-law has many books you can borrow," she said. "Some are in Yiddish and some are in Polish. He would be happy to share them with you."

"You would like my Uncle Shlomo," Lillian said. "But you will have to speak Yiddish with him even though we are in America." She grinned at Anshel, reminded of their first meeting at the picnic table when he had insisted they speak English.

"Now you tease me," he said, and smiled back.

After the tea had been poured, and the plate of cookies placed on the table, Clara said, "Lillian told me you moved here from Chicago."

"I lived in Chicago with my uncle for many years, but it was very cold there, and it was better for me to move here."

"He must miss you."

Anshel broke a cookie in two and took a bite from one half. "I am sending him money every week to pay him back for having me in his house. Soon it will be paid, and all my salary will be mine."

After lunch, Lillian walked Anshel to the bus stop and waited with him until his bus came. "Thank you for coming to lunch," she said. "My mother was glad to meet you."

"I am happy to meet her, too," Anshel said. "She is a nice lady and a good mother."

The bus arrived as he added, "Maybe soon I will meet your father."

Lillian waved as the bus pulled away. She didn't know her father's reasons for leaving home, but she was sure he had had a series of girlfriends while he was still living with the family. It was a scandal they chose to ignore, and nobody was so cruel as to mention it to them. So it had been years since Lillian had spoken about her father to anyone. Now Anshel was looking forward to meeting him. You aren't the only one with something you'd rather not talk about, she thought, as she watched the bus turn the corner at the end of the block.

Lillian came home to find her mother at the kitchen table sipping coffee and leafing through the latest issue of *Life*. She glimpsed pictures of baby animals before Clara closed the magazine and a blonde smiled at them from the cover.

"Well?" Lillian said. "Did he pass?"

"He's nothing like our family."

Nothing like our family? Is she comparing him to Aunt Thelma's choice of a man who fled before their second anniversary? Or is she thinking about Ada who still behaves like an outsider after so many years married to Douglas? Before Lillian could respond, Clara went on.

"But maybe that's the best thing about him."

"The best thing about him?"

Clara sighed. "I worry sometimes that you think all men are like your father. Maybe that's why you found a man who is so different."

Lillian was shocked to hear her mother talk about her father. No matter how often Lillian had tried to pry information from her as a child, Clara had always refused to talk about him, and Lillian had long since stopped asking. Until Anshel asked about him, Lillian hadn't thought about her father for years.

"But none of that matters, Lil. What matters is that even though Anshel seems to be a good man, something bothered me." Clara hesitated and looked down. "So I called Ida Schottenstein to see what she knows about him. I hope you aren't angry."

Lillian did feel angry. Her mother was taking her role as matchmaker too seriously. Hadn't she said she trusted Lillian?

"Why did you do that?"

"I could see that this is serious between you and Anshel, but I also saw that he is a man with secrets. I can't let you marry a man with secrets."

"You would stop me from marrying somebody I chose?"

"How could I do that? You're an adult. But I would find out what I needed to know to warn you."

"Is that what you're doing now? Warning me?"

"No. I'm not warning you not to see him. But I am telling you that he has secrets, and if he doesn't share them with you, there will come a time when they will share themselves." Clara began to cry. "Don't be angry, Lilly. I know what I'm talking about."

"Don't cry, Mom. I'm not angry, and I don't want you to be sad. Come, let's eat cookies."

Lillian put the plate of cookies from lunch on the table and they each took one. I'm getting to be exactly like her, she thought. A cookie is the answer to all life's difficulties.

"Well?" Lillian said after Clara had had a chance to dry her eyes and they had both munched cookies for a few minutes. "Are you going to tell me what Mrs. Schottenstein said?"

"First, I should say that I don't think Ida knows everything. I'll tell you what she told me, but I think it's important for you to hear what Anshel has to say, too. If he won't talk to you, that will be another story."

Lillian nodded, and nibbled her cookie.

"Ida said that Morris didn't want to hire Anshel when he showed up without any references except the name of his sponsor and a vague story about living in Chicago for three years. But Morris decided to let Rusty meet him, and Anshel was hired."

"So far, so good," Lillian said. "What's the bad part?"

"Ida said that after Morris saw Anshel with you, he followed up a little more on his own. He called the sponsor who turned out to be Anshel's uncle, his mother's brother. His uncle said he is a good boy who worked hard, but they had an argument and Anshel left. It was nothing that should worry Morris because it had nothing to do with his willingness to work. It was a family matter. But when Morris said he was calling because Anshel was seeing a girl who had no father to look out for her, the uncle became more serious."

Clara looked at Lillian and added, "Ida said she's sorry Morris referred to your father that way, and she hoped I would forgive him."

"Mom, you're scaring me. What terrible thing did he find out?"

"It's a sad story, Lillian." Clara sighed. "When Anshel's uncle heard why Morris was calling, he switched to Yiddish, and said, 'In the matter of a *shidduch*, I must tell you everything.' He said that Anshel's a good boy, but he won't talk about where he was in the war or what happened to the family. The uncle and his wife did everything they could to make Anshel happy, but still he was quiet and sad. Then his uncle arranged a *shidduch* for him with a widow lady. She was a little older than he is, and she had two children, but what else could a refugee expect? Anshel heard about the marriage proposal, and the next thing they knew, he was gone. Ida said that's when the uncle started to cry, and said, 'We don't see a letter, and we don't hear his voice. Only money he sends.' They don't care if Anshel didn't like the widow, but his uncle can't forgive him for never saying a word about his parents or the other children. By the end of the conversation, Ida said that Morris and Anshel's uncle were both crying."

Lillian didn't say anything for a long time.

"I don't know what to think, Mom. I like Anshel, and I like going places with him. So what if he doesn't tell me about the widow in Chicago or about the war? Maybe those things will never come up."

"Don't believe that, Lillian. It may not matter what he tells his uncle, but it matters what he tells you."

After they cleared the table and washed and dried the dishes, Clara said, "Don't worry, Lillian. This will turn out for the best. I feel it in my bones."

Lillian sat alone in the kitchen. She did not feel it in her bones, and she was worried. Anshel was the first man she always looked forward to seeing; the first man who didn't bore her after one or two dates; the first man she didn't feign interest in or work to amuse. It's true he was often quiet, but he did talk to her, and he listened to her, too. And even though they never touched, every time he looked at her, Lillian felt embraced. She never thought she would like such an old-fashioned man, but she did, and she couldn't imagine not seeing him again. I'm the one to decide if I know enough about Anshel, she thought. I can't expect him to tell me about every minute of his life before we met. Nobody does that. And it would be cruel to force him to relive painful memories, especially if he wants to put them behind him. If that's his choice, I'm not going to force him to look back. We can go forward from here.

But even as she worked to convince herself that her mother was wrong, Lillian worried that she might be right.

By the time Lillian walked to the little park the next day, Anshel was already there, and he was already standing. Even before she sat down, he asked, "Did your mother like me? Did she say this is okay?"

Lillian wasn't quite sure what he meant by "this," or what, exactly, he hoped was okay.

"My mother did like you," Lillian began and then hesitated. How to continue? Should she voice Clara's concern? No. Even if her mother was right, this was surely the wrong time.

"I'm glad." Anshel smiled and lit a cigarette. "I'm very glad. Maybe next time your father will be home, and he will also like me."

Lillian was silent. You aren't the only one with secrets, she thought. How can I expect you to speak if I won't?

Anshel looked worried by her long silence. "You think he won't like me?" he asked.

"My father doesn't live with us." Lillian stopped, unsure how to explain his absence to Anshel. "He was not a good husband, and my mother asked him to leave, or maybe he left on his own. I don't know. I was a little girl, and I'm not sure what happened."

"I'm sorry. It must make you sad."

"At first, I missed him. But it's been so long since I've seen him that I don't feel sad now." Lillian looked at Anshel and knew her mother was right about one thing. Not all men were like her father. "It doesn't make me sad today," she said.

They chatted for a time, and Lillian agreed to meet him at Thornden Park on Saturday afternoon.

That night Lillian lay awake longer than usual before she began to fall asleep. She loved the feeling of drifting when her thoughts took on a life of their own and roamed through her memories, making connections and taking fanciful turns that often surprised her. She called these moments her pre-dreams. Tonight, she saw Anshel sitting on the bench in the little park and drinking tea. She was wearing her process yellow dress, and he was dressed in all his favorite colors, his outfit so dazzling that she laughed and had to look away. Then he pointed to the sky and turned to talk to her. She didn't understand his words, but she saw the thunder clouds gathering on the horizon. She and Anshel ran behind the bench and into the little park where the clouds overtook them and bled the colors from their clothing until everything turned gray, the color of the clouds themselves.

Lillian sat up in bed. This was not the pleasant drifting into sleep she typically experienced. And how annoying to have such an obvious pre-dream.

THORNDEN PARK WAS, AS USUAL, LITTERED WITH SMALL children, harried mothers, and university students carrying big books they used as headrests when they stretched out on the grass. Anshel carried the blanket Lillian brought for them to sit on. After they walked for a time, she chose a quiet spot in the deep shade close to the trunk of a big tree, and he spread the blanket on the grass. They sat side by side leaning against the tree.

"Why are you so quiet today?" Anshel asked.

Lillian hesitated. She was afraid to have this conversation, and she was afraid not to. I'm not the timid sort, she reminded herself. But what will I do if he won't talk to me? And what will I do if he will?

"Lillian, what are you thinking? You look so sad. Did I say something wrong?"

"No, you didn't say anything wrong. I've been thinking about something my mother said." Lillian turned to face him. She felt sorry for what she was about to do. "My mother was surprised when I told her that I don't know why you left Chicago. She said we can't be happy if there are secrets between us."

Anshel didn't speak, and Lillian saw that his hands shook when he took out a cigarette and lit it. He smoked and looked out across the lawn, and she waited.

At last, he said, "Your mother is right. I will tell you, and I hope you will still like me after." Anshel finished the cigarette and turned to face her.

"My uncle is a good man, and I know he wanted the best for me, but I couldn't live in his house anymore. He wanted me to talk about Poland, and that I cannot talk about.

"He made a *shidduch* for me, and I also thought it might be best. But when I heard that the lady was twelve years older and had two children who were almost my age, I couldn't marry her. I told my aunt I had to leave, and she gave me money for the bus and a little bit more. She also gave me Mr. Schottenstein's name. She knew somebody he helped years ago, and she thought he might help me. So I left, and I didn't say goodbye to my uncle. I am sorry for that." Anshel didn't say anything more for several minutes. "Do you think it was a terrible thing to do?"

"No, I don't think it was terrible. But why can't you tell your uncle what happened in Poland?"

"I'm afraid to tell. I don't want the story to come to this country. I want it to stay in Poland."

Lillian didn't know what to say. Finally, she asked, "Does it stay in Poland?"

"No. In the night I see it."

"Maybe we should see it together in the daylight. I don't think you should be alone with the story, no matter how terrible it is."

Suddenly Anshel looked like a little boy. He turned away from her and rubbed his cheek with his hand. It was several minutes before he spoke.

"They took my father first. Before he went down to the street with all the other men, he kissed my cheek and whispered, 'Take care of Mommy and the little ones,' and then he was gone. We never saw him or any of the other men again.

There was just me, my mother, and my three little sisters. And there was a Polish boy, Jozef, who lived in the basement with his grandmother. When she didn't ignore him, she beat him, and he was always filthy and hungry and covered in bruises. My mother took pity on him and gave him food and sometimes even bathed him. He was ten, two years younger than I was, but we were the same size, so my mother let him wear my clothes. I remember how he would laugh in my face and show me he was wearing my shirt.

"When they came for us, I was in the backyard with other neighborhood boys. Some of them stayed in the bushes, but I went running to find my mother. She was already out in the street with my sisters, and Jozef was with them. I saw that she was carrying his jacket, and he was wearing my jacket with the yellow star. He grinned at me and took her hand. Then she looked up and saw me running toward them. 'Go home,' she yelled. 'I'm sick and tired of having you hang around me and my family,' and she threw Jozef's jacket at me, 'Leave us alone. Go away.'

"I stopped running. How could she choose Jozef and leave me behind? How could I take care of her if she didn't take me with her? All the women were screaming, and the children were crying, and my mother was still shouting at me. 'Put on your filthy jacket and get out of here!' That's the last thing she ever said to me. The Germans rushed in and forced the women to run, dragging their children to the trucks waiting at the end of the street."

Anshel rested his head in his hands, and Lillian wondered if he was going to say anything more.

"I put on Jozef's jacket. I didn't know what else to do. Suddenly, somebody grabbed my arm and turned me around. It was Jozef's grandmother. She was drunk, as usual, and she slapped my face before grabbing my wrist again and pulling me after her. I could hear her muttering in Polish, '*Ona obrocie syna dla syna*,' and she laughed. 'I don't mind trading. This good-for-nothing boy might be better than the other one.' She dragged me down to her basement and told me not to go out or she would sell me to the Germans.

"Now I was filthy and hungry and bruised all the time. When we were too hungry too often, we left the city and walked or begged rides on carts until we came to her sister's farm. It was better there. Her sister fed me if I worked, so I worked. I don't know if the sister knew I wasn't really Jozef Dabrowski, but she never looked closely enough to find out. They needed me to work on their little farm, and they fed me enough to keep me alive. I was there for years. When I heard the church bells ringing one morning, I didn't know what had happened, and it was months before a soldier who wasn't German leaned against the fence I was fixing and told me the war was over.

"The next day, I left them and stopped the first soldier I saw. He helped me find a place for orphans and they looked for my family, but my mother and my sisters were gone, all dead. It was more than a year before they found my uncle and I came to this country."

Anshel covered his face with his hands, and Lillian sat quietly next to him. She wanted to hug him and had to turn away to calm herself and dry her eyes. Finally, she spoke.

"It is so sad that all this happened to you. That there was no one to help you and protect you."

"How can I tell my uncle that my mother went by herself with the Germans? How can I tell him that I let them take her away? How can I say that I hid on a farm with two old ladies while other people were heroes? How could he ever forgive me?"

"You couldn't save her, but she could save you and she did. If he knew that, your uncle would be proud of her. And he would be proud of you, too. That you survived in spite of everything."

Lillian and Anshel walked silently back to her house. If she had known how inadequate her words would be in the face of his tragedy, she never would have forced him to speak of that terrible time. Lillian worried that she had failed him.

When they reached her door, Anshel handed her the blanket. "It's only since I know you, Lillian, that I'm sorry my mother never had the chance to hear me say, 'I forgive you for saving me.' Because it's only now that I would mean it." He left without another word.

THE NEXT DAY, LILLIAN WALKED TO THE LITTLE PARK AT lunchtime. Anshel was not there. She sat on a bench, hoping that he would come, afraid that he wouldn't. Before, he had always arrived first, and it seemed odd to be sitting there alone, waiting for him. When he appeared at the end of the little street, squinting into the sun, she saw what she must have looked like when their roles were reversed. As he walked toward her with the sun in his face, she knew he couldn't see her clearly. But Lillian could see him, so brightly illuminated that he seemed to glow, and she saw her shadow covering his heart. His shadow must have been imprinted on her heart in the same way every time she joined him, and he must have seen it there.

"I had to help Rusty wash two vats before I could go out," Anshel said. He sat down on the bench. "I was afraid you would not be here." He rubbed his hands together and smoothed his hair. "I'm glad you waited. I told myself that if you were here, I should tell you right away what is in my heart."

Anshel looked so serious that Lillian wasn't sure she wanted to hear what was coming next.

"I think God was right to show me that I should know you. I think you are the reason I moved here, the reason I lived when no one else did. I hope we can be happy together for a long, long time."

Lillian lowered her eyes and waited. When she realized that Anshel had stopped talking, she looked up and found him watching her, anxious and expectant. After an instant of confusion, she understood that this was a marriage proposal, and there was only one right answer.

"I also want to be happy with you for a long, long time," she said and heard Anshel let out a long sigh.

"I feel like I could dance right here," he said, "and invite everybody to make a *l'chaim* and tell me mazel tov! We need a bottle of vodka."

Anshel jumped up and took three, long, slow strides around the bench, before throwing his arms in the air and dancing a lively jig across the grass. Lillian laughed and clapped in time with his steps.

# A Married Woman

## *1965*

MELISSA MET RICK AT A PICNIC TO CELEBRATE THE engagement of his college roommate to her best friend. She liked his blue eyes, his easy conversation, and his quick laughter. She also liked the way he dealt with the crowd at the picnic table and returned to her with a piece of cake for each of them. Rick drove her home, and when she introduced him to her mother, Melissa was relieved to see that he made a good first impression.

"He seems like a nice boy with good manners," her mother said.

"I'm glad you like him," Melissa said, "because I do, too."

The morning after their first date, her mother was eager to hear all about it.

"He took me to see that new movie, *Shenandoah*," Melissa told her. "It was about a family, but it was also about the Civil War."

"I wouldn't want to see a movie about war. That's all you hear about these days, the draft and the war. It's enough to make me glad I don't have sons."

Melissa didn't want her mother's attitude toward Rick colored by her fear of war. "Don't be gloomy, Mom," she said.

Her mother smiled. "Who could be gloomy with you sitting here, so cheerful and bubbly?"

Melissa blushed, and they both laughed.

Several weeks later, Rick came to dinner and, as far as Melissa could tell, her father and her little sister, Phoebe, liked him, too. As the year went on, Rick joined them on day trips to the lake and helped her father plant strawberries in the backyard. One afternoon, when Melissa had to work late and her mother's car was making a funny noise, he took her mother to the supermarket, and insisted that she rest at the kitchen table while he carried in the groceries.

With so much goodwill in the air, Melissa believed there would be nothing but cheers and congratulations when she announced that she and Rick were engaged. They decided to tell the family at dinner on Saturday night.

"During dessert," Melissa suggested, "when everybody's feeling well fed and content. And I'll tell them, okay?"

Rick agreed.

Melissa was bursting with the news on Saturday night, but she restrained herself until the small cups of peach slices swimming in sweet syrup and the plate of sugar cookies were on the table.

"Rick and I have news," she began. Her mother looked up and stared at her, and Melissa knew immediately that she had misjudged her mother's reaction. After a lifetime of vigilance, Melissa had, at this crucial moment, failed to anticipate her mother's mood.

"We want to tell you...we want you to know..."

Rick took her hand, stood, and continued for her. "What Melissa's trying to say is that we are engaged to be married, and I think I must be the happiest man alive."

Phoebe clapped and cheered. "Nobody else in my class has a married sister. Pretty soon I'll be an aunt."

"Let's not get ahead of ourselves," her father said as he walked around the table to give Melissa a kiss on her cheek and shake Rick's hand. "This is wonderful news. Ada, where is the Chivas Regal? We need to make a toast."

"I'll get it, Douglas," Ada said and left the table.

"I remember when your mother and I got engaged," her father told Melissa. "Your grandmother brought out a bottle of Scotch that had dust on it. It hadn't been opened since your grandfather died. We all drank a toast and the ladies cried. I thought they were overcome by emotion until I tasted the Scotch and almost cried myself."

"I can't find it, Douglas," Ada said, returning empty-handed. "The toast will have to wait."

"I know where it is," he said and went to look for it himself, only to return a minute later, puzzled. "I remember putting it on the second shelf of the cupboard, but it's not there now."

"We'll have the toast to look forward to," Rick said. "I'm glad you are all so happy for us, and that you have confidence in me to take care of Melissa. Now we'd better leave if we're going to catch the early movie."

"Didn't you notice that she never said congratulations?" Melissa asked as soon as they were outside.

"She was surprised."

"My mother doesn't like to be surprised."

"Your mother thinks I'm great," Rick said. "She won't be a problem. You'll see."

MELISSA CAME INTO THE KITCHEN THE NEXT MORNING wishing she shared Rick's optimism. Typically, the family ate breakfast quickly, but on Sundays, Melissa and her mother lingered over their tea and toast and chatted. It was usually a calm, pleasant conversation, but Melissa had a feeling that the conversation this morning would be different.

Her mother was standing at the stove. "Good morning, Melissa. Have a seat. These will be ready in a minute."

"What are you making?"

"You'll see. I brewed a pot of tea. Pour yourself a cup."

Melissa did as she was told, and a few minutes later, her mother set a stack of blueberry pancakes on her plate, put a little pitcher of warm maple syrup on the table, and served herself a cup of tea.

Melissa poured syrup on her pancakes. "Yummy," she said. "My favorite kind."

"I know," her mother said. "You used to call them booberry pancakes when you were little, and after that, I always made them for you on Halloween. Do you remember?"

"I do." Melissa took another mouthful. "Aren't you going to have any?"

"No. I made them for you."

Melissa grew increasingly self-conscious as her mother watched her eat. "Please have some. They're delicious."

"You know how much I want you to be happy, don't you?"

Melissa nodded and began to feel like a small animal being fattened for slaughter.

"It's because I'm worried about your happiness that I didn't sleep a wink last night. I couldn't stop thinking about the announcement you made at dinner."

Here it comes, Melissa thought, and filled her mouth with pancakes. Maybe if I choke right now, this conversation will end.

"Sorry we surprised you, Mom."

"Being surprised is not the point. The point is the announcement."

"I know…I'm sure…" Melissa wished that Rick was at the table. She put down her fork, took a deep breath, and sat straighter in her chair. "We should have told you and Daddy privately, but we knew you would be happy for us, and we couldn't keep the news to ourselves any longer."

"You've just graduated and started working. You should meet more people before you make such a big decision."

"The decision is made," Melissa said in the same calm, firm voice she imagined Rick might use and looked up to see how her mother reacted.

"Maybe you think you're sure about Rick, but you must see that this isn't the right time. It will be years before he earns a good living. In my day, a man didn't marry until he could support his wife. It's selfish of Rick to ignore your needs."

"What I need is to be with Rick."

"But Melissa, he could be drafted and sent to Vietnam."

This was a possibility she and Rick had discussed, so it was easy for Melissa to respond with the conclusion they had reached. "We think that's a good reason to marry right away."

Her mother stared at her in apparent disbelief. "I would expect such behavior from Margaret, but you were always the sensible twin. Now you're starting to sound like her. Promise me you'll think this over before you do anything rash."

When Melissa did not respond, her mother pushed away from the table so abruptly that her tea splashed onto the tablecloth. "I'm not going to say another word," she declared and left the kitchen.

Ada's silence on the subject did not break Melissa's resolve to marry Rick. When she told her mother that she and Rick would plan the wedding themselves, Ada relented and helped them select a date nearly a year away. Three months before the wedding, Rick was drafted and sent to Fort Gordon, Georgia. His basic training would be completed five days before the ceremony.

"This is impossible, Melissa," her mother argued. "We can't plan a wedding under these circumstances."

"Rick will be back in time, and I can manage the rest of the planning myself," Melissa insisted.

The next twelve weeks passed in a haze of anxiety. Every day there was a crisis that seemed small to Melissa but not to her mother. Margaret precipitated the worst one when she refused to come home from San Francisco more than three days before the ceremony, too late to have her dress fitted and altered.

"It's just like her to make everything difficult for everybody," Ada said. "First she runs off to California and I never hear a word from her, and now she refuses to come home in time for her sister's wedding. There's no alternative. You'll have to postpone the ceremony."

"What?" Melissa responded. "You want me to postpone my wedding because Margaret's dress might not fit perfectly?"

"We can't have her dress falling off her as she walks down the aisle, can we?"

The irrationality of her mother's position made it easier for Melissa to respond calmly. "Margaret and I have always been the same size. I'll wear her dress for the fittings."

"You aren't exactly the same size. And what if Margaret's put on weight?"

"Don't worry, Mom. It will work out fine." But what did "fine" mean? For the first time in Melissa's life, working out fine for her did not mean working out fine for her mother.

It was a perfect wedding. Melissa wondered if all brides are beautiful, if all grooms are handsome, if all mothers cry, if all fathers cry, if all sisters behave themselves, if all arguments are forgotten in the joy of the moment.

There were more tears when she and Rick drove off in their new Dodge Dart, a gift from their two sets of parents, with everything they owned packed into the trunk and the backseat. As they left, her mother said, "I expect you to send me a long letter every week. You can write a little every day and mail it on Tuesday so that I get it before the weekend. I'll do the same for you."

In a rush of relief and gratitude, Melissa agreed.

IT WASN'T EASY TO LIVE IN GEORGIA IN THE SUMMER. Melissa had never seen such a place before. Their home was a converted chicken coop filled with old furniture Melissa was sure the farmer had found in his grandmother's attic. Rick bought a little fan for every room, and Melissa kept them on all day because, once overheated, it was impossible for her to cool off until nightfall. She usually spent the daylight hours inside busy with projects like sewing curtains for all the windows and embroidering a tablecloth to cover their scratched and scarred kitchen table. She was proud of her work and pleased that Rick noticed and appreciated her efforts.

She also wrote the daily section of her letter to her mother. That took time because it was hard to find something to write about every day. Melissa would have liked to write about the difficulties of living in Georgia and about her loneliness, but she didn't want to hear her mother say, "I told you so," and send her train fare home. So she wrote about how instructive it was to read Flannery O'Connor's stories while actually living in Georgia, and about the new kitchen curtains while being careful not to describe their apartment itself.

Rick mailed Melissa's letter from the fort on Tuesdays, and they picked up her mother's weekly letter on their way to the PX on Saturdays. True to her word, her mother wrote a section of her letter every day and filled the pages with bits of family news and advice. Advice about recipes and shopping and laundry and ironing. Advice to put some of the money she was given for household expenses in her own secret nest egg, just in case. Just in case? Did her mother have a "just in case" secret bank account? It didn't matter because Melissa couldn't follow that advice anyway. There was no household money. Melissa went to the PX once a week with Rick, and they did the shopping together.

Much of her mother's advice had to do with how she should behave toward Rick now that she was a married woman. Always put him first, her mother admonished; never let him know you are unhappy or worried; greet him with a happy face and a welcoming smile every afternoon so he looks forward to coming home; never be moody; cajole him to get your way, and never, never yell at him.

"Above all," her mother wrote, "don't ever get angry. Your father made me furious in 1943, and even though I didn't show him I was angry, nothing was the same after that." Melissa read and reread that sentence. Did her father have any idea that her mother had been angry for twenty-two years and counting?

In her letters, Melissa tried to include examples of all the ways she followed her mother's advice. But she learned that if she was a little lonely, Rick was comforting, and if she was a little moody, Rick could handle it. So she didn't have to be quite as cautious as her mother advised. But she was still careful not to become angry at Rick and yell at him, even when he yelled at her.

The first time Rick yelled, it was because Melissa spent too long assembling the lasagna. This was a side of Rick that

Melissa had never seen, and it frightened her. Then there was the time he yelled because she suggested they ask for directions, and the time he banned her from his garden at the back of the chicken coop because she was too slow planting the bean seeds. That time she had cried. Then he was contrite and confused because everybody in his family yelled and he didn't know what had upset her. Since then, she knew he was trying not to yell. Until one Tuesday morning when everything changed.

Melissa wasn't even sure how it started. All she did was ask Rick to buy her a root beer on his way home from the fort. She was surprised when he refused and more surprised when she didn't let the matter drop.

"All I want is a root beer and, as long as you're there anyway, the mail. Is that too much to ask?" Melissa said.

"As a matter of fact, it is. All I want after a day at the fort is to get out of my uniform and into the shower. A root beer is the last thing I want to worry about."

"You have the car and it's only another two miles up the road. The whole thing takes five minutes. I'm the one stuck here all day long by myself."

"You're the one with the time. You want a root beer? You go get it."

"You know it's too hot in the afternoon to walk so far in the sun, and if I go in the morning, the mail won't be there yet."

"And you'll miss the letter from Mommy and have to wait till Saturday to see it. How terrible is that?"

"She writes every week and expects me to pick up her letter and mail mine on Tuesdays. What's so bad about not wanting to make her mad?"

"Who cares if she's mad? She's a thousand miles away. You don't live with her anymore. You live with me, your husband, remember? And I want a shower after a day in the dust and the heat. I don't want to be driving out of my way for letters and root beer. I'm the one you should be thinking about, not her."

"And I'm the one you should be thinking about. The one who lives with you in a chicken coop without air-conditioning. I don't see why it's too much trouble for you to bring me a soda on your way home." Melissa's voice had lost its usual conciliatory tone, and it sounded strange to her ears.

"It's not on my way home, and it is too much trouble." With that, Rick left, slamming the door behind him. He gunned the car engine, bouncing from rut to rut down the dirt path to Route 88.

Melissa stood at the window and watched him drive away. "You unreasonable man," she shouted. "You horrible person. You terrible husband. You nasty thing."

When she ran out of steam, Melissa wondered what had happened to the calm Melissa, the pleasant Melissa who was never angry. What had happened to all the reasons Rick had married her? What had happened to her determination to follow her mother's advice? In one unguarded moment, she had ruined everything.

Melissa sat at the kitchen table and cried most of the morning. She sat there through lunchtime but didn't eat. Maybe her mother was right. Maybe she wasn't the right woman for Rick; maybe she had been too young to get married and move so far from home. This morning certainly made her mother's case.

At three o'clock, when Rick still hadn't called to apologize, Melissa buckled her sandals and filled an old soda bottle with water. "I can do this," she told herself. "I have to do this. He didn't even take my letter to the fort this morning. I'm on my own." Then she stopped talking to herself because her tears threatened to return, and she didn't want to go out with a red nose and swollen eyes. She brushed her curls into a feathery cloud, checked her face in the mirror, shoved the letter to her mother into her pocket, and took the key from the saucer on the kitchen table. The sun burned as she stepped outside.

Even as she locked the door, Melissa knew it was a silly gesture. There was nothing inside worth taking. Did anybody really want her other pairs of shorts, the blue Wedgewood candy dish from her mother, or the tiny bottle of English Lavender perfume Rick had given her on her birthday? But Rick's uniforms were probably worth something, and locking the door kept her nosy neighbors out. That was worth something, too.

Gloria was in her yard hanging clothes on a line strung from the corner of the roof to the tree in front of her unit. Her husband had put it up for her, and she let Melissa use it on days she didn't. Melissa thought she was a nice lady but had little to say to her. It didn't help that Gloria spoke almost no English, or that her husband was career army while Rick was a draftee who just wanted to get out alive. Still, they were always pleasant to each other, and Gloria waved as Melissa went by. Melissa thought Gloria looked surprised to see her setting out, but maybe that was because Melissa was surprised herself and assumed Gloria must feel the same way.

Farther down the path, she came to two trailers parked in the grass and rented to two young couples, both newly married and both still teenagers. The husbands had enlisted, and the wives spent all day together drinking coffee, trading recipes, listening to music on the radio, and dyeing and perming each other's hair. When they first met Melissa, one of them had laughed and said, "The first day you were here we saw you from the back, and with your curly hair and your brown arms, we thought you were a colored girl. We couldn't imagine that Mr. Dorsey would rent to a Negro, and then we realized that you were wearing a brown shirt!"

Melissa remembered how that first encounter had intensified her shock at finding herself living in the South. More than two months later, she still felt uneasy. The relentless sun, the relentless squalor, the relentless bigotry were almost too much to bear. But not quite. Being married to Rick had always saved the day. Until today.

Patty, newly blond, came to her screen door as Melissa walked by the first trailer.

"Where ya goin', Melissa?" she called out.

"To the post office for the mail and a root beer," Melissa answered.

"That's dumb. It's more'n two miles and over a hundred degrees. You'll never make it. Come in and set a bit and have a Coke."

"I'll make it. And I want the mail, too."

"Why don't Rick get it for ya on his way home?"

"See ya, Patty."

Melissa waved and kept walking. The highway looked wet and shiny, and her eyes refused to focus clearly on approaching cars. She had to remind herself to stay at the edge and walk in the dust at the side of the road. The slow, shuffling pace she remembered from movies about the South was the only way to keep from becoming too overheated to continue. In no time, her sandals and her feet were caked with red clay dust. Her T-shirt clung to her, and sweat streamed down her back, pooling at the waistband of her shorts. Her underpants were soaked and her legs glistened. She could imagine herself melting into a puddle of water like the Wicked Witch of the West.

Even though she sipped water and walked slowly, Melissa could feel the top of her head becoming hot and realized, too late, that she had forgotten her hat. Sweat matted her hair and stung her eyes, and her water bottle slipped from her hand. This is Rick's fault, she thought, and I'll never forgive him. One day I'll tell my daughter that her father made me angry in 1965, and nothing was the same after that.

By the time she reached the post office, Melissa was walking even more slowly than she had when she left the coop. Her curls clung to her neck and her cheeks; her mouth was dry, and her face felt hot. Gripping the wooden railing, she pulled herself up the steps to the porch. When the porch shook with the footsteps of somebody mounting the stairs at the other end, Melissa nearly lost her footing. She squinted into the glare of the sun and made out the dark silhouette of a soldier coming toward her.

"Melissa?" the soldier said. "Is that you?"

"...Rick?"

Melissa was so unprepared for his sudden appearance she could only hold on to the railing and stare as Rick rushed to her. Slowly, he came into focus. She saw his army crew cut standing up sharp and fierce, his boots covered in red dust, his fatigues bloused and his shirt open at the neck, his hands and face browned by the sun. She saw his blue eyes and the thin scar on his lip where his brother had hit him with a shovel when they were little boys.

Rick picked her up off her feet to hug and kiss her, and she nearly slipped from his arms.

"Mel, what have you done?"

"Ricky," Melissa said and leaned against him. "Ricky, it's you." She reached up and held his face close to her own. "Don't be afraid. I still love you."

Rick looked at her closely. "Are you okay, Mel?"

"And there's more." Melissa took a breath. "Everything is still the same."

"I'd better get you out of the sun. C'mon inside. I'll buy you some water."

"No," she said. "I want root beer."

Mr. Devers, the old man who called himself the postmaster and ran the little store, insisted that Melissa sit in his wicker chair in front of the fan and drink her root beer slowly and eat some potato chips while he went to the back for her mail, one letter from her mother. He frowned when Rick came to the register to pay for a six-pack of root beer and a candy bar and scolded him as he rang up the items.

"You Northerners don't know a thing about the sun, boy. Don't you be letting her walk around in the afternoon like that. You tryin' to kill your wife?"

"No, sir. I'll be sure she's more careful from now on."

"I'll take your money for the chocolate bar and the root beer. The chips is my gift to her."

"Thank you, sir."

"She's a pretty little thing when she's not bright red and sweaty. You gotta take better care of her if you want her to last."

"Yes, sir. I do want her to last. I'll try to take better care of her."

Melissa finished her drink in the car on the way home, and they shared the candy bar for dessert after dinner. The root beers were for her to have with her lunch every day for the next week.

"No more walking to the post office, okay? Mr. Devers thinks I'm trying to kill you. Please don't convince him he's right."

"Okay, Rick."

"And look, if you need me to pick up the mail on Tuesdays, I will. But I wish your mother's letters weren't so important."

MAYBE THE WALK IN THE HEAT MUDDLED MELISSA'S MEMORY because she didn't think at all about the letter to her mother until the next day when she found it, wrinkled and stained, in the pocket of her shorts. Much too messy to put in the mail, she told herself, and answered her mother's latest letter with a note written the following week. Like a married woman would.

# The Muse

*1971*

PHOEBE CHOSE AN EASEL IN THE BACK OF THE ROOM, pushed aside the brush and paints she found there, and set out her own materials. A tall student approached. He had lank, blond hair falling to his shoulders, fingernails crusted with paint, and jeans stained and stiff with linseed oil and turpentine. Phoebe thought he looked just like an artist.

He introduced himself as Kenneth, the teaching assistant for Painting 101. "The assignment today is to use the two-inch brush and the paint already at your easel. Experiment with bold brush strokes and vivid colors, and be sure to fill your canvas." He glanced at Phoebe's materials and moved on to the next student.

Phoebe spent the afternoon painting a tiny house in the center of the canvas. It was white with green shutters. Minuscule animals peered out of every window. At the end of class, Kenneth looked at her painting for several minutes.

"What an extraordinarily detailed house," he finally said. Phoebe smiled when he added, "I'd like to live there."

Week after week, Phoebe continued to produce pocket-sized pictures using nothing larger than a number-one brush regardless of the assignment. Anyone looking closely at her work would have recognized Greta, the girl at the easel next to hers, swinging from a trapeze; and Ron, the redhead at the front of the class, hiding in a treetop with the blond who painted next to him; and Cecilia, who painted at an easel facing the windows, picking strawberries in an open field. In fact, nearly every student was portrayed in one guise or another and hidden in Phoebe's little paintings.

The painting instructor, Professor Lustig, stopped at her easel the third week of class.

"Miss Kessler, what do you think you are doing?" he demanded.

"I'm painting," Phoebe said.

"Why do you ignore the assignment?"

"I'm painting in my own style."

"Ah, the problem at last. You think you are a painter with a style. Listen carefully. You do not have a style, and you are not a painter. You are a student. I don't want to see another of these ridiculous miniature menageries or flower gardens or dance troupes on your canvas. Nobody is interested in insignificant, Lilliputian paintings. You still have the first assignment to complete, so take a two-inch brush and get started." With that he walked away.

Phoebe packed up her brushes and paints, left class, and walked to the registrar's office where she dropped the course. That evening, Kenneth brought his dinner tray to the table where she was eating with her roommate, Darla. After Darla left for the library, Phoebe told him what Professor Lustig had said and that she had dropped the course. Kenneth looked surprised.

"I hope you don't believe Professor Lustig. Your pictures aren't insignificant; they're beautiful." Kenneth paused. "I'll miss seeing you in class."

Phoebe was flattered. "I'll miss you, too," she said.

"I've seen your paintings. Would you like to see the picture I'm working on?"

As a fine arts major completing his last graduation requirement, a one-man show, Kenneth had been assigned a small private studio. Rolls of canvas, wooden stretchers, tubes of paint, a hair dryer, jars of brushes, gallons of gesso, and cans of turpentine, varnish, and linseed oil overflowed a long table and covered much of the floor. A large easel stood near the window, and a stack of paintings rested against one wall. The studio also included a hot plate on a small table and a bed.

"I've tried to make it more homey," Kenneth explained. "Sometimes I paint half the night. Or I might wake up at three in the morning to paint, and I don't want to have to walk across campus to get to my easel."

Phoebe wasn't sure that was the whole explanation but was happy to believe him. She accepted his offer of a cup of coffee and looked through his paintings while he boiled water and put a teaspoon of instant coffee in each of two mugs.

"These are beautiful mugs," she said when he handed one to her.

"A gift from a pottery major," he said.

Phoebe sipped her coffee. Some comment about his paintings seemed expected, but she didn't know what to say.

Kenneth pointed to the large canvas on the easel. "I don't know what to do with that painting. It's lifeless. I need to start something new tomorrow." Phoebe agreed, but said nothing.

From the evening of that first visit, Phoebe spent most of her free time with Kenneth at his studio. He told her that she was perfect in every way. She wasn't short; she was petite. Her breasts weren't small; they were flawless. Her hair wasn't wispy; it was finespun. Her quiet nature wasn't boring; it was soothing. And Kenneth was an artist who needed a lot of soothing. His work was not going well, and he had yet to complete a single painting he could use in his show.

Darla was waiting in their dormitory room one Saturday morning when Phoebe came back from the shower. "We never have breakfast together anymore," she complained. "And last week you missed the dance team tryouts after we agreed to go together. I never see you, Phoebe."

"Sorry," Phoebe said and began to dress.

Darla sat on her bed and propped her pillow behind her back. Oh dear, Phoebe thought. She's settling in for a serious talk.

"I know it's because you're at Kenneth's all the time, but do you really think that's smart?"

"I need somewhere to paint, Darla, and Kenneth set up an easel for me in his studio."

Phoebe dug around in her closet until Darla asked, "Are you looking for your green shirt?" Phoebe nodded.

"It's in the second drawer of your dresser."

"Thanks, Darla." Phoebe laughed. "You must know that because you were the last to wear it."

Darla laughed, too. "Caught again. But you know how much I love that shirt."

"I know, and I'm thinking of giving it to you. But today, I'm wearing it." Phoebe pulled the shirt over her head.

"Does Kenneth like it?"

"As a matter of fact, he does. He says this shade of green is my color."

"Don't let him flatter you, Phoebe, and don't forget that he's a senior, and you're just a freshman."

"I know he's older, but I don't see how that matters. It isn't like he's ancient."

"He might not be ancient, but I think he's dangerous." Darla's voice rose as she warmed to her argument. "Did you know that he had a long relationship with another art major, and one day he gave her up, just like that? A girl in my history class knows her and says she was really upset. I think you need to be careful."

"Thanks for the warning," Phoebe said. "After midterms, we'll be sure to get together more." She tied her hair back in a ponytail. "Now I need to finish reading *Middlemarch* in a big hurry or I won't be ready for the test tomorrow."

Phoebe started out for the library but decided to go to the studio instead. She hoped she would be able to resist the temptation to paint. The small canvas on her easel was covered with little portraits of Dorothea, Celia, Rosamond, and Mary and the men in their lives. Despite George Eliot's descriptions, loyal and devoted Dorothea looked much like Phoebe herself, and all of the men, except Casaubon, Dorothea's self-centered husband, looked remarkably like Kenneth.

Phoebe spent the entire afternoon curled up on the bed, reading and watching Kenneth paint. She loved the mess on the table, the smell of the paints, and the sight of Kenneth squinting at his canvas, wiping his hands on his jeans, flicking his hair away from his face and standing back to scrutinize his work, his body tense and poised for his next approach to the easel. He looked like a dancer performing a strange pas de deux with a painting. What a beautiful man, she thought, a real painter.

The quiet intensity in the room helped her focus on her work and convinced Phoebe that Darla was wrong. Maybe she'd been fishing for information, Phoebe thought, and hoped not. One meddlesome person in anyone's life was enough, and Phoebe's meddler had always been her mother.

The spring before Phoebe's senior year of high school, students were shot at Kent State, and her mother began a campaign to have Phoebe live at home and attend their local college. When a building was blown up at the University of Wisconsin three months later, her mother declared any college, other than the local campus, too dangerous to consider. Only a reckless parent, she insisted, would permit her child to live far from home at a time like this.

"I don't know what's the matter with you, Phoebe. You've always been such a sweet, sensible girl, and now you won't listen to reason," her mother said on more than one occasion. "Where's my lovely little girl? Where's my precious baby?"

That was Phoebe's cue to answer, "I'm right here," and hug and kiss her mother and make her laugh.

While she understood her mother's worries, Phoebe was grateful when her father's intervention won her permission to go away to school. Her mother responded with a demand for a weekly letter home. "I wrote to my mother every week, and there is no reason why you shouldn't write weekly, too. I told your sisters the same thing when they left home, and now I'm telling you."

Her sisters might have been told to write home weekly, but Phoebe knew that Margaret had never complied, and even Melissa had not kept it up for long. So, while her sisters were invoked as precedent for writing every week, they set a different precedent in Phoebe's mind. To guard against her mother's calling the dorm or forcing her to transfer to a school closer to home, Phoebe compromised and sent a sketch or two every week. She knew her mother would be charmed by little pictures of her studying or sitting in class or having breakfast with Darla. Although she didn't like to think of herself as secretive, Phoebe was relieved that her mother didn't press for more details of her life at college.

One afternoon when Kenneth was out, Phoebe visited his studio and saw his most recent work. It was blocked in charcoal, and she looked at it for a long time before deciding that the balance was off. This painting would fail for the same reason his other paintings had. Phoebe moved her materials to his easel and, using her favorite number-one and triple-zero brushes, she painted a jungle lush with flowers, and hid a tiny heart in the tall grass. She carefully covered her painting with varnish and dried it with the hair dryer.

Kenneth laughed when he returned to find her jungle on his canvas. "How am I going to use this canvas without smudging your painting?" he asked.

"Don't worry," Phoebe answered. "I covered it with aged varnish and quick-dried it. You can paint right over it."

When Phoebe saw the canvas again, the painting was good, different in every way from his earlier work. Her jungle had been painted over, of course, but she knew it was under Kenneth's painting, concealed but essential.

That became their work pattern. Somewhere on every new canvas, Phoebe painted a detailed image and Kenneth created a painting that covered it. He said that she was his hidden muse, and he was her bold statement.

At the beginning of their collaboration, Kenneth scrutinized each of her images carefully, seeking every detail and standing back to gaze at the little painting as a whole. Then, slowly and deliberately, he would paint, covering her picture with his last brush strokes. Eventually he worked more rapidly, acknowledging her contribution with a nod and covering it quickly as his own painting took over the canvas.

The paintings for Kenneth's one-man show accumulated against the wall of the studio until there were fifteen of them. Then he and three friends hung them in the student union gallery.

The following afternoon, the painting faculty evaluated his show. Phoebe and several of his friends waited with him in the lobby and watched through the gallery's glass doors while the committee moved solemnly from painting to painting, examining each one and taking notes. After the committee conferred, Kenneth and his friends were invited in. When Kenneth's adviser announced that the committee had voted to award his degree with honors, his friends cheered and everybody offered their congratulations.

Noticing Phoebe, Professor Lustig said, "Miss Kessler, the paintings you see here are the work of a fine, young artist. It is possible that you could have learned to paint like this. I'm sorry you dropped my course. "

Phoebe stiffened, but made no reply.

ON THEIR WAY TO HIS STUDIO FROM THE GALLERY, KENneth grabbed Phoebe's hand. "Tomorrow is the opening of my show, and Lustig invited newspaper reporters and bigwigs from the museum. Did you hear him call me a fine, young artist? It doesn't get any better than this."

Kenneth pulled Phoebe close and walked so quickly she had to trot to keep up. "No one will ever know that you paint only for me. We're an inspired team, Phoebe, baby. Promise me that will never change." Kenneth didn't seem to expect an answer as he hurried along.

Phoebe was quieter than usual that evening. After Kenneth fell asleep, she packed her little painting and her belongings into her knapsack along with cotton swabs and a can of mineral spirits and walked to the student union gallery. The room was dark and silent. Using the illumination of the emergency lighting, Phoebe worked painstakingly through the night. Near dawn, she took a moment to look at each painting and admire the result. Then she gathered up her materials and her knapsack and slipped out of the gallery, unnoticed.

Art critics praised Kenneth's show, but his work raised a controversy among them. Some held that the big painting was the point, and the intricate little painting revealed in its midst was simply a counterpoint to the larger message. Others maintained that the bold colors and shapes around each small image were a frame designed to heighten the impact of the exquisitely detailed little picture.

The next sketch Phoebe sent her mother showed her walking to class with Darla. Among the other students on the sidewalk was Casaubon, looking quite a bit like Kenneth and very much out of place.

# Clara's Legacy

*1973*

Clara Mae Kessler (nee Gantz) died at 4:48 p.m. on Friday, March 23, 1973. She was alone at the time. Clara had hoped to die quietly in her own bed some night when the house was dark and silent, and she blamed herself for the fainting spell that alerted everybody to her condition and caused her to be whisked off to the hospital just after midnight. As the mother of the Head of Obstetrics, she was assigned a bright, shiny room that made her feel like a window display, in the spotlight and peered at by everybody who walked up the hall. Clara turned her face away from the doorway and watched the wind ruffle the leaves of a large tree outside her window. She had thought she had more time, but now she knew she would not sleep in her own bed again. There were three people Clara needed to see before she died, and she prayed for enough time and strength to speak with each of them.

After a complicated early morning delivery, Douglas visited his mother. "I'm sorry I couldn't meet you in the ER. It was twin boys this morning, and that took a while." He held her hand and simultaneously took her pulse. "Do you like the room? Have the nurses been good to you?"

"Sit down," Clara said. "I need to talk to you." She whispered to him for almost an hour while Douglas listened carefully, nodding and patting her hand throughout her long monologue. Clara seemed peaceful after their talk, but Douglas hurried away without his usual jokes and instructions for the nursing staff.

Clara's daughter, Lillian, arrived at nine o'clock, overflowing with apologies for not coming sooner and stories about her hectic morning getting Anshel, her husband, off to work and Zalman, their son, off to school.

"Can you believe it, Mom?" she said. "Not one, but both of them forgot their lunches this morning, and I had to drive from the ink factory to the high school delivering lunches to men who can't be bothered remembering anything." Lillian leaned over the bed and kissed Clara's forehead. "I'm so sorry I'm late."

"Sit near me now and listen," Clara said. "I need to talk to you."

Lillian sat in the chair Douglas had left next to the bed and took her mother's hand. She had had these talks before and already knew where her mother's favorite necklace was hidden and about the jar of quarters in the back of her mother's bedroom closet.

Clara talked for a long time, and Lillian listened without interrupting her. Then Lillian talked a bit. Clara nodded and Lillian leaned far over the bed so that Clara could kiss her cheek.

"There's not a daughter in the world like you, Lilly."

"Or a mother like you."

"Zalman's a wonderful boy, but I wish you'd also had a girl so you could know the joy of having a daughter."

"One day, Zalman will marry, and then I'll have my daughter," Lillian said.

Clara didn't answer, and Lillian wondered if Clara's experiences with her daughters-in-law, Ada and Fay, had been anything like having more daughters. There had been some talk at one time of Clara's living with Ada and Douglas once Melissa and Margaret moved out and Phoebe was off at college. Their house was certainly big enough, and it seemed fair since Clara had taken them in when they were newly married. Ada had said that it was a lovely idea, but she was sure Clara would be happier being cared for by her own daughter. So Clara continued to live in her crowded little house with Lillian, Anshel, and Zalman in the downstairs apartment and Harold and Fay and their children living upstairs. Still, Ada had agreed to visit this afternoon so Lillian could drive Zalman from school to his music lesson without leaving Clara alone. She had even agreed to be at the hospital by three o'clock.

Clara closed her eyes and seemed to nap. She said she wasn't hungry when her lunch arrived, but did accept a little apple juice.

"Do you think Ada will be here today?" Clara asked.

"She said she would come at three o'clock. That's when I have to take Zalman to his music lesson. I didn't want you to be alone." Lillian expected her mother to protest that there was no need for everybody to change their schedules just because she was in the hospital.

Instead, Clara said, "Good," and was quiet for the rest of the afternoon.

Clara was sleeping at three o'clock when Lillian tiptoed out of the room, telling herself that Ada would be there any minute.

Clara woke at four o'clock and saw that the chair next to her bed was empty. She called out Ada's name. It was a moment or two before she realized that she was alone. "Any minute, any minute," she said. "She'll be here any minute." Clara watched the tree and tried to stay awake, but it wasn't long before she fell asleep again.

Clara was mistaken. Since nothing was expected of Fay, Harold's wife, Ada had concluded that she didn't need to spend hours sitting with her mother-in-law, either. I'll visit tonight with Douglas, she decided, and missed her last chance to see Clara alive.

THE NURSE CALLED DOUGLAS AND DOUGLAS CALLED LILLIAN and Ada. Lillian called Anshel and her brothers, Harold and Ira. Ira was overcome and in tears when he heard the news, but Harold was angry.

"Why wasn't I told earlier?" he demanded. "I would have left work to be with her."

"I'm sorry, Harold. But I didn't know she would die this afternoon."

"You might not have known, but Douglas is a doctor. He must have known. It's just like him to keep something like this to himself."

Harold's outburst reminded Lillian of all the childhood jealousies and quarrels she had witnessed between these two brothers. "I don't think he knew," she said, "and he wasn't there, either. We're all very sad right now, Harold. It's not a time to say harsh things. Think how Mom would want us to act."

"I'm not mad at you, Lil. I know you're only the messenger here, but it's frustrating just the same. I would have wanted to say goodbye, and I didn't get the chance."

"It's alright, Harold. Mom knew how much you loved her, and you know how much she loved you. Will you take care of calling Fay?"

Harold called Fay and told her how that son of a bitch, Douglas, had denied him his last chance to see his mother alive, and Fay called their children to say their grandmother had died. Ada waited until the long-distance rates went down at nine o'clock in the evening and called Phoebe and Melissa.

She told Melissa that she wasn't going to bother Margaret with the news because Margaret lived too far away to attend the funeral anyway. Melissa called Margaret.

Phoebe flew home from college on a ticket that Melissa paid for after Phoebe called her to say that Ada had not offered to pay, and she didn't have enough money to buy the plane ticket herself. Margaret managed to book a flight across the country, arriving at her parents' house in plenty of time to ride with the family to the funeral home. They arrived early as requested by the rabbi and were led to a room next to the chapel. The rest of the family had arrived even earlier.

Ada noticed that all the women wore somber colors except Fay, who looked like she was dressed for a party. Yet another confirmation of how foolish a woman she truly is, Ada thought, and turned her attention to the men. All of them wore suits. Even Ira, who hated to dress up, had made an effort, though his suit was old and rumpled. Ada couldn't decide if Ira's outfit showed he had some understanding of appropriate attire or proved he had no fashion sense at all.

Now that the mourners he had been told to expect had gathered, Rabbi Baumgarten joined their group. "This is a sad occasion. Clara was a fine woman and a loving mother and grandmother. We will miss her."

Lillian wiped her eyes and leaned on Douglas, who put his arm around her. Lillian's adoration of her oldest brother annoyed Ada. "It feeds the God's-gift-to-mankind complex your mother gave you," she complained once, and was further annoyed when he laughed.

"I need the mourners to gather here with me," Rabbi Baumgarten continued.

Ada watched Clara's four children step forward. The rabbi clipped a black ribbon to the jacket of each of the men and to Lillian's blouse, and made a snip in each ribbon. Then the mourners repeated a prayer, word for word, after him as they each ripped the ribbon, leaving the torn pieces clipped to their clothing. Lillian covered her face with her hands, and Douglas patted her arm.

One of the funeral directors who had been watching from the edge of the room stepped forward. "If the family is ready, we will open the doors so your friends and relatives can pay their respects before taking their seats in the chapel."

Douglas nodded, and the doors were opened. Immediately, two men rushed into the room ahead of the group gathered in the hallway. Max Kessler and Sol Pinsky.

It had been more than thirty years since Ada had seen Max, and now that she saw him again, she realized how odd it was that their paths had never crossed in all that time. Max didn't seem to have changed a bit. He was the same short, slight man for whom the word *dapper* fit perfectly. He carried a cane and wore a three-piece black suit and a somber tie. Everything looked new. Once inside, Max leaned on his cane, and looked around quickly. Then he slowly made his way to Douglas. Ada wondered why Douglas looked more resigned than surprised.

"My boy, my boy," Max said. "Such a sad day. How could you leave me standing outside while my darling Clara lies in her casket? A man needs his family when the love of his life is gone." Max embraced Douglas and then Harold and Ira, who both looked shocked to see him. "I'm a fortunate father to call these grown men my sons," he said before turning his attention to the women.

"Ada, my sweet, and my dear daughter, Lillian." Max stood taller and instantly his cane became more a fashion statement than a means of support. "This must be the lovely Fay. And are these my beautiful granddaughters?" Max opened his arms as if to embrace them all. Only Fay stepped forward and responded to Max's enthusiastic hug.

Ada drew herself up into what her children called her Queen of England pose, regal and imposing, and designed to make her appear impregnable, like the display of a peacock or the warning of a rattlesnake. She didn't know what she would do if Max tried to touch her, and she took a step back only to bump into Lillian who was suddenly standing behind her.

Lillian put her arm through Ada's, as if to say that the two of them together were more formidable, yet. Their united front was not tested because Douglas stepped between them and Max.

"What do you want, Dad?"

"To be with my family, of course. To mourn my wife as any husband would." Max took his handkerchief from his pocket and wiped his eyes.

"You want to be at the funeral?"

"Of course."

Douglas seemed at a loss, and Rabbi Baumgarten stepped close to him.

"Your father must not be shamed," he said. "He deserves the opportunity to honor his wife and be comforted."

"I agree," Harold said. "I had no idea where he lived, or I would have called him myself."

"My sweet son," Max said, smiling at Harold.

Douglas looked at Ada and his daughters and Lillian, but he didn't speak.

It was Anshel who finally said, "He can stay and sit between Harold and Ira."

Douglas nodded, and it was decided.

Rabbi Baumgarten clipped a black ribbon onto Max's jacket, and, as Max ripped the ribbon and sobbed, they said the prayer together.

The rest of the crowd at the door filed in, the men shaking hands with the male mourners and the women hugging the female members of the family and sharing memories of Clara and sadness at her loss.

Ada steeled herself to hear all sorts of nonsense about Clara, a woman whom Ada had always found loud, crude, and uneducated. Still, she had to admit that Clara had never been unkind to her, and she knew that her children loved their grandmother without reservation.

Ada kept her daughters around her and quieted their questions about the unexpected appearance of a grandfather they had never met. "Later, later. We'll talk later," she said, hoping the time to talk would never come. She had some thinking to do.

The family filed into the chapel and filled the first bench. Max leaned heavily on his cane, and Harold had to help him to his seat. Behind them sat Clara's friends and large extended family and the friends and colleagues of her children and grandchildren. Rabbi Baumgarten stood at a podium on the stage, and a simple, pine casket rested below him on a low, raised platform.

The service was in Hebrew, so Ada had a few moments to herself. As long as Clara lived, she thought, Max never showed himself. As soon as she's gone, he's back. Ada looked over at Lillian who was crying quietly and wondered why Lillian had moved to stand next to her when Max came in and why Douglas had spoken up so quickly to put an end to the hugs and greetings.

The rabbi extolled Clara as a woman of valor while Max sobbed loudly and nearly slipped from the pew. Ada thought that Douglas looked almost amused as his father's weeping and laments nearly drowned out the rabbi's voice. After the memorial prayer was sung, the service was over.

The funeral directors in their black suits, black ties, and black shoes swooped down and stood next to Clara's coffin. Ada wished for a drop of color to relieve the dark tones, the way Clara's laugh would have dispelled the solemn mood. Clara's laugh? Imagining Clara's laugh reminded Ada how much those loud guffaws had irritated her.

The names of the pallbearers were read, and Clara's sons, son-in-law, and grandsons took their places beside the coffin. Max reached for Lillian and the two of them walked directly behind the casket as the procession left the building, first the family and then everybody else. Max continued to hold on to Lillian while the casket was placed in the hearse.

As soon as the doors of the hearse were closed, the men spoke quietly together. At first it seemed to Ada that Harold and Douglas were arguing, but then Douglas said something that must have appeased or flattered Harold, and he nodded. Ira looked confused but signaled his agreement, and the conversation broke up. Anshel hurried to his wife's side.

"I'll help him now," he said.

"I need to hold on to her. I don't feel so steady," Max said.

"Harold will hold you up," Anshel replied, and Harold came over to take his father's arm.

"Come with me, Dad. I'll take care of you," he said.

"Lillian told me the grandchildren will ride in the second limousine. That's wonderful because there will be room for me with them," Max said.

"We've changed our minds," Douglas said. "The men will ride in the first limo, and there's room for you with us. The women will ride in the second car."

"I want to be near my daughter." Max dropped his cane and clung to Lillian. "Only she can comfort me, she's so like her mother."

"Ride with the men or go with Mr. Pinsky in his car," Douglas said.

Max reluctantly released Lillian. Douglas handed him his cane, and he went with Harold to the first limousine.

Fay and the granddaughters took seats in the second limousine, but Ada decided to go to the ladies' room before the trip to the cemetery. After a minute, Lillian hurried after her. As they washed their hands, Lillian looked at Ada in the mirror over the sinks.

"Don't worry, Ada, my father's not coming back into the family. Mom left instructions with me and, apparently, with Douglas, too."

"Instructions?" Ada said.

"About Dad and what he might try after she was gone. She's been right so far." Lillian shook her head and laughed in spite of the somber mood of the day. "I wasn't supposed to talk to you about this, but you looked so frightened when he showed up that I need you to know that you're safe."

"I don't know what you mean." Ada took a paper towel from the dispenser and dried her hands carefully. "What did Mom say?"

"That he'll try to come back, but he must not be allowed to. And he's never to touch you or any of her granddaughters."

"Did she tell you why?" Ada was afraid of the answer, but she asked anyway.

Before Lillian could respond, Phoebe came into the ladies' room. "Hey, Mom, Aunt Fay sent me to find you. The hearse can't leave until the procession is formed, and since we are the second car, everybody's waiting for you and Aunt Lillian."

Lillian and Ada hurried to take their places, and the long procession left for the cemetery. The women were quiet in the car.

Max wanted to walk to the grave site between Ada and Lillian, but Douglas insisted that he help carry the casket. The rest of the funeral party followed, pausing seven times while the rabbi read Psalm 91. The casket was slowly lowered into the ground, and Clara's sons took shovels from the mound of dirt next to the grave.

The first thud of earth on the wooden casket echoed in the still, morning air and sent a shudder through the group. It was as if Clara's presence on earth made one final effort to be heard before she was removed from the sight of the living.

IN KEEPING WITH TRADITION, DOUGLAS, HAROLD, IRA, AND Lillian planned to spend the seven-day period of mourning together in their mother's house, while other family members and friends visited and provided food and comfort. By the time the family arrived to begin the week of shiva, neighbors had prepared a special meal for them.

The mourners were fed first, and Douglas took the seat at the head of the table. Max arrived after Clara's children were seated and was led to a chair between Harold and Ira. "Don't you know you shouldn't sit in your father's seat?" he asked Douglas. "Your mother would never have allowed it."

"I'm doing what she told me to."

"I don't believe you," Max said and turned his attention to the food. It was the simple meal traditionally served all mourners: bread, hard-boiled eggs, lentils, and tea.

"Ah, Mrs. Handleman," Max said, taking the hand of one of the ladies serving the family. "Our wonderful neighbor all these years. We'll miss our Clara, won't we?"

Mrs. Handleman nodded and hurried to the kitchen for another basket of rolls.

After the mourners had eaten, Ada, Anshel, Fay, and the grandchildren had their meals. The adults said little, but the grandchildren enjoyed the opportunity to chat. Melissa, who lived less than an hour away, told them about the last weeks of their grandmother's life, and soon they were all sharing stories about how funny she was and how generous she had been and the miracle of her sponge cake, which most of the granddaughters had tried to replicate without success in spite of having her recipe.

People came and went all day until Rabbi Baumgarten led a brief prayer service in the early evening and the last of the visitors left. As tired as they were, the family sat together into the night, the five mourners on low stools and everybody else piled onto armchairs and sofas and seats they dragged in from the dining room.

"Remember how she would sniff when she came into a room and know if you'd had a cigarette there in the past week?" Douglas said. "I got caught more times than I can count before I understood that I would always be caught, and I might as well stop trying to smoke in the house. Even leaning out the window didn't help."

"I remember when she found Douglas giving wine to Ira," Harold said. "Ira was a little boy, and Mom was really mad. She chased Douglas around the house with a wire hanger raised in her hand until she fell laughing into a chair. I don't know what she would have done if she had caught him. She never hit any of us."

"Remember when Ira gave his class ring to a girl who wouldn't give it back? That ring cost twenty-five dollars, and Mom wasn't about to let her keep it. So she went to the girl herself and got it back for him."

"Remember how she used to say, 'You have trouble with anybody, you tell me, and I'll clean up for you'? I never understood what that meant."

Slowly the family became silent as the room grew dark around them. When Fay offered to make sandwiches, the granddaughters went upstairs with her to help.

"Where will I sleep tonight?" Max asked.

"Wherever you live now," Douglas answered. "You can't stay here. There's no room."

"I can stay in her room. The room where my darling Clara slept."

"That's a good idea," Harold said, looking defiantly at Douglas. "You're going to double up with Ira in Zalman's room, so nobody was planning to sleep in Mom's room."

"No, it's not a good idea," Lillian said firmly. "I haven't cleaned that room, and it's full of her things. Nobody can go in there."

Harold looked at Lillian in surprise. Ada was surprised, too. She rarely heard Lillian speak so resolutely or contradict Harold except in jest, and Lillian clearly wasn't joking now. Ada was confident that Harold would have taken on Douglas, but everybody knew there was no arguing with Lillian once she took a stand.

"This can't be you talking, Lilly," Max said. "Talking like that to your old father."

"I'll drive you wherever you need to go," Anshel said, "and we should leave now."

"I want a sandwich, and I want to be properly introduced to my grandchildren. We've hardly had time to talk with each other."

"I'll get a sandwich for you to take in the car," Anshel said and went upstairs. When he came back, Max was wearing his coat and looking unhappy.

"I'll be here tomorrow," he said, banging his cane on the floor. "The door is always open at a shiva house, and this is my house now, anyway."

Before Douglas could answer, his father was out the door with Anshel.

Douglas shook his head. "He's in for a surprise about the house."

The rest of the family came downstairs with a platter of sandwiches and a tray of drinks. After they ate, nobody had the energy for more conversation. Ada and her daughters left for home; Zalman went upstairs to sleep in his cousin Bobby's room, and Clara's children went to bed in Clara's house.

ADA ALWAYS LOVED DRIVING WITH HER GIRLS IN THE BACK seat because they talked to each other during the car ride as if she wasn't there, and she learned things about their lives they didn't tell her, otherwise. On the ride home from the shiva house, they were full of news for each other. Melissa described the latest escapades of her children. Margaret extolled the beauty of San Francisco and told Melissa to bring her family for a visit. Phoebe shared her decision to be an English major with an art minor, though she had changed her mind about her major so many times that her adviser now wrote her choice on her forms in pencil.

"Are you still reading *Les Misérables* for your literature class?" Melissa asked Phoebe, and Ada wondered how Melissa knew what Phoebe was reading.

"I am. I have it with me so I won't be too far behind when I get back."

"When I heard what you were reading, I started it, too," Melissa said. "We can talk about it at breakfast."

Maybe I'll read *Les Misérables*, Ada mused. Her thoughts were interrupted when Phoebe remembered she was there.

"Hey, Mom," Phoebe said. "What's with this grandfather who suddenly shows up and nobody wants around?"

"He moved away for a job and never reconnected with the family."

"Looks like he wants to reconnect now. Why all the resistance?"

"I think everybody is sad about Grandma, and he's been gone so long there's no place in the family for him anymore."

"There has to be more to it than that."

"Not as far as you're concerned."

"Uh-oh, family secrets," Margaret said. "And what about that creepy guy who drives him around?"

"That's Mr. Pinsky, his oldest friend."

The girls seemed ready to speculate about their grandfather's long absence, but they had arrived home and, as Ada carefully pulled into the garage, she said, "No more talk tonight. It's been a long day."

The habit of obedience was so well ingrained, and the chances of learning anything from their mother so slim, that Ada's daughters went off to bed without another word. In a short time, the house was quiet.

ADA LEFT FOR THE GROCERY STORE AND THE BAGEL SHOP early the next morning. She had taken responsibility for the mourners' first breakfast; Fay had agreed to provide lunch and dinner. By the time Ada reached the shiva house, Lillian had already set the dining room table and was filling the kettle.

"Lillian, why are you up so early? You aren't to be doing anything for yourself, much less for anyone else, this week."

"I couldn't sleep, and there's no point in sitting around. I can feel just as sad while I'm fixing breakfast."

"Sit down, and I'll make a bit of breakfast for the two of us before anybody else is awake," Ada said and set out places at the kitchen table.

Lillian let her take over and sat quietly while Ada made tea and put bagels and cream cheese and jelly on the table.

"My favorite breakfast since I was a little girl," Lillian said, and helped herself to a bagel while Ada poured the tea and put a small pitcher of milk on the table. "You've even trained me to like milk in my tea, the way your mother made it in Scotland. It must have been a shock to come across the ocean and join this family. And lonely, too."

"That was a long time ago, Lillian." Ada chose a sesame seed bagel and cut it in half. No matter how little she wanted to hear what her mother-in-law had told Lillian, Ada knew she had to take this opportunity to ask. "We were interrupted yesterday when you were telling me about a conversation you had with Mom. What do you know about why your father left home?"

"Probably more than you think I do." Lillian spread cream cheese and jelly on her bagel before continuing. "When I was little, I loved sharing my room with you on the nights that Douglas slept at the hospital. One night I heard my father come into the room and try to kiss you good night."

Ada was silent. There was nothing for her to say.

"I heard everything," Lillian continued, "and I was angry with you for not letting him kiss and cuddle you. And I was jealous because he used to come in and kiss and cuddle me before you moved into my room." Lillian sipped her tea and cradled the cup in her hands.

"A few weeks later, Dad was gone. I told Mom it was your fault, that Daddy went away because you wouldn't give him a good night kiss. I said I wasn't mean like you, that I always gave him good night hugs and kisses."

Ada took a bite of her bagel to keep herself from pointing out that Clara must have kept Max away for what he did to his own daughter, not what he tried to do to her. I wasn't the one who mattered, she wanted to say, you were.

"I'm sorry that I misunderstood completely what was going on. How could I have been so stupid?" Lillian began to cry.

"No sense in crying now, Lillian. It happened long ago, and you were a little girl."

"Mom said that Daddy moved away because he found a job, and we were not to talk of it again, and we never did—until the day she died."

"She talked about this in the hospital?"

"Yes. She told me that what my father did with me was wrong, and she hadn't wanted me to realize it when I was a child. But Mom was much more worried about what he tried to do to you and what he might try to do in the future."

"She worried about me?"

"She said he was a greater danger to you than he would ever have been to me, and she wouldn't be here to protect you anymore. So now we need to."

"She was protecting me?" Ada said. She sat back in her chair and stared at Lillian. "All these years, she was keeping him away from me?"

Lillian nodded. "She did what had to be done."

Ada's eyes filled with tears, and she looked down. "She was protecting me."

"She must have told Douglas something, too." Lillian said. "And I told Anshel that Dad was never to touch you or the granddaughters. I didn't explain, and he didn't ask me to."

Ada looked up to see Douglas and Harold come into the kitchen. She hastily dried her eyes on her napkin and said,

"You boys are up early. Go to the dining room, and I'll bring you some breakfast. Do either of you want eggs?"

"Scrambled would be good," Harold said, but Douglas wanted only coffee, as Ada knew he would.

"Lilly," Harold called, "come sit with us. You and Ada have cried enough."

Ira joined the family at the dining room table and after they had eaten, the mourners took their places on low stools in the living room.

It was still too early to expect her daughters to be awake, so Ada made herself another cup of tea and sat down with it at the edge of the dining room table. Suddenly, she saw the front door fly open as Max rushed into the house.

"You didn't think I'd be back so early, did you?" he said. "And I brought some things so I can stay here tonight. I'm not going to be put out of my own house again. Your mother would not have stood for it."

Ada placed her teacup on the table and shrank back in her seat. She would have liked to retreat to the kitchen but was afraid of drawing attention to herself. So she sat very still and hoped to go unnoticed. What's wrong with me? she thought. I didn't do anything wrong. Clara might have thought I needed her to protect me, but I can take care of myself. Ada sat up a little bit straighter.

Max took his suitcase from Mr. Pinsky and shooed him away. "No need for you to stay, Sol. I won't need a ride again today."

"Stay, Mr. Pinsky," Douglas said. "My father will need a ride sooner than he thinks."

But Mr. Pinsky had already backed out the door and could be seen through the front windows hurrying down the sidewalk to his car.

"He left quickly and right on cue, Dad," Douglas said.

"I don't know what you're talking about." Max looked around the room and smiled when he saw Ada sitting at the dining room table. "If you send me away now, Ada will have to drive me. Unless Fay is here, and I don't see her." Max sat on a low stool, resting his cane against his leg and placing his suitcase on the floor. "I'll put my things in my darling Clara's room after I eat breakfast."

So much for my hope of going unnoticed, Ada thought.

"You'll leave when I tell you to if I have to call a cab," Douglas said.

"You may be a grown man and a big-shot doctor, but I'm still your father, and you will treat me with respect. This is my house now, and you can't send me out of it."

"You may be my father, but this isn't your house," Douglas said with obvious satisfaction.

"You don't know what you're talking about."

"It never was your house. Mom bought it with the money she inherited when her father died and left you off the deed."

Max looked around the room. "You all knew about this?"

"Only I knew," Douglas said.

"It doesn't matter. Now that dear Clara's gone, I'll inherit the house. I'm her husband."

"The house is left to Lillian."

"You cheated me?" Max roared. "You son of a bitch. I'll take you to court! You can't keep me out of my house or away from my family."

"I'm going to do both," Douglas said.

Max looked at Harold. "Aren't you going to stick up for your old man?"

"This has gone far enough, Douglas," Harold said. "Just because you're the oldest doesn't mean you get to call the shots."

"On the day she died, Mom and I had a long talk, and she told me what to do," Douglas said and seemed pleased by the shocked look on his father's face.

"Spell it out," Harold said. "I want to hear exactly what she said."

Ada's composure evaporated, and she looked anxiously at Douglas.

"I'm not supposed to talk about it."

Max smiled and nodded.

"So," Harold said, "we're supposed to take your word for it? I don't know why everything has to be a secret. Dad deserves an explanation."

"Is that what you want, Dad?" Douglas said. "Should I tell everybody the story that Mom told me?"

"It doesn't matter what the story is," Max said. His cane punctuated every word as he stood and paced around the room. "Can't you see that he's being a bully, Harold? Remember how he used to boss you around when you were kids? Well, he's doing it again. Don't let him get away with it."

"You're not interested in hearing the story, Dad?" Harold shrugged when Max remained silent. "That changes everything."

"You always were a gutless wonder, Harold." Max stumbled to his seat. "I can't believe this. How can you be so cruel to a sick, old man? I didn't want to go away. It was your mother's idea."

"I know that," Douglas said. "And what's more, I know why you had to leave."

"I knew it!" Max yelled, pointing at Ada. "This is your fault! You made a mountain out of a molehill and ruined my life. It's all because of you and the stories you spread." He wiped his face with his handkerchief. "You turned my whole family against me."

Ada stared at Max. To deny that she had said anything would seem to admit some wrongdoing worth hiding. To say nothing would seem to admit that she had told. Ada had never felt so exposed and helpless. Now she understood what Clara's protection had meant.

"Don't yell at my wife!" Douglas shouted. "Never, never raise your voice to her."

Everybody in the room recoiled. Max looked stunned, and his cane clattered to the floor. Even Douglas seemed startled by his own behavior, and for a moment, the room was silent. Ada was as shocked as anyone. She had never heard Douglas take her part or come to her defense before.

Douglas took a deep breath before he spoke again. "Ada said nothing to me or, as far as I know, to anyone else. I wish she had told me so I could have taken care of you years ago. Mom is the one who told me the kind of man you are, and unless you want everybody to know, you had better end this conversation now."

"You aren't the only one who knows," Lillian said quietly.

"Are you against me, too?" Max said. "My sweet, little Lilly, the light of my life?"

"Mom also talked to me before she died. She knew Ada wasn't the only one you wronged. I stand with Douglas. You can't come back here."

"Did Dad hurt you, Lil?" Harold asked.

Lillian didn't answer and put up her hand to stop further questions.

"Don't be stupid, Harold. How could I hurt my own daughter? Don't you see what they're doing to your poor old father?"

Harold watched Lillian rest her elbows on her knees and cover her face with her hands.

"I don't know what's going on, Dad," he said. "But maybe Douglas and Lillian are right. Maybe you should stay away."

Ira, looking sleepy and confused, nodded his assent.

"You've all been turned against me," Max said. "I can't believe my Clara did this. She loved me."

Nobody responded.

"Did she tell you that she gave me money?" Max said. "She saw that I'm sickly, and she made sure I had what I needed."

"She did, and it made me angry to hear that you have been taking from her all these years," Douglas said. "But she made me promise that I would continue the monthly checks. I'll do that, but I set the same condition she set. You must stay away. If you come around, or if I hear that you are spreading tales, the money stops. That condition starts right now."

Max made no reply.

"Are you going to call Mr. Pinsky, or should I call a cab?"

ADA DIDN'T WAIT FOR MAX TO LEAVE BEFORE SHE SLIPPED back into the kitchen and sat at the table. Her tea had cooled, but she hardly noticed as she sipped from the cup. *What if I'd visited the hospital when she expected me? Would she have told me not to worry, that I would still be protected? Would I have understood what her protection meant?* Ada couldn't control her tears. *I lost my chance to thank her.*

After the door closed behind Max, Ada heard Harold turn on Douglas. "I don't know why you always get your way," Harold said. "We just sent our father away because of Ada. Why don't we treat her the way she treats us? She's always looking down her nose at everybody. Why should we care about her feelings? It should be about Dad. I don't know what you're accusing him of, but maybe it wasn't all his fault."

"You don't know anything about Ada," Douglas said. "Nothing was her fault, and don't ever suggest such a thing again. I did what I was told to do, and I was glad to do it."

"Maybe he changed," Harold said.

"Does he look like he changed?" Douglas asked.

Lillian's voice put a stop to their argument. "Dad never hurt me or Ada, but what he did was wrong. Even so, this isn't about us. It isn't even about Dad. This is about Mom. It's about the kind of woman she was and the kind of mother she was. It's about honoring her by seeing the truth the way she saw it and doing what she would have done."

The mourners began to talk quietly. Dealing with Max seemed to have drained their animosity, and their voices were soft. Ada roused herself and made a new pot of coffee and arranged some pastries on a platter. She carried the snack into the living room.

When he saw her, Douglas placed a little stool between him and Lillian. "Come sit with us, Ada," he said.

Ada was surprised and almost declined, saying she wasn't a mourner. Instead, she took her place with them, grateful that she was included and that nobody objected.

The room was quiet until Ira suddenly spoke. "I never knew that Mom sent Dad away. I always thought he left because of me."

Because of you? Ada thought. You think you sent Max away? Ada looked down. On any other day, she would have scoffed at such an outrageous claim, but she felt no inclination to scoff today. The mourners must have been as incredulous as she was, and a moment of complete silence followed Ira's remark.

"You thought you sent Dad away?" Harold finally asked. "What were you? Fourteen years old? How did you think you managed that?"

"One night after Ada moved upstairs, I heard Dad go up the back stairs and knock on Mrs. Brotkin's kitchen door. I knew we weren't supposed to go up there and bother Ada, and I guess Dad found out, too, when Mr. Brotkin made him leave.

"The next day, I had a sore throat, and Mom let me miss school. I was home alone when Dad showed up. I stopped him at the front door and said, 'I know you've been bothering Ada. You better leave right now.'

"He looked shocked and said, 'And if I don't?' in his nastiest voice. 'What are you going to do about it? Tell your mommy?'

"'No,' I said. 'I'll tell Douglas, and he'll kill you.'

"'You think so? How's he going to do that?' he said.

"'I'll help him,' I said."

Ira looked down. "I don't know why I said that, but he must have believed me because he left and never came back. I didn't know Mom knew anything about it. I thought he left because of me."

Ada looked up at Ira. "Thank you," she said. "Thank you for watching out for me."

"I should have been paying better attention," Douglas said, shaking his head. "Thank you for taking care of my wife, Ira. She was lucky you were there."

Only Harold seemed amused, but a warning look from Lillian was all it took to calm him down. "You were brave to stand up to him," Harold said.

Lillian went to hug Ira and kiss his cheek. "My strong, silent brother," she said.

Ira blushed bright red.

After a moment, Douglas said, "It's been quite a morning, but we aren't going to speak of this again. Mom didn't want a lot of chatter, and she's right. She said I'm not to waste any words talking about him or any time missing him." Douglas looked at his siblings. "Please assure me you will do the same." Each one nodded, and Douglas wiped his eyes. "It will be easy to forget him, but I'll never stop missing her."

When Fay came through the back door carrying shopping bags, she found the family in quiet conversation. "How about a helping hand," she called out, and Ada went to help her carry the rest of the groceries in from her car.

"I'll come back to help with lunch," Ada said. "But now I think I'll run home." She scooped up some bagels and a tub of cream cheese and told the family that she would bring her girls with her when she returned.

ADA PULLED INTO HER GARAGE AND SAT IN THE CAR FOR A few moments, too close to tears to go into the house. Pull yourself together, she scolded, and took several deep breaths.

Melissa was at the stove when Ada came in. "Where are your sisters?" she asked.

"Margaret went jogging, and Phoebe is in the shower."

Ada took the bagels out of the bag and arranged them in a basket.

It wasn't long before Phoebe appeared in the kitchen and poured herself a cup of coffee. Margaret sprinted in the side door soon after. "I'll take a quick shower and be right down," she said. As soon as Margaret reappeared, the four of them sat down to breakfast.

"Delicious, Melissa," Phoebe said. "And the bagels are a big treat, Mom. It's so nice to have all of us home that it's hard to remember we're here for a sad reason. It's like our last gift from Grandma."

Ada felt like a guest with nothing to add to the conversation as her daughters chatted about their cousins.

They agreed that everybody had grown up or gotten old but them. Only Phoebe, at nineteen, was eager for her next birthday.

"Was turning thirty easy for you, Melissa?" Margaret asked.

"Knowing that you turned thirty on the same day made it bearable," Melissa answered, and they both laughed.

"You guys are really old," Phoebe said. "I don't think anybody at school has sisters as old as mine."

"It used to be that we had the edge, and you were the little kid. But I see the tables have turned," Margaret said. "No need to rub it in."

"Are you really reading *Les Misérables*, Melissa?" Phoebe asked.

"Yes, and I'm enjoying it."

"How far are you?"

"I'm up to the part where the priest forgives Jean Valjean."

"What did he do to the priest?" Margaret asked.

"He stole from him," Phoebe explained. "He wasn't used to people being good to him, so when the priest forgives him, he doesn't know how to react. After he steals again, he vows to be good like the priest."

"I bet he can't change," Margaret said.

"That's what the people who know him think, so he has to find people who didn't know him when he was a thief before he can live a better life."

"He won't be able to keep it up. People are the way they are."

"That's gloomy," Phoebe said. "I think people change all the time."

"Not in my experience," Margaret said.

Ada checked her watch. "We need to clean up here and go back to Grandma's house. I told everybody I would bring you over for lunch, and it's almost time, even though we just finished breakfast."

"Wait a minute," Phoebe said. "You didn't tell us about this new grandfather of ours."

"He's gone home, wherever that is. We won't be seeing him again, and we won't be talking about him again, either." Ada carried her breakfast dishes to the sink. Everybody helped clear the table and wash the dishes, and they were soon on their way, Margaret in Melissa's car and Phoebe with Ada.

THE PERIOD OF MOURNING LASTED SEVEN DAYS. THE FAMILY spent the mornings sharing stories about Clara, tales from their own childhoods, and news of their children. The grief in the house softened each of them and opened them to the healing that families manage at such times. By the fourth day, when their conversation included politics and sports, they realized they were feeling less sorrowful.

In the afternoons, aunts and uncles and cousins came to visit; in the evenings, colleagues, patients, and clients stopped by. Clara's grandchildren came and went bringing news and stories of their own; her great-grandchildren brought noise and running feet.

Ada spent her time organizing and preparing meals. Her daughters helped their Aunt Fay shop and their mother cook.

Douglas noticed that Ada didn't complain when people came in at all times of the day expecting food. "Thank you, Ada. You're making it easy on everybody," he said, giving her a hug and a kiss.

Ada smiled and kissed him back.

On the last day of shiva, Rabbi Baumgarten came to the house early in the morning. Ada had been worried that Max might appear, but there was no sign of him, and nobody mentioned his name.

"Today," the rabbi announced, "the mourners are escorted

outside for the first time in a week. Though we will never forget Clara, we must put our sadness in perspective, and resume our ordinary lives. When we go outside, it is as if we are taking her spirit with us, remembering the lessons she taught us and dedicating ourselves to fulfilling the promise of her long and fruitful life."

Margaret grinned at Melissa. "What are the chances of that?" she whispered. "We can't even duplicate her sponge cake."

Ada overheard her and found herself unexpectedly moved to tears. As she fumbled for the tissue in her pocket, she missed seeing the look of surprise and disbelief that passed between Melissa and Margaret when they noticed she was crying.

"Is everybody here?" the rabbi asked.

"Yes," Douglas answered.

"You're sure?"

"I am."

Rabbi Baumgarten looked around the room, but when nobody challenged Douglas's statement, he had to be satisfied that the children and spouses and grandchildren who had gathered made up the complete group. "The family and friends will accompany the mourners on a walk around the block," he said and led the way.

Lillian reached for Douglas and Harold took Ira's arm. Fay and Anshel walked together. Several neighbors followed.

Ada looked for Phoebe and saw her far ahead, walking with Melissa and Margaret. But a few steps in front of her, Becca, Melissa's little girl, was walking alone. Ada caught up to her and took her hand. Becca seemed surprised.

"Hello, Grandma," Becca said. "Do you think Mommy and I can really visit Aunt Margaret in California?"

"I don't see why not," Ada said, and held on to her.

# EPILOGUE

# The End Is in the Beginning

*2007*

ADA WOKE IN THE MIDDLE OF THE NIGHT. NOTHING unusual about that. Except there was no urgency to pee. In fact, there was nothing but a heaviness in all her limbs and a flutter in her chest that seemed quite new. Something was not right. In fact, something was quite wrong.

She tried to look at the clock on her night table, but her head refused to turn. Maybe I've had a stroke, she thought. I'd better take an aspirin right away.

Some time later, Ada woke again. I dreamed I couldn't move, she thought, and pushed herself upright until she realized that she couldn't push, and she certainly wasn't upright. Not a dream.

Her right arm refused all commands, but she could manage a bit of movement with the left. Just enough to press the middle of the necklace they made her wear, the one that was supposed to bring help anytime of the day or night.

"May I help you?" a bright, wide-awake voice said.

"Yes," Ada said. "I can't get out of bed."

"Hello? Is anyone there? How can I help you?"

"Yes, help me," Ada said.

"Hello? Hello?"

Stupid woman, Ada thought. Must be the only one they could find to stay up all night answering calls from a necklace.

"I'm sending help," the voice said.

Finally, a reasonable response. Ada sighed. I don't have the energy for more conversation, anyway.

Ada stared at the ceiling and felt herself slipping back to sleep. It seemed as if the world was slowing while she rushed forward. Or was it the other way around? Was she slowing and the world rushing on ahead?

Ada woke and wondered why it wasn't morning yet. Her head still wouldn't turn enough to let her see the clock. It's very quiet, she thought. And then announced, "It's very quiet," just to prove that she could. Will people say I died peacefully in my sleep? Is that what this is? Well, I'm not sleeping and it's not peaceful. It's annoying and it's unfair, that's what it is. I want to be the first woman in the family to reach ninety. I want a big party, an elegant affair in the late afternoon on a Sunday, and a cake with so many candles there's a danger of setting the curtains on fire.

Phoebe will have to come from Chicago with all her daughters. She won't be able to say she's busy if it's my ninetieth birthday party. And Margaret will have to show up, too, even though she's a fancy San Francisco lawyer. And Melissa, of course. And Fay and Lillian hoping to reach ninety themselves and feeling a little jealous that I got there first. And all the aunts and cousins and second cousins whose names I can't remember. And a newspaper reporter and a photographer and an article in the Sunday paper with quotes saying how I don't look a day over seventy and how nobody in the family ever got to ninety before.

And presents. Lots of presents piled on a big table waiting to be opened later. Somebody will have to help me with the thank-you notes. Melissa, probably. Or Becca, if she's back from vacation. Imagine selling the most of whatever she sells and winning the big prize of a two-week vacation cruise. Can't remember where she is, but she's touring somewhere. Sends me postcards. I know she's buying me a present. I'd rather have her here.

Ada closed her eyes. If I can't have another birthday, at least they'll all have to come for the funeral. But it won't be the same. No presents.

I didn't say goodbye.

So what. Why should I be sorry to leave? Even after I picked up and moved to live closer to Melissa, she still doesn't visit more than once a week. It's her husband who changed everything. I never liked that boy, rushing her into marriage the way he did. Never hear from Margaret, and Phoebe always has some excuse. All I wanted was for everything to be perfect. The way I imagined it would be when I left Scotland. But I couldn't make it come out right.

Ada worried that tears were gathering at the corners of her eyes. Foolish old woman. No sense crying now.

Becca. Sweet Becca, the best of the lot. She let me love her and she loved me back. We cooked and baked and planted flowers together. She gave me another chance to make it perfect. I don't want to leave without telling her I love her and saying goodbye.

Rose. Standing on the platform, waving to me and holding Mama up. The train sped by, and she was gone forever. I never wanted to see her again, and I never did. Biggest mistake of my life. There never was a sister like Rose. Then she died. Left a little girl. What is that child's name? Can't remember.

Isn't there supposed to be a bright, white light, and aren't I supposed to feel wonderful about the whole thing? And my mother is supposed to greet me with hugs and kisses. Oh, no. Not my mother. She'll tell everybody I'm doing this wrong. I want Rose to come for me.

It's Addy, Rose. Come take me home. We'll have tea with our baby dolls under the apple tree. I'll let you have the doll with the curly, yellow hair.

ANGELO ADJUSTED HIS EARBUDS, SETTLED BACK IN THE chair, and closed his eyes. Second night on the job. Not a bad gig. Next track, "Moment's Notice." He smiled, tapping his left foot on two and four, and swinging the band with the ride cymbal he played on the desktop.

Angelo's father sang arias in the shower and berated his son regularly for his musical preferences. "You're Italian, act Italian."

"Half Italian. The other half digs jazz." His father didn't know that the other half also hung out with a kid up the block who said he was picking up stuff real fast. Sometimes he even had a chance to sit in at Charlie's when the kid played there. Earlier tonight, he'd overheard a guy at the bar say, "That Angelo's getting pretty good for an Italian kid," and wondered if he should change his name to Buddy or Max or Elvin.

Suddenly Angelo heard the wail of a horn he hadn't noticed before. It grew louder and more insistent until it seemed to be coming right into the lobby. He opened his eyes and saw swirling red lights in front of the building and two paramedics pushing a gurney loaded with equipment through the front door.

"Emergency call from 502," one of them said.

Angelo checked the emergency protocol, handed them the keys, and phoned the on-call administrator.

A sleepy voice answered.

Angelo read the message. "This is Angelo at the front desk. It is," he paused to check the calendar, "Tuesday," and again to check the clock, "at three forty-seven. I gave the keys to 502 to two paramedics who arrived in an ambulance responding to an emergency call. The resident is," he checked the resident list, "Mrs. Ada Kessler."

"Thank you, Angelo. I'm on my way."

The paramedics reappeared in the lobby twenty minutes later. The male said, "Hey, man, you're new, right?" He leaned over the counter and peered at Angelo's name tag. "Don't worry about a thing, Angelo. She had a valid DNR posted. We made the necessary phone call, and she's been pronounced." Noting Angelo's look of confusion, he added, "Pronounced dead. We don't transport dead people, so we're leaving her here. Your people will get her ready for the family or the funeral home, and they'll take it from there. You're all set, man." He handed Angelo the report.

Angelo flipped the pages in the protocol book. "Thank you," he read. "I'll take care of all necessary arrangements." Then he looked up and said, "Really, thank you."

The ambulance crew left Angelo hoping he wasn't one of the people expected to get the dead lady ready for her family.

"Hey, Cindy, was that your work?"

"Shhh. Don't wake Mom. I have to go in for an emergency."

"Why don't they call the social worker? She's trained to deal with emergencies. You're the assistant marketing director. You're trained to show people around and get them to admire the flowers in the lobby."

"It's my turn to be on call. Go back to sleep."

"Cynthia, why are you girls talking this time of night?"

"Sorry we woke you, Mom. I have to go to work."

No use reminding her mother or her sister to call her Thea, a name much better suited to her than Cynthia, too old-fashioned, or Cindy, too juvenile. Thea was a dramatic name with a hint of sweetness. And as it was the last half of her given name, she believed she had a right to claim it as her own.

Thea dressed hurriedly in the dark, brushed her hair and teeth and rushed out the door without makeup to show that her concern trumped her need to look good. When she arrived twenty minutes later, Angelo was sitting at the desk, wide-awake, no earbuds in sight, and a copy of the EMT's report and 502's emergency instructions and numbers on the desk in front of him.

"Thank you, Angelo," she said, taking the papers he handed her.

Following the instructions in her protocol handbook, Thea called the designated funeral home and read the report from the ambulance crew to the man who answered. He checked their records and assured her that the family had made all the necessary arrangements. Their staff would see to the death certificate and transport the body as soon as possible.

Her next task was to call the next of kin, Ms. Margaret Kessler, Esq., in San Francisco. Too bad, she thought, that the old lady lives here and the next of kin lives in California. But maybe that's as close as they wanted to be to each other.

That done, Thea went out to the front desk and sat next to Angelo.

"You new here?" she asked.

"Second night."

"Don't worry. It's not always this exciting."

"Have you been here long?"

"Only a few months. I work for the marketing director. Mostly I keep the flowers in the lobby looking nice."

"They're beautiful. You must be doing a good job."

"Thanks, but really I'm an actress, and I consider this my first role."

"I'm not really a night security guard," Angelo said. "I'm a musician—a drummer."

They smiled at each other, and Angelo offered to make a new pot of coffee.

"Sorry that I only have the stuff they leave out for me," Angelo said. "I bet there's something better in the locked cupboards."

"Everybody guards their stash around here. It's really quite an unpleasant place to work. But don't worry, anything strong and hot will be perfect."

They sipped their steaming cups of coffee and agreed that it was not very good.

"But it helps me stay awake," Angelo said. "So I don't plan to complain."

When the morning shift came in, Angelo nodded to Thea and left. Thea worked a half day since she was not perky enough to show anybody around.

Margaret was wakened by Thea's phone call and took care of everything. She called her sisters, Melissa and Phoebe, and arranged to have Ada's apartment dismantled and the furniture and clothing donated to charity. Afterward, the apartment was cleaned as required by the rental agreement.

The funeral home arranged for immediate burial. No family member attended. Melissa had bronchitis and couldn't leave her house. Becca was on vacation, and Melissa didn't bother her with the news of her grandmother's death. Margaret was too busy at work to take the time, and Phoebe was overwhelmed by her girls' dance recitals and a new litter of kittens. So the cemetery workers hired to close the grave and the rabbi paid to officiate were the only mourners. There were no presents.

Unless you count the small bouquet of daffodils Angelo put on Thea's desk the next night because he thought she was pretty, and he knew she liked flowers. And the packet of Starbucks Caffè Verona Thea left at the front desk with Angelo's name on it because she thought he was cute and deserved a better cup of coffee at night. And the silver necklace Becca bought for her grandmother while she was on vacation and buried under the sod at the corner of Ada's grave to say she was sorry she hadn't been there to hold her grandmother's hand and say goodbye.

# ACKNOWLEDGMENTS

MY GRATITUDE TO ALL THOSE WHO ENCOURAGED ME TO write. I have been blessed with gifted and supportive writing teachers including Margaret Osborne, Tim Johnston, and Faye Moskowitz. Special thanks to Michelle Brafman for her helpful comments on "Bottled Sunshine," Clifford Garstang for his critique of "The Muse," Bill Black whose generous mentoring guided this book through its final revision, and Jean Graubart for her devotion to the Summer Retreat writing community.

My thanks to Susan Helsel, Sarah Arno, Gloria Neubert, and participants in workshops at Johns Hopkins University, The Writer's Center, and The George Washington University for reading and commenting on drafts of the stories. Particular gratitude to Beth Greenfeld and Carol Solomon for their careful reading and rereading of these pages and for their incisive and helpful comments and suggestions.

Thanks to Kim Stone, Director of Communications at the Flint Group, who referred me to the National Association of Printing Ink Manufacturers and to George Fuchs at the association for his informative description of ink factories in the 1950s, to Matt Levinson, Sol Levinson & Brothers, for information about funeral practices in the 1970s, to Abby S. Kasowitz-Scheer, Learning Commons Librarian at the Syracuse University Libraries for information about the Everson Museum, and to Jon Ochs, Mervis Diamond Importers, for information about diamond rings popular in 1952.

Finally, thanks to my family, Tim, Jen, Fran, Aley, and Maya for all the ways they enrich my life, and to Andy whose love sustains me every day.

Made in the USA
Middletown, DE
15 May 2021

39572460R00172